BYRON'S SHADOW

Further Titles by Jason Foss from Severn House

SHADOW IN THE CORN

BYRON'S SHADOW

Jason Foss

SEVERN
SH
HOUSE

This first world edition published in Great Britain 1994 by
SEVERN HOUSE PUBLISHERS LTD of
9–15 High Street, Sutton, Surrey SM1 1DF.
First published in the USA 1994 by
SEVERN HOUSE PUBLISHERS INC., of
425 Park Avenue, New York, NY 10022.

British Library Cataloguing in Publication Data
Foss, Jason
  Byron's Shadow
  I. Title
  823 [F]

  ISBN 0-7278-4700-7

Typeset by Hewer Text Composition Services, Edinburgh.
Printed and bound in Great Britain by
Hartnolls Ltd, Bodmin, Cornwall.

Chapter One

London rain lashed the windows of the houseboat. Warm rain, true; it was summer. Flint tapped a small invitation card against his left hand as he sat on the bed, watching raindrops obeying the rule of gravity. He would rush to the tube, then make his way to a reception given by the Hellenic Society in Gordon Square. He rarely thought of what had happened in Greece and spoke of it less: it had been seven years ago, he had been unprepared for tragedy and ran away from it at the first opportunity. The card drove a stiletto into his conscience. Some face would emerge from the crowd and a voice would begin to say 'Didn't you used to know...?'

He groaned. Soul-searching over the Greek tragedy had been abandoned years ago; a party was a party and the past was deeply buried. Flint fell back onto his bunk, thinking of a blazing summer's afternoon and a woman in flaming red.

A dot in the distance resolved into a dust-covered coach approaching Palaeokastro in low gear. The road swept up from the Gulf of Argos, through the charmless

1

village and beyond into the hills. Pitted and potholed, it had not seen a new surface since American engineers had re-routed and upgraded the donkey track which had existed in 1949. The coach passed the petrol station, with one hull-red petrol pump and an inattentive attendant, then emerged from the jumble of stucco-faced buildings. It began to slow down.

There was a time when English archaeologists were stern pith-helmeted ex-army men but these had given way to radical, bearded, and impoverished youngsters. Jeffrey Flint had been twenty-five, not quite free from University as he squatted by the roadside in his straw hat and John Lennon glasses. Trowel stuffed into his hip pocket, he felt the very model of a modern archaeologist.

Once the coach had come to rest, the door hissed open and out poured an inquisitive flock of tourists, hot from another day of concentrated culture. The archaeologist rose to his feet, dusting himself down to little effect as he searched for one red-skirted figure.

'Hi there,' he called.

Lisa, the courier, marched up to his side, clipboard at her waist, blonde hair pulled away from her face into a pony tail. 'Sorry we're a bit behind.'

Flint shrugged off her apology in his usual relaxed manner. The world could wash away and it would leave him unperturbed.

'Okay for tonight?' he asked, establishing his priorities immediately.

'We'll see,' she teased, turning to face her charges.

Greece is at its kindest in late afternoon, when the

savage heat of noon has mellowed, the sunlight no longer glaring back from the grey stones. Lisa took a few moments for the stragglers to catch up, then launched into the courier's routine.

'Now, as a special favour, we are going to be shown around a real archaeological excavation. This is Jeffrey Flint from Central College, London, who is assistant director of the Palaeokastro field survey. Although he won't admit it, he's also something of an expert on the Romans in Greece.'

Flint fidgeted at the accolade, then grinned through his beard as she handed over charge of the tour. He spread his arms, 'Welcome...'

So the show began, with Flint as conjurer bringing the site back to life. He spoke quickly and excitedly about Palaeokastro – there was no castle – it was just one of those folk names. With a sparkle in his eyes and histrionic emphasis in his voice, he coloured the drab picture presented by tired stones and scattered ruins.

'First it was a Greek town, then in 146 BC the Romans thought they would improve the place by burning it down – planning regulations were a little hazy in those days.'

This was the third time Lisa had heard his routine, his jokes and logical tricks. Flint thrived on attention and he knew he held Lisa's; she was as firmly hooked as her paying public. Excited and animated, he led a rapid march past stunted remains of walls barely distinguishable from the natural grey rocks which littered the valley side.

'The town was re-founded by the Romans around

40 BC and survived until it was deserted in the sixth century. The site was hacked about by German archaeologists in the nineteen-thirties and all the loot went back to Berlin. We're not really sure what they found, thanks partly to the crude techniques in use at the time and partly to the activities of the Royal Air Force . . .'

Sweat- and grime-smeared co-workers were introduced and persuaded to pose for the photo opportunity. Flint could also be induced to stop beside a Doric capital, remove his hat and grin for the camera.

'Where's the diggin' then?' It was a fellow Yorkshireman, gruff and practical.

Flint had spent seven years studying at University and now it was his turn to educate. 'Excavating is slow and never gives you the big picture. I'm trying to do as little digging as I can, this is a field survey. The Germans dug up all the sexy bits of the town, such as the temples and public buildings, so what I'm looking for is evidence for the economy: field systems, aqueducts, outlying farms and so on . . .'

Anecdotes were sprinkled amongst the hard facts and the loose speculation. He'd studied college lecturers, separated the stimulating from the pedestrian, and rehearsed his own technique to keep back the yawns. Flint led his verbal dance towards a herders' hut of breeze blocks and corrugated iron. A lightly-built woman emerged at his approach. She was in her early thirties but a whole generation separated her philosophy from the ebullient Flint.

'Emma will show you our goodies,' he said, remaining breezy, but inwardly waiting for the tension to show.

Emma narrowed the small hazel eyes that hid behind her glasses, then turned from Flint to the assembled tourists. She wore a floral head scarf, but the rest of her clothes were a shapeless jumble of cloth and dust. The contrast with buxom, well-groomed Lisa reminded Flint what a sexless occupation he'd chosen. Flint took a seed box from Emma, who immediately launched into her own, slightly shrill, slightly too rapid explanation of the meagre finds: well-weathered potsherds, fragments of brick, bone and tile. She made an effort to rival Flint's enthusiasm, trying to make something of the assemblage and possibly succeeding. The tourists had seen far greater treasures at Athens, Mycenae and other halts on their lightning tour, yet were prepared to pick amongst the finds and appreciate them for what they were. Still damp from washing, or still dusty and awaiting cleaning, the immediacy of the collection made up for its poverty.

'Have you found any gold?' A red-faced Essex woman in bright white sunhat was first to race out the obvious question.

Flint interrupted whatever Emma was about to say. 'Ah, popular misconception number one; archaeologists are only after treasure. Nothing could be further from the truth.' He injected a little irony into what he was saying, preparing the audience for his next trick. 'However, it just so happened that this morning, I found this.'

From the hip pocket of the cut-down jeans, Flint produced a chunk of glittering metal. The gasp was instant and even Lisa was fooled. She took her turn at fondling the golden artefact, half amused, half disappointed. It was a fountain pen, gold plated, of dated design and rather crushed.

'Did the Greeks have biros?' One wag thought he was being funny.

The remark was ignored, 'I found it in a water channel, close by the road,' Flint waved up-slope towards an olive grove. 'I was investigating an anomaly in our resistivity survey.'

The Yorkshireman demanded details and Flint gesticulated heavily as he explained how a resistivity meter was able to detect features such as walls and pits just below the surface. 'Or that's the theory. Personally, I hate the thing, today is the first time I managed to get it working. When we located the anomaly, we did a little digging, but found a tip of modern rubbish at the edge of the road. Hence, modern treasure.'

Sensing that maximum joy had been squeezed from the jaunt, he raised his eyebrows to draw Lisa's attention. Immediately, she made a pro-forma speech of thanks then began to usher her charges back aboard for the drive to Nauplion.

She cast a look over her shoulder, her ponytail whipping around. 'Are you coming?' she asked.

No question. 'Sure!' One obstacle to surmount, then he was free. 'Emma, I'm off.' Flint dodged past Emma into the hut.

'Where?' the woman asked his back.

'Town, back tomorrow.' He avoided her eyes and grabbed a bulging army surplus satchel.

'Who's clearing up?' Emma demanded.

He avoided her glare and the inevitable argument. 'Andy, he knows what he's doing. Bye.'

Lisa was waiting for him, directing a practised, insincere smile towards Emma. He followed the courier onto the coach, then sat down beside her in a cloud of dust.

'If looks could kill,' she mused.

'Emma? Don't worry about Emma, she hates everyone and the feeling is mutual.'

The coach bumped into motion.

'Well, you changed your story again . . .' Lisa began.

'. . . we make it up as we go along.'

'Intellectuals . . .' She shook her head, never completing her criticism. 'Still, our arrangement is working out very nicely.'

'How nicely?'

She lowered her voice, 'Last week's tips were very good. They should run to dinner plus wine.'

'Suits me.'

But did he suit her? Flint wondered.

'I thought I'd take you to Andreas' place,' she said, 'Do you know Andreas? He's a real character, his bar's always full of locals.'

'Sounds great, I'll need decontaminating first.' He brushed at a little more dirt.

'I'll sneak you into the hotel and you can use my shower. There may still be warm water if you're lucky.'

Lucky, yes he felt lucky. Lisa was leading him from

Purgatory to Paradise. Dimitris the driver hummed to himself as he urged the coach uphill towards the village of Anatoliko, where he could find space to swing the vehicle around. On the right lay the olive grove, on the left, the grey hill rose sharply, its slopes dotted with brambles and scrub. The coach crossed an embankment over the dry gully where Flint had found his 'treasure' and continued in low gear for another mile.

Anatoliko clings to a sharp spur of the hills, its low white houses tumbling from the heights where a bell tower points the way to God. At the summit is a small square, with the church forming the eastern side. Dimitris slowed almost to a halt and heaved at the wheel, the coach turning around a lifesize bronze statue flanked by a pair of needle-pointed conifers.

'Who's that old bird?' Flint asked.

'Someone asks the same question every week,' she replied, 'Stylanos Boukaris, schoolteacher and local hero,' Lisa recited, 'He had his leg shot off fighting the Germans and was killed by the communists during the Civil War.'

'That's what, 1948?'

'Somewhere around then; history was never my best point and you'll never get the Greeks chatting about the Civil War. It's not a polite topic of conversation.'

Flint had taken only a glance at the statue, but its image remained with him; a balding man with flowing moustache and eyes fixed on infinity. Dead heroes and secrets of the past were the stuff which kept him in business.

Chapter Two

The rain had eased and Flint could raise an umbrella and stroll to Camden Town tube station. Smalltalking with academics normally appealed, but that night, he wanted something more, something exotic, like dinner for two outside a small backstreet taverna in old Nauplion. One day he'd go back there, to that heap of houses surrounded on three sides by the sea and surmounted by a low Venetian fort. From a distance, Nauplion reminded Flint of one of his childhood sandcastles, encrusted with limpet shells, about to be swept away by the tide. The smell of burning fat carried from the doorway of a Kebab house and Flint had to stop, watch the greasy meat turning, cast his eyes on a faded print of the Parthenon and feel the shadow of the past creeping towards him.

Andreas ran the sort of small, outwardly squalid place which was frequented solely by Greeks and the wily tourists who take pride in avoiding other tourists. Nauplion had not yet been overrun by foreigners; Lisa's clients were on an expensive and highly select tour programme, but she seemed to want to escape from them whenever she could. She would send them to eat along Akti Maouli with its holiday brochure harbour views, whilst she led Flint into the enchanting maze of Venetian buildings and Turkish fountains which lay beyond.

Only three small tables had sneaked from the taverna onto the sloping alleyway. All were occupied, whilst seated in half the chairs within the yellow-flushed interior were local men, lingering over ouzo or coffee. Others lounged over the counter.

Gently, gently, Flint could unwind. A scene with Emma had been avoided, his getaway had been clean and the night was his. Between the overhanging balconies, a long slit of sky was passing through China blue into shades of night. Lisa had been retelling her latest batch of tourist horror stories, adjusting her voice to mimic unfortunate victims of circumstance, using slow hand-motions to illustrate the catastrophies. Flint responded with one of his wild and unlikely diggers' tales. He made her laugh, which was good, even if she refused to swallow the yarn.

'It's true!' he implored.

'Alright,' she said, dismissing him with a laugh, 'I believe you.'

Her eyes were a wholesome nut-brown, but at night, with pupils dilated, they seemed almost black. Lisa wore very little make-up, just a little mascara to thicken up her eyelashes, but Flint liked the natural look. She had washed and let down her hair; now Lisa was toying with her wineglass, swirling the contents around and around, watching the red liquid and flicking her eyes up to meet his.

'I've always been amazed that anyone with brains can spend a whole summer picking around in the dust,' she said.

'I wouldn't do anything else. Travel the world, meet people, play in the dirt. It's like joining the army without the snag of having to shoot people. In truth, it's an excuse to have a good time.'

Lisa leaned forward, demanding intimacy. 'So how did you get into it all? Somehow, I just can't picture you as a six-year-old saying, "Daddy I want to be an archaeologist".'

'Oh but I did; by seven the man is made. My dad loved old films and I got hooked on epics: Fall of the Roman Empire, Cleopatra, and of course,' he laid on an American accent, '*Spartacus*. I stood no chance of making it in movies, so with a name like Flint, it was archaeology or nothing.'

As he trotted out his life story, Flint assessed Lisa under the irregular lighting. At first glance she might have been taken for a Greek, with her tanned skin, brown eyes and dark, partly plucked, eyebrows. Only the bottle blonde hair and its black roots betrayed the image.

'So, is that grotty old pen the only treasure you have found?'

Her accent was educated southern middle class and she tended to speak lethargically, giving her words a relaxed, sultry tone. It did not seem to belong to a travel courier; something deeper and richer must lie

11

in her past. Flint withdrew the pen from the breast pocket of his lumberjack shirt and rotated the find, watching it glitter in the light of a failing bulb.

'Gold! Treasure! Riches! An archaeologist's dream!'

Lisa snatched it from him. 'Your sponsors are going to be very, very disappointed my boy, if this is the best thing you take home.'

'We are not treasure hunters!' He was far from sure about the 'boy', she was no more than four or five years his senior.

'So you're not a treasure hunter, but you were digging for something. What were you hoping to find?'

'Nothing, it was only a quick sondage.'

'Stop. You're doing it again,' she warned.

'What?'

'Bullshitting. What's a sondage?'

'A little hole.'

'Isn't saying "little hole" easier?'

'Less precise.'

'Well, it's precise enough for me. What else did you find?'

'All sorts of boring modern junk. It's what we call made ground; rabbits are disturbing it and bringing this stuff to the surface.'

She rubbed her fingers along the casing, 'Hmm, this must have been expensive, does it still work?'

'No. The inside's all rotted and the casing is too far gone to repair.'

Lisa had found the inscription etched in flowing letters across the frosted gold surface. Leaning back to catch the light, she read it aloud. 'Byron F. Nichols: I bet he was sick losing this.'

She pushed the pen back towards him, then gave a long, relaxed, deliberate sigh. Flint wondered whether she truly thought him too young and cringed at the thought of their first meeting, three weeks before. Fresh from England, with two undergraduate diggers he had hitched to the coast and gate-crashed a hotel beach party. Whilst the others had found a pair of giggly nurses to impress with their tales along the lines of 'the last time I got drunk', Flint had sat beside Lisa and helped her whip life into the over-forties. A Greek guitarist strummed his way through transatlantic folk classics, but could master only the first two lines of each. Flint had begun to fill in the words, perking up the party and raising that full-cheeked smile on the courier's face. Their deal had been struck by the light of a driftwood bonfire, since when the relationship had remained strictly business. Still, the night was young and he had every intention of correcting the situation.

A large moving shadow indicated Andreas, the bar owner, emerging from within, approaching Lisa from behind and laying a hand on both shoulders.

'Lisa the lovely, you have brought the great explorer?'

'Yes.' She gently wriggled from the grasp and took up the pen. 'He finds buried treasure too.'

Boredom had cast the die. Andreas examined the pen in unnecessary detail, then carried it inside, passing the trinket to all his friends, relatives and customers, repeating Lisa's repetition of Flint's story. Hands were waved, voices called from inside, people wanted to know more. Go away, thought Flint, fearing to lose Lisa's attention amongst the mass of men, thinking of nothing beyond consummating their relationship.

One man came back to them slowly, glancing at the pen, passing a courteous nod to Lisa. He was dressed in an open white shirt and black trousers, his face and hands betraying half a century as a peasant. Flint was unprepared, too late in sensing a purpose in his manner.

'Pretty thing,' the man said, choosing the wrong inflection for his English words. 'Which Palaeokastro you are digging? The one of the Romans? Up in the hills?' He inclined his head landward.

'That's right.'

'Ah,' said the man, still looking at the pen. 'You're digging in the olives now?'

Flint nodded, wondering how the man knew and whether he cared.

Andreas called from the next table. 'Costas, do you know this man Byron Nikola?'

Costas shrugged and thrust the pen back, with cold resentment in his expression. 'You should look for Roman things, not dig up a poor man's olives.'

Flint suddenly felt uncomfortable, very foreign and very out of place. He avoided the Greek's eyes and slid the culprit pen back into his breast pocket. Costas said nothing else and trotted away down the steps towards Stakiopoulou.

'Glad I didn't find the mask of Agamemnon,' Flint said, disgruntled. 'It was only a little hole . . .'

'Sondage' Lisa corrected.

'Whatever. We were a good ten feet away from the nearest sodding olive tree.'

Lisa put her finger to her lips. 'Shush, remember where you are. Greece is full of foreigners trampling over every ruin they can find, throwing their money about, goggling at the peasants and their cute donkeys. It offends their honour, even the poorest have honour, they have a word for it – *philotimo*.'

Flint's *philotimo* had been badly dented and the mood had been broken. 'Look, let's just disappear before our fame spreads. It's time to party. Lead me to the hot spots of Nauplion.'

'Hot spots?' she asked, with just a hint of innuendo. 'You don't strike me as being the disco type. They don't do Bob Dylan...'

'I'm not fussy.'

'But I am,' she said, 'We'll stay here if you don't mind, it's a little early for anything else.'

A gentle Sithaki drifted out into the night and the odour of fried mullet wafted across from the next table. Worse ways could be found of spending an evening, he mused.

'We'd better order more wine then,' Flint said, hiding his regret. 'Come Friday, I feel the need to unwind.'

'Ah, so now you are finally admitting that digging is not just fun and games from morn 'til night. Admit it, Jeff, something odd is going on up there isn't it?' Lisa's voice was slowed even more by the wine.

'Odd?'

'That long-nosed cow gave me a filthy look. Is she your secret admirer?'

'No, not Emma, we don't get along. She's thick with the Dalek, I'm not.'

Lisa giggled slightly, 'The Dalek?'

'Our esteemed director: Sebastian T.D. Embury MA (Oxon) F.S.A., alias The Dalek.'

'Why do you call him the Dalek?'

Flint picked up the empty Demestica bottle and stuck the mouth onto his forehead, croaking 'Excavate! Excavate! Resistance is useless!' The bottle came down again, 'It was Andy's idea, he's a space opera freak. Nicknames are one of those puerile things that keep us all sane.'

Lisa giggled again. 'How beastly is he?'

'He's just an alien, my mate Andy is perfectly correct. We're all red-blooded human beings fresh out of college, full of ideas, full of enthusiasm but he's a robot from the planet Tedium. He has no comprehension of modern survey techniques, plus, he's an old-fashioned right-wing autocrat and I'm an anarchist, so there is a minor philosophical gulf between us. His latest strategem for keeping me out of his hair is to send me out surveying the edge of that miserable olive grove. He's hoping I won't find anything and he's not going to be disappointed! Meanwhile, he messes about on the juiciest parts of the site, pretending to be the great antiquarian.'

'Take it from me, the boss is always a shit. Every boss I've ever had has been a first class shit.' Lisa turned to attract the attention of the weighty Greek taverna owner and ordered a bottle of Nemea in impeccable Greek.

'I wish I could do that,' Flint said. 'All the Greek I can manage is "yes", "beer", and "chicken".'

'The secret is to have a Cypriot mother,' Lisa confessed. 'My father was stationed in Cyprus. He was a Squadron Leader.' She shaped her fingers into goggles around her eyes to mock her parent, 'He runs a dog kennel on Dartmoor now. How the mighty have fallen.'

He heard the resentment in her voice, but Lisa was a little old to be a teenage runaway. 'Fluent Greek is a useful skill for a courier.'

'Yeah, but I'm not going to be a courier all my life.' She ran the neck of the empty bottle up and down between forefinger and thumb as she dreamed, 'I'm just learning the travel trade. One day, I'm going into business, perhaps set up a little hotel around here. What's your ambition Jeff?'

'To be an archaeologist.' The word 'ambition' ranked as low as 'profit' in his personal philosophy of life.

'So you've no ambition then?'

He spread both hands, 'It's better than working.'

'You really are an old hippy at heart, not a care in the world.'

'And why not?' he asked. 'Someone has to be happy.'

She pointed to his calloused palms. 'Hippies never had to do hard labour.'

He rotated his hands to show the knuckles scarred and scabbed from wielding a trowel. Lisa took his hands

17

briefly to inspect the damage, playing at sympathy. The Nemea bottle clunked onto the table top.

'Try this,' she said, 'It will take away the pain.'

A London taxi almost took Flint's pain away for good and he skipped back onto the kerb. That night with Lisa had tainted his mind and warped his attitude to women for the intervening decade. He had put aside left-wing hypocrisy about sexual equality and women's rights and focussed on rampant sex, with tender sex as a back-up option. He had been so dedicated to the pursuit of wine, woman and song that his mind had closed to the darker motives of those around him. Who was Costas and what had his angle been? Somewhere in a box of momentoes lay that crushed and rotten pen. Somewhere back in time lay a mystery that was not going to go away.

Chapter Three

London Underground was liberally plastered with threats aimed at fare-dodgers and the busker's attempt at 'Annie's Song' was further off-key than usual. Given good weather, Flint would have walked. Instead he stood for half an hour on the platform, waiting for a 'passenger incident' at Waterloo to be resolved. The vision of a sticky corpse being wiped off a subway track was difficult to avoid.

Sticky corpses, yes. Flint the student had been gauche, inexperienced, naive, or any of the other insults the Dalek had fired in his direction. He had been keen to run at the first opportunity, save his own skin and try to forget the whole gruesome episode. If the death had occurred now, he could have handled it, he would have fought back and imposed a solution. Okay, there had been no witness, no motive, no suspect, and not even the certainty that the murder had been deliberate, but the past was always an imperfect puzzle and Flint had grown to find puzzles irresistible.

The smartly dressed West Indian woman who sat opposite was turning the pages of a Ruth Rendell whodunnit. A good plot had a beginning, a middle and an end. Flint was aware of having witnessed one confused chapter of a mystery, but he was ignorant of how it had begun, and knew it had never been resolved. Until that moment, he had always believed his involvement had been incidental, and he had been absent from the critical scenes. Coldness crept across his skin as he realised how much he had missed in his rush to be militant and get laid.

It had been the Monday after the weekend of unparalleled lust and the young Flint was both tired and elated. Two of the students had laid out survey squares in the lower valley, and five of the team then formed a line and walked methodically across the gridded area, slightly down-slope towards the sea, picking up artefacts which lay loose on the surface. Flint watched them from his exile on the hilltop, as a lightly overcast sky kept work cool.

Sebastian Embury was deep in thought, quiet and introspective. He walked along, holding his grey-black beard down as if to keep his eyes on the ground, but his mind was elsewhere. He had once nurtured the dream to be an Evans or a Schliemann, but at fifty-eight, he had encountered a beast called The New Economic Reality. Early retirement had saved his face at College, but the promise of funding for his field work in the Argolid had been a blatant bribe. Flint supposed that his own presence was a deep irritant, tearing wounds wider with his near-completed doctorate and his fresh, Marxist interpretations of the past.

Embury straighted up to stretch his back, a symbol

of an endangered lifestyle. His pipe, his ouzo, his young followers, and a token academic standing were all he had asked. Now, suddenly, he seemed to have acquired a purpose: irrational for someone who had arrived at the cul-de-sac of life. Frenetic phonecalls and hyperactive direction of site work would leave him breathless and distracted. The distant figure glanced upwards, as if wary of being watched. Flint felt deep pity for the old man, but knew the void between them was too great. One day, the generation of Old Imperialists would die away and the New Archaeologists would step into their shoes, no doubt with a further rank of itchy youngsters pressing their backs. Flint's mind returned to Lisa, and his body to the pretence of work.

Each day on the excavation ran into the next, with seams welded tight by the sun. In the mottled shade of the olive grove, Jeffrey Flint and Andy Ernshaw were talking nineteen-fifties Sci-Fi movies whilst the latter dabbed at the lens of the dumpy level with a damp tissue.

'"Invaders From Mars," now that was right bad.' Andy's Geordie accent had not yet been overridden by his education. Once an engineering student, he had dropped out and drifted into archaeology. He had already cultivated overwhelmingly bushy hair and a contiguous black beard, and one day, he threatened, he was going back to college to study the subject seriously.

'Did you ever see "Santa Claus Defeats the Martians"?' Flint asked idly.

'No, is it worth a miss?'

'Definitely.'

Andy finished wiping the lens and stood the battered orange instrument back on its tripod. He stopped and grunted a warning. Flint saw the Dalek striding through the trees towards them.

'How goes the battle?' Embury called.

He seemed cheerful, even friendly, so Flint was instantly wary. Embury came up close and glanced at the plan in Flint's hand. 'Are we finished?'

'No, it will take another day,' Flint said cautiously.

'So, what have we found?'

'Zero.'

The Dalek scoffed, so Flint began mechanically to list his non-discoveries. 'The road embankment at the top messes up the readings so there's no joy in that direction. Over towards the gully, there's just made ground and modern junk. Elsewhere, too many trees and old root-holes to gain any sort of sensible results.'

'We're very close,' Embury said, shaking his head.

'To what?'

'Yesterday you thought you detected walls lower down the hill.'

'Yes, but it won't be anything exciting.'

The Dalek clicked his fingers. 'Excavate, we'll excavate tomorrow.'

'Excavate?' Flint felt his hackles rise and his hopes fall. 'Sebastian, we can't...'

His protest was ignored, Embury was already strolling away from him, sweeping his hands. 'Yes, just here I think, over your wall line. A two metre trench should be just about right.'

'A six foot hole would be just about right,' Flint muttered to Andy. The bearded radical was taking over from the silent pacifist. Andy smirked.

'Yes, that should verify our findings,' Embury continued to act like the native of another planet.

'What findings?' Flint protested, 'There's nothing here Sebastian; just trees and rocks and ants and rabbit holes.'

'Pardon? You're questioning me again.' The friendly tone was suddenly replaced by hostility.

'We're wasting our time up here. There's acres still to survey down there...'

'Look Flint, this is my excavation.' The Dalek snapped, pointing a spiteful finger. 'I don't like other people interfering and telling me where to dig.'

'You have this whole new plan to survey the valley bottom.'

'I need you here,' Embury snapped, then spelled out detailed, patronising, instructions for a new sondage, which was greeted by insolent silence.

Flint watched the Dalek march away, ears burning, trying to recall a few words of songs preaching love, peace and non-violence. Andy stuck out both hands, robot-like, and began to march stiffly around squawking 'Excavate! Excavate!'

The joke had ceased to be funny. Flint's ego had once persuaded him that Embury exiled him for daring to be radical. As the tube train rocked its way towards Goodge Street, an idea slowly forced its way through the dust of ages.

'The silly old duffer.'

Dark eyes left Ruth Rendell and met with his.

'It explains the murder,' Flint said to the West Indian woman.

'Don't tell me how it ends!' she implored angrily.

Flint shook his head with an excess of nonchalance. 'Different plot. Embury was onto something and wanted to make damn sure I had nothing to do with it.'

Chapter Four

Of course, Emma Woodfine was at the reception. A degree in Classics, an MA in Greek archaeology and twenty years playing second fiddle to a variety of menopausal male academics bought her a place at all such gatherings. Turning slightly grey now, she was dressed smartly in charcoal grey waistcoat over floral blouse and blue skirt. He'd heard she had married that fool Hubert Yarm; they deserved each other. Emma had her back turned, yet Flint could hear her shrill voice across the room, using the word 'naturally' far too often. He noticed she'd given up smoking and drank only mineral water. Hubert Yarm had always been a desperate prig.

'It's Doctor Flint, is it not?' asked a voice from behind his shoulder. 'Didn't you once know.?'

Of course he did, and everyone in the room knew he did.

His mind sought a familiar retreat. Green-framed plate glass windows ran all along the side of Taverna Mikos and gave ample views out into the street, and off down towards the Roman town, although the first thirty yards of slope were chiefly strewn with builder's rubble, Evian bottles and oil cans.

Mikos furnished the room sparsely. One long counter followed the internal wall, facing an airy space, across which a mere six square tables were scattered. The team of English excavators had pushed three together by the far windows and were sipping beer, awaiting the day's gastronomic delight.

Sebastian Embury sat in his chair, pipe in hand, passing around some of the dullest sherds of pottery imaginable for discussion or delight. Emma Woodfine sat by his left elbow, fascinated by every word the would-be great man had to say. The pair shared a man-and-wife resemblance. On him, black hair mixed equally with grey on both head and chin, and merged with the thick rims of his glasses, masking the subtlety of his expressions. She was slight and plain beyond description, large tortoiseshell glasses straddling the unfortunate nose and matching her hair of indeterminate brown. Action and reaction matched perfectly; Emma tried so hard to be indispensable.

Anthropological observations ceased at the sound of a car drawing up. Lisa was coming. Lisa would lift the evening above pottery typologies and anecdotes about Sir Arthur Evans. The courier strode in, scarlet uniform drawing all eyes her way. Flint was on his feet to meet her, conduct introductions and find a chair. Mikos came over and made a show of hospitality.

'I shall cook you my special moussaka,' he said with a flourish, then retreated towards the kitchen.

'Moussaka. Just for a change,' Andy observed.

'What's special about it?' asked Lisa.

'Dunno.' Flint said, 'Perhaps he's going to warm it up.'

From the corner of his eye, Flint saw the Dalek fidget and tap his pipe, clearly displeased. He seemed in worse humour than usual and most of the group were trying to ignore him. Emma muttered darkly, just loud enough for Flint to hear.

'That woman will be moving in soon.'

Flint closed his hand around a piece of cutlery, then released it slowly. How dare they? Lisa caught his eye. She had a vivacious mischief in her smile.

'You'll curdle the milk,' she said.

'Drinks,' Flint responded. He stood up and clapped his hands, 'Drinks!'

Quivering wads of lukewarm moussaka came and went, with a portion to spare. The five youths clustered around Lisa, trying to impress and amuse. Emma and the Dalek were quickly excluded from the circle and moved away to play cards at a side table. Cheap and aggressive wine, plus fizzy beer, were brought to the table. Mikos sensed the mood, and dropped his one Bob Dylan LP onto the functional gramophone.

Six Greek men by the far wall shook their heads silently.

Flint hummed along, content. Life just carried on getting better. The Dalek might have a hidden agenda, but this was his own payoff for the sweaty toil of archaeological fieldwork. It was his heavenly reward for turning the other cheek and absorbing all those insults.

'Mister Embury!' Mikos called from the door. 'Some persons to see you.'

The director rose and carried his trail of pipe smoke towards the taverna owner. He went outside, and was gone for ten minutes. Socially isolated, Emma drifted back, making token forays into the party. Lisa was retelling tourist stories, each improving with telling, as did caricatures of her clients' mannerisms.

Emma cut across the conversation, 'He's not going to put that record on again is he?'

Three times through, 'Gawd on mah side' was enough even for the would-be hippies in the bar. Lisa agreed with the complaint.

'I'll go talk to Mikos.' Flint rose reluctantly and padded to the bar. Mikos was whistling and wiping out a glass.

'Another drink Jeff?'

'No, Mikos, another record. I love Dylan, for me you can play it forever, but there are barbarians who refuse to be converted. Be a mate, find something different.'

A car door slammed somewhere outside. Sebastian Embury strode back into the bar in a deep, black mood. He placed both his hands on the bar, without looking directly at Flint. 'Are you going to pay for that girl's meal?' he rasped.

Flint was wrong-footed and was still thinking of a reply when the director attacked again.

'Are you listening to me Flint?'

'Pay who?'

'This food is funded by the project.'

Fumbling around the objection, the youngster blurted,

'But does it matter? Who cares?' He turned to Mikos, 'how much?'

'Eh? What for?'

'Six cubic inches of moussaka, three chunks of feta and half a slice of stale bread. Lisa has dined royally at our expense.'

'Is paid for' Mikos confirmed, he too was confused.

'Insolence!' Embury breathed, 'You insolent . . .'

Dispute dissolved into chaotic acrimony. Embury was all beard and invective. Flint refused to be cowed with Lisa at stake, meeting ire with ire, enjoying the chance to let rip. When he next glanced towards Lisa, she was pulling herself around the chair back and shouldering her handbag.

'It's okay, I'll move in another day,' she pushed between Flint and his oppressor, 'One can tell when one's not wanted.'

Flint reached out a hand to stop her, then withdrew it.

'See you, Jeff,' she winked at him.

He followed her out of the bar, but she would say nothing else. Lisa climbed into her car with just a twitch of her chin. The single tail-light receded into the night, then was extinguished. Flint returned inside, ready to resume the fight, but The Dalek was taking Emma upstairs, deep in conspiratorial discussion.

'Mikos!'

'Jeff?'

'Another beer. And stick the Dylan back on.'

*   *   *

29

The Dalek was away for most of Tuesday, finding a pressing need to see some crony at Epidauros which conveniently kept him away from real work. He brought the minibus back to Palaeokastro before supper, speaking to no-one, except to grudgingly surrender the keys to Flint. Within minutes, Flint had gathered the other four male students and was urging life into the minibus, christened 'the shuttlecraft'; a Ford Transit conversion, painted yellow with the College Logo on its door. It had already seen 90,000 miles of travel on excavations, field trips and beer runs. The left and right wings were different hues of mustard, whilst the bodywork was pitted by stones and splattered by the corpses of flies.

Flint negotiated the potholed road down to the highway and into Nauplion, where the cinema was within a converted mosque. It often showed dated English language releases with Greek sub-titles and that week it was 'Clockwork Orange': as scratched and noisy as the minibus. The expedition soothed Flint's nerves and served to compensate for weeks of cinematic deprivation; his exposure to London's glut of cinemas had spoiled him. Kubrick had withdrawn the film from British Cinemas, so Flint settled down for a treat in an island of empty seats. Trying not to read the sub-titles, he allowed his mind to wander. How had they translated 'malenky bit of cutter' into Greek? What picture of England did the film transmit to the local audience? What did the locals think of 'Zorba the Greek' or 'Guns of Navarone'? How long would it be before one of the digging team stabbed The Dalek to death with a trowel?

*　　*　　*

Breakfast normally consisted of bread and coffee, sometimes with a little cheese, sometimes with yoghurt and honey when Mikos was feeling sweet. Little was eaten next morning, everyone was outside the taverna by seven, standing around an empty patch of ground.

Flint and The Dalek argued over keys, handbrakes, security and amnesia. No-one could remember hearing the minibus driven away, no-one could confirm that Flint had indeed locked all the doors and put the brick under the back wheel.

The Dalek might have been a shade of purple behind the glasses, the facial hair and the squashy hat, 'You see, it was easy for them. You left the door unlocked. The thief just had to climb in and let off the handbrake, then roll it to here . . .'

Flint watched the director pace to the roadside, '. . .and he could freewheel for half a mile before starting the engine.'

He should have been a detective, thought Flint, maintaining a neutral expression. But then, all archaeologists were detectives, of a sort.

'It is your fault, of course . . .'

Fault lay with Flint, of course, further argument was futile. He adopted a penitent pose and half-listened to the rebukes. If it were not for the unnecessary jaunt, the minibus would still be rusting quietly behind the taverna. Instead, some colour-blind hooligan with no sense of value had saddled himself with innumerable garage bills and the digging team had been marooned. Breakfast was cancelled.

Flint was sent back to the olive grove with a list of

trivial tasks to perform, whilst The Dalek waited for the police, muttering about hiring a car. For once Flint suffered a crisis of confidence. Was he to blame? Had he been too sure in himself, too arrogant? The young archaeologist's morale began to tip towards the abyss. One bus per day made the round trip to Nauplion, and there was no link to the beaches further south. His future held the prospect of dust and more dust. It seemed a long way to the top of the hill.

Down on site, the four-letter word count was high that afternoon. When the director returned from talking with the police, he embarked on a campaign of systematically needling his workers one by one. From the edge of the olive grove, Flint could see the green blob strutting round the site, bawling at unfortunate students. The arm waved, the voice grated derision, random words of reprimand drifted on the still air. It was possible to approximate the moment at which he and Andy would take a turn as victims of approbation.

Flint braced himself, laying down his trowel to avoid temptation. Embury was approaching. 'Klingons on the starboard bow,' he quipped.

'Deflector shields on maximum, Mr Sulu,' Andy responded.

'So? What have we here?' Embury seemed to be panting from the exertion of climbing the hill, but otherwise, was quite calm and irritatingly chummy.

'It's a wall,' Flint pointed to the short stretch of crude stonework they had uncovered, 'See the cunning way one stone has been heaped on another, with all the precision of finest classical craftsmanship. The construction cut is tantalisingly sterile, matchless in its poverty.'

The director nodded, deep in thought, not seeming to hear the sarcasm. Flint gently suggested the hole be filled in and that he should return to the site. The director shook his head slowly. 'Another trench I think, ten metres to the north, following this wall.'

Flint remembered the excavation as a blur of useless toil. Holes were dug, and filled. Grubby finds cleaned and marked. Embury seemed to have had means, but no ends. It had been Wednesday, in a week with six Wednesdays and an infinitely distant Friday and Lisa as his only link to sanity. If he had not been so hooked on Lisa he might have seen what was coming.

The crowd of grey suits parted and the mature Emma Woodfine looked his way. Her lips set thinner than usual, she involuntarily straightened her glasses and slowly sauntered towards him.

Chapter Five

'Jeffery Flint,' Emma said, with her expression totally neutral.

'Hello Emma, how's tricks?'

She threatened to smile. 'My sister was talking about you only last week. It's her museum now, in Kingshaven. What's left of it.'

Typical Emma, straight for the kill. Flint tried not to recall old animosities. 'I was thinking about you too, Emma.'

'How sweet.'

'You never forgave me did you?'

'You never even tried to tell me what happened,' she retorted.

The party was already thinning out. 'Ready now?'

Emma looked around for her husband. 'Hubert wants to leave soon.'

'Pack him off to bed, and I'll get you a taxi later. Give me twenty minutes and we'll lay all the ghosts. You can't hate me forever.'

'Watch me.'

Flint had avoided alcohol that Wednesday evening.

His stomach rebelled against something greasy which had swum around in the bottom of Mikos' frying-pan and he was wishing he had stayed vegetarian. Emma emerged from the stairwell, with her hair combed back and swathed in a scarf. She was wearing a severely plain blue dress, and made a show of departing for dinner with Doctor Dracopoulos, the site guardian, whose name she repeatedly dropped to impress.

Flint had been lounging against the bar, drinking soda water and showing Mikos the pen which had caused all the excitement in the Nauplion taverna. Mikos said the local grapevine had already been chattering with stories of gold and old bones at Palaeokastro. It was a pitilessly small world, thought Flint.

As Emma was about to leave, the Dalek came into the taverna and she moved towards him. 'Oh Sebastian, there's still time, do come.'

'It's business,' he dismissed her plea and walked towards the bar.

'Business, ha, ha,' Emma tightened her grip on her handbag and ran for the door.

The Dalek gave one glance towards his rebellious assistant, then addressed another. 'Don't drink too much, Flint. I've hired a car: I want you to drive me into Nauplion tonight.'

'Tonight?'

'Important business. I need a driver, you know how the Greeks do business.'

A table crowded with empty bottles and choked ash trays came to mind. Flint simply nodded reluctantly.

Embury indicated the pen at the centre of discussion. 'What's that?'

Flint was saying, 'Nothing,' as Mikos handed over the pen, immediately retelling the story of its discovery.

'Nothing? This is your idea of nothing?' Embury held the pen in his quivering hand, gripping it by its crushed tip, 'You never told me about this.'

'I must have.'

'No, my memory is excellent, you never told me about this!'

'It came from down by the gully, in the olive grove, in with all that modern rubbish you had me search through.'

'You should have reported and classified it with every other find.'

'And a couple of wine bottles, half a dozen spent hunters' cartridge cases, sheep bones, an old boot, a brass button . . .'

'All right all right, but this is different!'

'Because its gold?'

'Well no,' The Dalek blathered, his breath stinking like a disaster in an ouzo factory. All the team knew a bottle lay concealed in the site hut.

'So, the pen is irrelevant.' Flint plucked it from the other's grasp and dropped it into his own top pocket. 'Just junk.'

The Dalek stepped back and levelled a wavering finger. He was certainly in no state to drive. 'You're insubordinate, you know? You're no good Flint, you're useless on my team. Why don't you go home?'

'Before or after I drive you to Nauplion?' Flint played

it cool. He was the only other person with a valid driving permit. It gave him a last lever of power; it offered an opportunity to escape into town and gatecrash Lisa's usual Wednesday Greek Cultural Evening.

'Half past eight: don't wander off.' Embury snapped out of the conflict, and went towards the stairs without another word.

The Dalek had hired a red Ford Fiesta, whose nearside bore a long white scar. He explained that it would serve as emergency transport, until the minibus was brought back. Flint thought this optimistic, but signed the papers and allowed the men from the hire firm to drive away. He sat in the driver's seat and fiddled with the gearstick before starting the engine.

'Right side of the road,' he reminded himself aloud.

'What?' The Dalek climbed in beside him.

'Nothing.' Flint hated driving. He crunched the gearbox and drove away into the night.

Not a word was exchanged on the ten minute drive to town. The sky was a deep, dark blue by the time they rounded the black mass of the Palamidi rock, with its Venetian fortifications crenellating the skyline.

'Past the station, through the new town,' The Dalek said mechanically, as if following a script.

Flint did as ordered, passing the station, passing through and beyond the modern suburbs. As the houses faded into the night, they were replaced by industrial buildings and anonymous sheds.

'Slow down.'

A building site beside the railway track stood at the very northern limit of town.

'Stop by that cement mixer.'

Flint pulled off the road onto a rough rubble kerb where the yellow cement mixer stood. 'Picturesque,' he commented.

'This could take some time.' The Dalek said, climbing out.

'Who are we meeting?'

'I'm the one doing the meeting. You wait here.'

'How long for?'

'An hour, perhaps longer. You won't go anywhere, will you?' The Dalek leaned across and whipped the keys from their hole. With a thin chuckle, he pulled himself out of the car.

Flint was angry, 'Where are you going?' he shouted after the retreating figure. The Dalek offered no answer.

'Bastard.'

Boredom came in seconds, as did rebellion. Flint needed ten stiff beers, or a pair of warm arms, or both, to rectify his mood. He would seek Lisa out, have a talk and deploy his best chat-up lines. If successful, The Dalek could drive himself home and damn the consequences. If he failed, nothing was lost.

Ten minutes' brisk walk would bring him to the heart of Nauplion. The first stars were advancing on the heavens as he jogged around the football ground and took a short cut along Boubolinas to the seafront. Entrancing lights drew him on, whilst the road still radiated the day's heat. Squadrons of bugs besieged each puny orange streetlamp as he reached the lit area. Sea air and the scent of warm, dusky vegetation lifted his spirits. He need never go back, damn the Dalek and his mysteries.

Well within his ten minutes, Flint stopped to gather breath outside the ugly slab-concrete hotel where synthetic Greek Culture was being paraded for the tourists. The reception desk was unmanned so the archaeologist easily gained access to the enclosed courtyard behind.

Below a perfect night sky, a troupe of sad-eyed young people in national dress flogged their routine to the rhythm of an expertly played bouzouki. Lisa was in the process of rousing a table of eight to join in the dancing. Flint stood back and watched her work. After a minute, he caught her eye and she broke away from her people.

'Jeff, what are you doing here?'

'Couldn't keep away. Thought I'd just pop in and see you.'

'Well, I'm afraid fifty people have paid good money to have my attention tonight. I'll be up to here with fun and merriment 'til midnight.'

'Afterwards?'

'Afterwards is bedtime. It's jolly old Olympia tomorrow; it's a hell of a way and I'm on duty from seven. I need my energy, sorry. Stay around if you like, but I have to work.'

Her next 'Sorry' was surgical, not apologetic. Lisa turned her back on him and returned to her job. Perhaps he had been naive, certainly he had overestimated his own charm. The gamble had been in vain and he would have another row with the Dalek to no profit. Totally dejected, Flint walked down to Atki Mouri and looked out at the castle of Bourdzi, seemingly moored in the harbour and bobbing like a tug-boat below the moon. The sea lapped gently around fishing and pleasure boats whilst music drifted from half a dozen sources. What should have been an idyll was turning into hell. At that moment, he decided to desert. Damn the Dalek, damn Palaeokastro, damn Lisa. He was going home for the cricket and the rain.

A deliberately slow journey brought him back to the car, kicking at loose road chippings and swatting at flies to defuse his anger. The car was intact where it had been left unlocked. Only as he moved to open his door did Flint see that his passenger was already there, slumped against the other door. The Dalek had soaked up a skinful of ouzo with whoever he'd had to visit so urgently. The grubby construction site had probably been an unsubtle diversion to hide his real destination. Flint smiled to himself, imagining a furtive meeting with a woman, possibly the bored wife of one of his many acquaintances; it would explain why Emma was so miffed.

As Flint slipped inside, ouzo fumes flooded out. He congratulated himself on the accuracy of one prediction. At least, he might be spared an argument.

'Evening.' Flint took his seat, speaking quietly.

Nothing.

'Could I have the keys?'

Nothing.

'Come on, wakey wakey!'

The silence was deeper than he liked.

'Dalek, time to go back to the concentration camp.'

Nothing. Flint enjoyed a brief fantasy, in which the drunk was abandoned in a gutter whilst he drove off.

'Hello, can I have the keys, piss-head?'

The silence was so deep, not even disturbed by the other's breath.

'Oops.' Flint jabbed the horn, 'Sorry, did I wake you?'

He didn't, and suddenly Flint became aware of the overwhelming silence which followed the horn blast. He snapped on the map light. Sebastian Embury was still slumped against the door. His head was a mass of blood. Blood had dribbled from his mouth and splashed down the front of his check shirt. Flint's brain went numb, his own breathing seeming to stop. On reflex, he opened the car door and got out. Coming to his senses, he hastily got back in and felt for a pulse. Sebastian Embury was warm, but quite clearly dead.

Chapter Six

'I read all that in the newspapers,' Emma said as they waited for a taxi to pass the corner of the tree-lined square. 'I never believed it.'

'Believe it,' Flint replied. 'The police did – after a little persuasion.'

Emma said little more until they were seated in the taxi. For Flint, the conversation had brought back a nightmare of blood drying on his shirt. He had been convinced he would wake, but waking had not been an option.

'I don't suppose you know any basic first aid?' Emma stated.

'Emma, I tried,' the memory of mouth-to-mouth contact with bristles, blood, pipe-smoke and ouzo was not one to be savoured.

'I tried to flag down a car. Then I drove on the wrong side of the road through the suburbs.'

'Pronoia.'

'Yeah, I guess, but my Greek was pretty ropey. I couldn't read the signs and I didn't know whether Nauplion even had a hospital.'

'God that's feeble, try looking at a map.'

'I stopped to ask, but the only person who I could talk to was a German tourist. He was as confused as me.' Confusion overwhelmed his memory of that night.

A trio of national servicemen beside the car called out towards him. More people were approaching now, shouting questions across to the soldiers. Meanwhile, Jeffrey Flint stood on the kerb, no longer hearing German directions to a probable hospital. When the policemen came from behind, they pointed at his blood-stained clothing and asked unintelligible questions. It was the beginning of a pattern.

Flint had seen so many prison movies, so many grey detective films, so many blood-and-sweat features set in third-world jails, yet his first ten hours at Nauplion police station were a nightmare he could never have prepared for. Phrase books do not contain phrases such as 'When did you find the body' or 'I am innocent'. An officer from the Tourist Police spoke passable English and was drafted in to take his statement, but he was never sure whether what he said was understood, or whether what was written matched what he said.

'We found you a lawyer,' Emma stated in the dark of the London taxi.

'Thanks, that man kept me sane, he must have cost you a fortune. I couldn't even have afforded his taxi fares.'

'He did it for free.'

'Honest?'

'I don't lie, Jeffrey.'

'Lisa said he was the most expensive lawyer in Nauplion.'

'Lisa, oh, yes, Lisa.' Emma was so unsubtle once she extended her cat's claws.

'Emma, I'm curious. Why should whatshisname . . . Bokkis . . . work for free?'

'His name was Vassilis Boukaris, he was a good friend of Doctor Dracolopoulos . . .'

With whom Embury should have dined on the night of his murder – Archaeology in Greece was as incestuous as it was in Britain. Still, Flint mused, if Doctor D. were a long-standing friend of Embury, why should he pull strings to help someone accused of Embury's murder? Something very philosophical and uniquely Greek probably lay behind his motives. Flint needed to understand what had happened, and if he was going to gain Emma's trust he would have to tell her the whole story.

Mr Boukaris had been allowed inside the cell some time before noon and introduced himself in embarassingly correct English. Short, spreading, fifty-ish and neatly presented, he explained the situation carefully and correctly. Whilst he spoke, the lawyer would subconsciously touch the fringe of his thick mat of black hair, possibly checking for the first sign of balding.

Flint had never held policemen in high regard, and that day his opinion reached its nadir. Hungry and still in a state of shock, he was taken to another bare, nicotine-yellow room. Memories of Amnesty International reports on human rights under The Greek Colonels came to mind and depressed him further.

45

At the far side of the square table sat an officer whose face had been scarred by smallpox and whose sense of humour had vanished with his looks. His name was unpronounceable, even if Flint could have remembered it. A youth whose uniform seemed too large sat by his side, threatening Flint with a box of cigarettes.

'Smoke?'

'No.'

The other three did, continually, adding to Flint's discomfort. The two officers ran through his statement, with Boukaris translating and insisting that Flint write an English version as the interview proceeded. After two hours, the prisoner was taken back to his cell and offered a sliced tomato drowned in engine oil, plus bits of a chicken that had died of malnutrition.

At intervals, he was called back as the officers asked for clarification, verification and explanation. His clinical mind was still muddled, his memory was far from its photographic norm and Flint tried desperately not to contradict himself. The policeman with the scarred face was very agressive and reluctant to speak English. He would jab his finger and ask rapid, intimidating questions. The placid, smooth-talking Boukaris dissipated the impact of the vicious jabs, turning them into polite enquiries to be answered after consideration. Flint began to rely on that man to keep him from bursting under the strain.

'Miss Woodfine said you and the late professor argued frequently.' Boukaris translated the latest incisive question.

'We disagreed.'

The customary two-way translation followed, with a pause as Boukaris converted the barb into English. 'What did you argue about?'

'I don't know, it's hard to explain. We had professional disagreements about planning and surveying . . . you know.'

No, they did not know. He began to list areas of disagreement, one by one, deliberately keeping them technical, introducing jargon whenever possible to sound convincing. The one he nicknamed Scarface soon became irritated and returned to the attack.

'He would like to know what you argued about on the night of the incident.'

'Finds recording . . . I had omitted to tell him about a find.'

Each question and answer was punctuated by a hurried translation, some nodding and hand waving. Scarface glared directly at Flint, hitting the table top with his finger as he spoke in machine-gun Greek.

'Was this a valuable object you argued over?' asked Boukaris.

'No, it was a piece of junk, a crushed pen, worth a thousand drachmae or so.'

'You have this?'

'It's at Taverna Mikos.'

Scarface expressed dissatisfaction and continued to probe actions and motives. He asked why Flint had been to see Lisa, but showed no interest in the reply, confirming that she had corroborated the alibi. Alibi, the word, floated around in Flint's jaded mind. Only the accused have alibis.

'Why did Mr Embury want to go to that strange place?'

'He had a meeting.'

'They would like to know who he was meeting.'

'I don't know, he never told me anything.'

The two-way translations were making Flint dizzy, he had lost the sense of which question was being answered.

'Why did he leave you in the car?'

'I don't know.'

Scarface would interrupt Boukaris, Boukaris would break into rapid procedural dialogue, Flint would ask questions of his own and be ignored by all.

'Why did you walk away?'

'I was angry, no, I was bored.'

'Angry?' Scarface knew that word.

'I was bored, fed up at being left alone.'

Alone, yes, but never so alone as now.

'Why did you go to see the woman, Lisa Morgan?'

'I wanted to sleep with her. Happy? Will he believe that?'

Dirty chuckles, yes, that one got through.

'Why did you not take the injured man to the doctors?'

'I didn't know where the doctor was.'

Scarface grunted disbelief at this answer. He started to explain, slowly, and in great detail, directions to the medical facilities of Nauplion. As if every idiot should know. Question followed answer, lines of enquiry were built and demolished. Nauseous with the process, Flint began to speak mechanically, trying hard to keep his story logical, which was so hard, when little of it carried any logic.

By evening, the pace of interrogation slackened and Flint was allowed to have time alone with Boukaris.

'The police would like to have you as their suspect,' the lawyer said.

Flint was slumped back on his bench-bed, drenched with sweat and crippled by fatigue.

'There is much that points that way. You and Mr Embury argue. You go for this mysterious meeting, but you say you do not know who you were to meet. You drive a car with his dead body around the streets of Nauplion. Your clothes have blood stains . . .'

The suspect groaned, 'A few spots, I tried first-aid! If I had beaten the poor old bastard to death I'd be covered in blood. They had no right to take my clothes away.'

'Oh but yes they do. And what of your hands, Mr Flint?'

Boukaris pointed his pen at the scratched and scabbed knuckles. 'The Captain thinks you have been in a fight.'

'No, I've been trowelling. Look at any of my mates' hands and you'll find the same thing. All these cuts would have been ripped open if I'd even hit the Dalek once.'

'Who?'

'Mister Embury.'

Boukaris pointed his pen at his client. 'A very good point in your defence.' He made a note in his pad.

'What now?'

'The police will look for more evidence, all they have is,' he hummed for a word, 'circumstantial. The Prosecutor is very strict and what the police have is not sufficient to establish a *prima facie* case against you. I will ask for you to be released.'

'Can I go home?' A vision of green fields and village pubs swam before his eyes. 'Home to England?'

Boukaris fixed Flint with his deep set, almost black, eyes. 'In a few days. Trust me.'

'And I trusted him, and Boukaris was as good as his word. Damn good value for free,' Flint said.

The taxi drew up outside the semi-detached Victorian villa in Acton. Flint's pocket felt the impact of the fare. He supposed he owed Emma something, after all these years.

Death had come riding a heart attack the night Sebastian Embury died. The crime may have begun as a beating, or mugging, but it had ended as murder. Only one suspect had ever been named, but once Flint had been released, the case fell as dead as the archaeologist.

'We should have stayed, you know?' Flint said as Emma fumbled for her door keys. 'But the moment I held that passport in my hand, I gave it a great big kiss and scuttled for home.'

Emma was still reluctant to talk about it, not even it seemed, as therapy. She had always worked the system, had always been a string-puller and found joy in standing in the shadows of would-be great men. It was curious that she had never caused a fuss, never called in famous names in academia and law to delve deeply into Embury's death and demand answers from the Greek police.

He was half inside her hallway, dominated by a Grandmother Clock with the appropriate legend 'tempus fugit': time flies.

'I keep thinking that what I should have done was hang around and ask a few questions of my own.'

'I can't see what good that would have been.' Emma was about to close the door on him.

'Invite me in for coffee and I'll tell you.'

Chapter Seven

Emma had decorated Hubert Yarm's house in high Victorian style. Flint hated being impressed by interior decor, but the mahogany fireplace and matching overmantel had him emitting coos of admiration.

'Hubert's probably asleep,' Emma sang, 'but please remember I'm not a giggly undergraduate girl you can add to your score card.'

Flint cringed at the thought. 'Emma, hostility doesn't help.'

'Hostile? Why should I be hostile?' She became shrill.

He found himself a seat on the red, buttoned leather sofa. 'I know you adored him, we all knew, it was no secret and no sin.'

Tears filled her tiny, round eyes and Flint began to regret the suspicious impulse which had drawn him inside. 'Cast your mind back to the night of the murder. It was a murder, we agree on that?'

She gave a nonchalant downward twitch of her lips and sat in the Chesterfield opposite him.

'Okay, it was Wednesday night. You had a barney with Sebastian, just before you went out – we all witnessed it.'

Emma sensed his drift instantly. 'I was at the Dracopoulos', having dinner.'

'And why didn't Sebastian go too?'

She stiffened again. 'Sebastian had to see someone – I don't know who. He'd been very busy and he wasn't well. It didn't help when people kept winding him up.'

Flint's pulse began to rise, he was learning something, and detection always gave him a thrill. 'Have you any idea what his secret meeting was about?'

'Perhaps it might have been the minibus. Sebastian told me it had been found.'

By the time Flint had been released by the police, the mustard-hued 'shuttlecraft' had been back beside the taverna, apparently intact. Arrangements had been made for Andy to drive it back to England a week or so after Flint had flown home. Perhaps Embury had been asked to pay a price at the dark edge of town. A small ransom for a paltry prize, an argument and a scuffle with teenage car thieves leading to his downfall. The mystery could be that trivial.

'And what time did you get back?'

'How can I remember that? Midnight – why does it matter? You were always obsessed with trivia – that's why you never realised how great Sebastian was,' Emma said quietly.

Now she was starting on the panegyrics.

'He was almost there, after all these years, he was almost there.'

'Almost where?' Flint regarded the Paleaokastro survey as a kind of academic mystery tour lacking a planned destination.

'You never believed in him did you? All you did was argue and insist things were done your way. You never had the patience to understand his methods and his purpose.'

So much was true, Flint would admit. 'What was his purpose?'

'All he needed was another year, but everyone let him down.'

'Other people interfering', was the way Embury had put it, that day he tore a strip off Flint in the olive grove. Blaming others for one's failures was the mark of second-rate talent.

'Listen, Emma, I didn't kill Sebastian. I couldn't have, I was with Lisa.' The truth was stretched just a little. 'Honest, I did not kill Sebastian and you knew it or you wouldn't have arranged that lawyer.'

'Doctor Dracopoulos arranged him; I would have seen you hang.'

'Lovely.'

'You got away with it Flint, so why not just let Sebastian rest in peace? Why do you suddenly care what happened?'

'The time is right.'

'You hate Greece,' Vikki said, combing her hair into its short, stiff, upright style.

Flint lounged on the bed of her Docklands flat, all grey decor and black furnishings, a hundred years apart from Emma's Victoriana. 'I do not hate Greece.'

'You'll never take me.'

'I've never wanted to go back, until now. You

can come.'

'Lay off, I'm in Brussels three days a week.'

'Jules is going to be bone man on a dig near Marathon in August. I might just tag along.'

'Jules is a drunk. If you and him are off drinking Athens dry, who is going to excavate your precious villa?'

'Tyrone. He's been begging me to let him have a go at directing a site, now he has the chance.'

'He'll sell off your pottery, or charge people to look down the hole.'

'Doubtless he will, but that's the way archaeology is going, sweetheart.'

'Talking of sweethearts, what does this Emma look like?'

'A Gorgon.'

'And Lisa?'

Flint paused. Vikki stopped combing and threatened him with a glance.

'Open relationship?' he ventured.

'Open your skull,' she made a chopping motion with her comb.

'Can I scrounge your car?' He dodged around the subject.

'Where to?'

'Deepest Essex.'

A close, if erratic, relationship with Vikki had changed Flint. His beard was closely trimmed, his hair scarcely reached the collar and his clothes sense had improved one notch: shirt by Marks & Spencer, jeans by Levi, tweed jacket via Oxfam, shoes from Mr Gupta's hand-cart at Islington market.

He hated driving, but reaching The Rodings was impossible by any other means. All the way his mind tried to make sense of events that seemed far more distant than the third century, with which he was intimately familiar. Embury had not been the victim of a casual mugging as nothing had been stolen. The culprit must therefore have planned to meet Embury, possibly intending to beat him senseless even if not intending to kill him. Flint had seen enough thrillers to remember the old cliché that most murderers are known by their victims, so odds on Embury knew his killer.

Adam Sirutis had been a fine arts undergraduate when he had worked on the Paleokastro field survey, subsequently 'retiring' at twenty-six when his father made him the beneficiary of a sizeable Trust. Flint parked Vikki's new Rover in the gravel driveway of a chocolate-box thatched cottage. Someone else, it seemed, had attained Middle-Class Nirvana. The 'Adam S' studio was above a converted dairy at the rear, entered by an external stair.

Putting motives into the heads of the digging team, Flint recalled the many threats against the director's life. Violent, perverse and inventive forms of termination had been devised as a means of releasing tension, but all the lads had been in the bar on the night of the murder. Or had they?

'Jeffrey Flint, my man, come in, how are you?'

Adam was a tall ex-public schoolboy, once fresh-faced and still plum-voiced. After each man had exchanged a one-minute resumé of their lost years, Adam waved a hand towards his workshop.

Flint picked up a watercolour of a Rodings cottage peeking through a screen of foxgloves.

'They sell well. Owners place commissions,' the artist said. 'It kills time, don't you think?'

An emptiness was audible behind his words. How does one retire at twenty-six? Flint asked about Palaeokastro. They recounted the high jinks, relived the space opera jokes and ended with the tragedy.

'We wouldn't have called him the Dalek if we'd known what would happen to him,' Adam said. 'Remember how Andy used to mimic his voice. Exterminate, exterminate!'

'Excavate, excavate!' Flint recalled the games.

'That was it – I could never do the voice.'

Now that forgotten incidents had been dragged to the fore, Flint began to explore the purpose of his visit. 'Have you any idea what Embury was up to?'

'Don't ask me, I was only a *helot*, he never stooped to tell us a thing.'

'I'm trying to sort things out in my own mind. If you can remember the week before he died, he suddenly seemed to turn manic. Did you notice that?'

Adam twiddled one of his paint brushes and shook his head. 'I hardly even remember what he looked like, but I suppose that week stuck in all our minds. I found him okay at first, but he used to abuse us more and more often towards the end.'

Yes, the crisis had been marked by escalating tensions. Flint mentally ticked off points on his list of ingredients for murder. 'I've been asking myself why Embury sent me and Andy up to the olive grove. There was nothing up there, it was a complete waste of our time and he knew it. I just wonder if he'd stumbled on something and wanted us out of the way.'

Adam shook his head slowly.

'Nothing? No structures, graves, inscriptions?'

'No. I'd remember that.'

Flint tried a different angle. 'I met Emma last week, remember Emma?'

'Darling, sweet-scented Emma with the delicate nose?'

'The same. She seems to be under the illusion Embury was on the verge of discovering New Troy when he died.'

The hair had been cropped around the neck, but allowed to grow a little higher on Adam's crown, producing an effect similar in shape and colour to a champagne cork. The cork head nodded. 'He was very excitable that last week. He pulled everyone down to the bottom of the site, you know, where the old mill was. We worked an extra hour each day and had to show him everything we found, but as I said, nothing came up.'

Flint felt a surge of excitement. 'No, he was stopped before he found it, but he must have been very close. What I can't figure out is why, if it were so important, he didn't bring Andy and myself down too. Dammit, we were the best surveyors he had!'

'I advanced that thought, but you can guess the response.'

'Rude?'

'Bloody rude.'

They talked around the past, distant and more recent. Adam's failed marriage, Flint's continuing struggle to buck the system. Half the archaeologist's mind still toyed with his proto-evidence, believing he had almost found a motive. Next he needed a suspect.

'On that last night, were all the lads at the taverna?'

'I guess,' Adam thought deeply. 'Yes, certain, I was teaching them bridge.'

'Any idea what time Emma got back from her outing?'

'We were imbibing Mikos' newt's pee until one, as per norm. She staggered in a lot later. Andy kept us awake with some sort of stupid movie quiz and we heard the car drop her off.'

Was the timing relevant? Flint's mind began to whirr as he continued to talk over the old times. He wished he knew where Andy was, but he had drifted out of contact some years before. Adam was left to his stock-broker dream-cottages, with the promise of a postcard from Nauplion. As Flint walked back to the car, his mind walked slowly over the site of Palaeokastro, seeing nothing and sensing nothing he had not noticed before. Doctor Dracopoulos had been the site guardian, the man charged with monitoring the progress of the excavation on behalf of the Greek Ministry of Culture. He'd always looked sickly, was he still alive? If so, Flint ought to speak to him, or at least thank him for engaging Mr Boukaris.

In Greek? A fatal flaw suddenly appeared in Flint's

line of enquiry. If he was to return to Nauplion, he would need a translator. His thoughts turned immediately, and irresistibly to Lisa.

Chapter Eight

The window frames of Taverna Mikos had been painted a deeper shade of Green. The taverna owner was fatter, had one less front tooth and his face folded into frown lines as the bearded Briton strode in, rucksack hooked on his arm.

'Jason?' Mikos said, a finger poised in the air.

'Jeff.'

His eyes widened, 'Yes. Of course, now I remember. Bob Dylan?'

'Do you still have that record?'

'Yes, yes. I have a new record player, you like to hear it?'

'Not now.'

Over a glass of 'Fix' beer, Flint unrolled seven years of his life across Mikos' counter. Mikos told him of his wife, his two sons and baby daughter, and of his new expresso machine.

'Oh, Sebastian, that was such a disaster . . .' Mikos shook his head, 'For three years he came here . . .'

'Have there been any more excavations since then?'

Mikos shook his head. Buried secrets would still be buried, the trip need not be futile.

For old time's sake, Flint took a room at the taverna. It was the one at the front, overlooking the street; the one Sebastian Embury had occupied whilst the students had spread their sleeping bags on the floor of the airless side room.

It was another perfectly bright August morning when he walked from the taverna, through the screen of plane trees and onto the site of the silent city. He forgot the murder and was immediately drawn back twenty centuries. Even the brainless sweat of digging the bone-hard ground was forgotten as he remembered Andy's constant use of Star Trek jargon, Adam's laconic wit and Phil's habit of singing Genesis songs one after another to stave off boredom. He looked around to the point where Lisa would step down from her coach, then down towards an abandoned mill at the bottom of the slope, where a stream bed lay as a ribbon of dried reeds. He gazed around at the acres of scattered stones and dried thorns. What had Embury been looking for?

His eyes came to rest on a distant olive grove, oddly different from the picture he carried in his mind. Flint found one of the overgrown Roman thoroughfares and followed it uphill to the edge of the trees.

One of his trenches had never been filled in. The spur of a stone wall was still visible in what remained of the hole, overgrown and three-quarters silted by erosion of its edges. All that effort and the excavation had never even been published; the archive still lay somewhere at the British School in Athens. Embury had followed the golden rule of eminent archaeologists: die before you become obliged to write up your work.

He walked on, to the gully at the far side of the olive grove. Here, his memory had been thoroughly trampled. A dozen olive trees had been uprooted, a concrete apron had been laid close to the point where the road crossed the gully and a breezeblock building had been partly erected. He walked onto the apron – possibly intended as a small car-park, and looked inside the building – possibly a petrol station or kiosk that had never seen fulfilment of its owner's dream. The dream had failed some years ago, Flint noted from the depth of litter within the structure and the weeds in its wall.

Later, he asked Mikos about the unfinished building.

'That was Korifi; they build hotels. They wanted to put a taverna there to steal my bread, so I complained to your friend, Mr Boukaris the lawyer: he stopped it.'

Flint remembered hearing of some odd Greek tax loophole surrounding incomplete developments, but he soon forgot breezeblocks and concrete; Mikos had secured a telephone number. Within the hour he was driving to the beach resort of Tolon.

Hotel Sun was on the main street, fifty yards back from the beach. It was a five storey concrete building of forty rooms, built in the charmless style common to innumerable resorts from Benidorm to Bodrum. In the shaded lobby, with its aquamarine mural, Lisa Canelopoulos, once Lisa Morgan, held his attention with her wholesome, nut-brown eyes.

'You took your time coming back,' she said.

'I've been busy.'

She invited him into her office. Courier red had been replaced by managerial grey. Her hair was shorter, her figure possibly even more attractive to followers of Rubens. Lisa took the corner of a right-angled black couch and Flint sat opposite.

'You haven't changed at all – except for the "Doctor" bit.' Lisa reached for a packet of Marlboro's on the table.

'You didn't used to smoke,' he said.

'Still the same idealist out to change the world? You're going to tell me how I'm going to get cancer . . .'

'No, I'm going to tell you about capitalist multinationals and the crimes committed by tobacco companies in the third world.'

Lisa stopped mid-motion. 'I'm convinced. I'll quit, just for you. I don't want to be accused of murdering black babies.'

For a moment, former lovers stared at each other, then Lisa swept the empty packet into a paper basket. 'I'm winding you up; my friend Spyro is such a messy sod.'

Both burst into laughter and they were on their feet, exchanging hugs. 'You're bloody impossible, you always were,' she said.

'And you're still the most gorgeous woman to grace these shores since Helen launched the Trojan boat-race.'

'And you always were a bullshitter Doctor Flint.'

A war-weary orange Datsun pulled away from the hotel

the following day. Flint was at the wheel of his hired car, Lisa once more at his side.

'So you're here on a nostalgia trip?'

'Nostalgia isn't what it used to be.'

'Very funny. Where are you taking me?'

'Picnic.'

'When you said "lunch", I imagined an expensive beach-front restaurant.'

'I'm an impoverished archaeologist, bear with me. Call it a sense of romance.'

A ten-minute drive between the rolling grey-green hills and the sea, led to an unmade road where mimosa scraped both sides of the car. Perched on the cliffs a hundred feet above a crescent bay sat a chapel, deserted for some years. The roof had fallen and its low, whitewashed walls were sinking into decay. Flint and Lisa had once shared a picnic on that spot, the morning after their business relationship had been jettisoned for something more special.

'I was right about the nostalgia,' Lisa said.

'My sanctuary, remember it?'

'You saved me from a beetle crawling up my leg.'

'I saved the beetle from you – one second later and you would have had it with your sandal.'

'Are you still into peace and love?'

'Yes. I'm one of a dying breed.'

Leaving the car, the pair ventured into the tile-strewn interior of the ruin. Weeds and thorns already colonised patches of wind-blown earth whilst small green lizards darted into the shadows at the first hint of human approach. Lisa knelt and retrieved a length of brass chain from the dirt, pulling it taut in an explosion of dried earth. Jerking upwards into her grasp was a bent and broken censer.

'Gold!' she exclaimed.

'I'll make an archaeologist of you yet.'

She blew off the dust and rubbed away at the tarnished brass before dropping the worthless find onto a heap of tiles. The external wall of the apse cast just enough shade for the pair to retreat from the sun. Backs against the cool stonework, each contemplated the northern end of the gulf of Argos. A white blur indicated a ferry en route for Athens, and beyond it the sweep of the far shore. Far to the north lay ancient Mycenae, whilst in the west rose the mountains of Arcadia. A mile or two to the south lay the acropolis of Asine, one of many sites known as Palaeokastro. It was a small world, ancient or modern.

Lisa reached into a brown paper bag and withdrew a bottle of 'Fix' beer, opening it with a satisfying fizz. What more could a man desire? On reflection, thought Flint, there was one more thing many men might desire. He remembered a younger Lisa, body perspiring, honey-brown, her cleavage inadequately concealed, her proximity alluring as pheremones drifted in the still air. He had slipped an arm around the sticky shoulders from which her 'Coca Cola' singlet had hung.

Cold shower, Flint, look at the view. Lisa was freshly made-up to conceal the skin destroyed by unreasonable doses of sunlight and the age-lines which could be dated like tree-rings: his calculations made her thirty-six. Whilst Flint the academic had remained Flint the academic, Lisa had been married, mangled by miscarriages, then widowed. Her bouyant optimism had been repeatedly battered by the refusal of Fate to fulfil her dreams.

'Remember this?' Flint drew a glittering, if crushed, pen from a plastic zip-lock bag.

Lisa took the pen and once more read the name. 'You still haven't found Byron F. Nichols?'

Slowly, talk drifted back towards the murder.

'The survey was doomed from the start,' Flint said. 'Six men and one woman was a recipe for disaster. When I run a dig, it's fifty-fifty, with no virgins and no wrinklies.'

'Rule me out then.'

'You're not wrinkly.'

'Don't bullshit me!' Lisa said. 'All that was a long time ago; why are you here?'

'I met Emma Woodfine in London last month. Remember her? Small woman, big attitude problem?'

'The long-nosed bitch?'

'The same. I always wondered why she helped bail me out of jail – I put it down to enjoying the power.'

'I wouldn't have trusted that woman as far as I can spit, if you pardon the ladylike expression.'

'I had no choice. But it made me think, meeting her again. Someone killed Embury, probably someone he knew. Emma was the only one of our squad missing that night.'

Lisa's pupils dilated with surprise, even excitement. 'You think she did it?'

'It's possible, she'd stacked up a whole heap of grudges.' Flint broke off a hunk of bread and waved it. 'It's all tediously complex, but in short, my Prof at college had a hand in funding the project and I went with the money. Emma would have been the number two if I'd not come along.'

'That's hardly a motive for killing someone.'

'I know – it sounds silly. I thought that seven years ago; when I was released, all I wanted to do was go home. I wanted escape, not the truth. There were no clues, no suggestions of any dark motives on Emma's behalf, but with hindsight, the more I think about things, the more I start feeling uneasy.'

Lisa leaned over and pulled out a wad of dripping feta. 'This is fascinating, do go on. Convince me she did it, master detective. Give me a better motive.' She was not taking this at all seriously.

'Right, let's try sex.'

'Here?' She raised an eyebrow.

'As a motive! All the lads thought they were having an affair; she and Embury had a tiff just before she went out. Sex is always the best motive for murder.'

'She struck me as being sexually repressed,' Lisa mused, 'not a woman who feels like a woman ought to feel.'

'Which is?'

She turned away. 'These are silly games, Jeff, why have you come to see me?'

'Seven year itch. I wanted to see you for old times sake, if you forgive the cliché. Plus, I can't speak more than a few words of Greek.'

70

Lisa flopped her head over her shoulder, remembering the same night that he treasured so deeply. '"Yes, beer and chicken",' she quoted.

'That's right.'

'I've a hotel to run.'

'Emma had dinner with Doctor Dracopoulos on the night of the murder, or so she says. He lives in Anatoliko, you know, the place with the church and the statue.'

She nodded, her mouth set in a humourless line. 'And you need a translator?'

'And company.'

Chapter Nine

Flint was enjoying himself. If subjected to torture, he would have admitted that the long-dead mystery was little more than an excuse to see Lisa once more. She leaned on the open window of his hire car, allowing her hair to flutter in the slipstream, allowing all his bright memories to conquer the darker ones.

Christos Dracopoulos was physician to Anatoliko and neighbouring villages. He was also a noted antiquarian, specialising in Byzantine icons and had been appointed site guardian for the Roman town at Palaeokastro. His blank, inward-looking house was one of the largest and oldest in the village, lying just below the church, with its roof on the eye-line of the bronze statue.

In his shirtsleeves, Dracopoulos answered his own door. After a few moments passing a suspicious eye from one to the other, he remembered enough Greek hospitality to allow the visitors inside. He coughed once and adopted a slow, shambling gait. His wife was called into the cool, dark passage which bisected the house. Flint caught an odd stare, devoid of a glimmer of welcome. Dracopoulos gave her a rapid order, which turned out to be for fruit juice. With an expression of manic disgust, the woman disappeared through a doorway.

Not a happy household, thought Flint.

The doctor cleared his throat, then led them out onto the veranda, overlooking a walled enclosure that might have been called a garden, given a lawn. Orange juice arrived in a glass jug, service without a smile. Dracopoulos barely acknowledged its arrival. He would perhaps have been some years Embury's junior, now fifty-something and even more gaunt and sickly than Flint remembered. Dracopoulos lounged deeply into his cane chair as Flint reintroduced himself.

'Your hair is shorter . . .' Dracopoulos said. Perhaps Flint would not need a translator, after all. 'I remember you with Sebastian. Such a loss, such a tragic loss.' His English was imperfect, but his vocabulary stretched far beyond Flint's three words of Greek.

'We were old friends. For five, even seven years, Sebastian came to the Argolid. I suggested he works here at Palaeokastro . . . for three years everything was fine, but then . . .' He waved towards vines scrambling skywards up the grey stonework, indicating that his old friend was up there, somewhere in the ether.

'I have to thank you for arranging my defence.'

Dracopoulos frowned, requiring Flint to explain himself. 'Mr Boukaris, my lawyer? I thought Emma arranged him, but she said it was you. He never sent me his bill, I'll have to thank him one day.'

'Ah, Mr Boukaris; that is him all over. A big-hearted man. He was born here, you know? His father is our village hero.'

The statue, of course. Past and present cuddled each other very closely in small villages. Flint could imagine Mr Boukaris retained some paternalistic influence over local affairs. Perhaps he would hunt him out if the investigation ran dry.

'You invited Sebastian to dinner the night he died,' Flint began to cautiously advance his enquiry.

'Yes.'

'Have you any idea why he couldn't come?'

The doctor had obviously never read of the relationship between tobacco and health. By way of reply, he lit a small cigar and examined the burning end.

'Did Emma tell you why he didn't come?' Flint continued.

'I'm sorry,' Dracopoulos said, 'It was so long ago, I don't understand why you want to know this. I cannot remember.'

Flint looked towards Lisa for help, but she simply rolled her eyes upward. He was on his own.

'Could you try? I really need to know a few facts. I was the one who found Sebastian's body, I remember everything about that night, as if it were yesterday. You don't forget events like that.'

Dracopoulos shuffled. 'Why disturb the dead? Eh?'

The cane chair creaked as Flint fidgeted around his questions. 'Did Emma walk here?'

A hand waved away the irrelevance of the question. 'Yes, I think so, why is that important now?'

'She was here all evening?'

'Yes, with myself, my brother and his wife.'

'And who took Emma home?'

'She walked, it wasn't far,' The answer was rapid and automatic. Too rapid, perhaps. 'Greece was safe to walk at night, even for a woman. It still is, away from the tourists.'

A barbed edge was audible to his words and the contradiction threw Flint off-course. Adam had heard a car; was he mistaken, or was Dracopoulos' memory at fault?

'Any idea what time it was?'

'Seven years ago? It was late, I don't know, is that important?'

It was a detail too distant to check – perhaps Flint would never be able to ascertain the truth.

'Did Sebastian ever tell you about what he was looking for at Palaeokastro?'

Dracopoulos shook his head slowly, concentrating on the cigar. 'The city plan.'

'Emma seemed to think he had discovered something important, something unusual. Did Sebastian confide in you, as site guardian?'

'No, there was nothing extraordinary.' He checked his large wristwatch and muttered something in Greek.

Co-operation was about to cease, it was time to drop the subtlety. 'Would you say anything was going on between Emma and Sebastian?'

'I do not understand.' He may have understood, for the doctor's discomfort increased.

'Were they . . .' Flint fished around for words.

Lisa had been quiet so far, sipping at her drink and watching Flint play the bumbling amateur detective. 'Were they lovers?' She slipped into Greek and

76

emphasised the act of love-making with a few gestures.

'No, no,' Dracopoulos was emphatic, even offended. 'You are poisoning his memory. I thought this was a social call, a polite visit, do not insult my friend!'

Colour had flooded into the sickly complexion and the Doctor had lost all composure. Further kite-flying would only be destructive, so Flint nodded to Lisa, and thanked Dracopoulos, who dismissed him by clearing his throat again. As they retreated from the house, the icon in the hallway caught Flint's attention, with its soft-eyed Madonna framed by gold leaf. It had to be Byzantine, original and expensive.

'Thrilled?' Lisa asked him as they sat back in the Datsun.

'He collects antiquities,' Flint said, half to himself. 'Never trust anyone who buys or sells antiquities.'

'A tomb-robber is a tomb-robber,' Lisa said. 'Does it really make any difference whether that picture hangs on some bloke's wall, or in a dusty museum?'

'Yes. Archaeology and money don't mix. When they do, you have the opportunity for all manner of fun and games.'

He started the engine and pulled off sharply up the incline towards the square. Only two or three minutes' downhill ride would bring them to Palaeokastro. Stones and potholes rumbled beneath the car, jolting thoughts of all those questions Flint wished he'd asked. Emma should be able to answer most of them, if she'd been here.

'The Good Doctor wasn't a happy man,' Flint said.

'Would you be, if your friend had been murdered and the prime suspect called in for tea?'

'Prime suspect?'

'Yes. I asked around last night. The locals who remembered the story said you had been let off. The police never found anyone else to pin the blame on.'

That could prove tricky, Flint thought. 'Am I wrong, or was Doctor D. being evasive? I spotted at least one blatant lie.'

'I assume everyone is out to screw me unless they can prove otherwise,' Lisa said with deep conviction. 'He could just have a bad memory, it was an awfully long time ago.'

'But tragedy has an effect of fixing events in the memory. Everyone can remember where they were the day John Lennon died.'

'I can't.'

Flint sensed that Lisa was being deliberately obstructive, but pressed onwards. 'Lies are like London busses, you don't get one on its own. Just for a moment, let's fantasise that Emma was behind Embury's death. Let's say it was a *crime passionelle*. She couldn't have worked him over on her own; it needed at least one man and she needed two-way transport to Nauplion. The good Doctor D. just attempted to give her a perfect alibi, so if Emma did have something to do with the killing, he must have had a hand in it too.'

Chapter Ten

Flint met Lisa in the lobby of Hotel Sun after she had dealt with the aftermath of breakfast and weathered a stand-up argument with one of the travel company reps.

'Do you own this place?' he asked idly, as she sifted through the contents of her leather bag.

'I thought I did,' she replied, flicking her eyelashes to indicate betrayal. 'My plan was to marry an old man with pots of money, but dear George had pots of other people's money. Let's go and play Humphrey Bogart.'

'Hey, Lisa you don't have to help. This isn't a matter of life and death.'

'I thought it was.'

He had expected, irrationally, to find Lisa had been captured in amber and preserved intact. The reality was that Lisa was subject to the laws of time: she had passed beyond maturity into disillusion; she substituted his romantic attachment to the past with practical concerns of the near-future.

Suddenly, she pinched him on the cheek and flashed her eyes. 'Come on, day out. I'll treat you to lunch, and I don't mean a student picnic.'

The coast road swept through the shadow of Palamidi

and around into tree-lined streets opposite Nauplion station. Flint noticed more traffic, more development on the northern fringes of the town as he drove through the new suburbs, past the football ground and brought the car to rest in a strip of unmade ground beside the railway track. On that fateful Wednesday night, this had been an ambiguous spot: part industrial, part coastal, part wasteland, part development. He remembered heaps of gravel, the grey concrete skeleton of a new building and half-a-dozen warehouses which had marked the frayed edge of town. When Embury had last been seen alive, he was walking northwards, towards the building site.

Now the building site was an office, some of the warehouses had been replaced with more modern structures and buildings continued for a further quarter of a mile. Flint slid out of the car and adjusted his camera. He began to take photographs of the car in the position he remembered parking the Fiesta. A short jog brought him to the buildings of concrete and peeling wood which clustered haphazardly alongside road and railway track. Doorways, signposts, parked trucks and thoroughfares were quickly snapped. He recognised a few name-boards and was gratified to think there was some continuity. His film exhausted, Flint examined the ground on his walk back, as archaeologists do on reflex.

'Why here?' he mused.

It was no place for an illicit affair, or even for the backroom business meeting Embury had hinted at. His killers would have wanted Embury away from people and away from any clues to their identities; the warehouses advertised the owners' names and were thus no place for a furtive conspiracy. Perhaps the grey skeleton, the last structure in Nauplion, had been simply the first stage on Embury's final journey to the underworld. Embury seemed to have been reciting instructions: 'Park by the yellow concrete mixer, then walk northwards'? Embury must have met someone in a car; the car drove away – perhaps – but the killers certainly returned rather than dump the body over a cliff, or throw it across the railway track.

'Any clues Humphrey?' Lisa had remained in the car, listening to the radio.

'If I were Bogart, I'd have found a book of matches leading me to a seedy nightclub and a dancer who knew everything.'

'And did you?'

'Life's not like that.'

Tourists of all nations pack into the great theatre of Epidauros at dusk to witness the peddling of ancient Greek culture. These tourists would never pay attention to a square, red-roofed bungalow that sat forlorn in a wasteland beyond the coach-park. Only the British could have built that house, which would have been more in place on a Burmese rubber plantation.

Flint had recited a ten-minute life history of Juliette Howe during the drive.

'Do you know everyone in archaeology?' Lisa asked.

'Enough; they fall into distinct categories, so its easy to pigeonhole those I've only heard about by repute.'

'So Juliette Howe is in the frumpy spinster pigeon-hole?'

'Loosely.'

The sunbleached verandah had seen happier years and the front door opened at a touch. Approaching forty, dressed in a wide matching set of khaki t-shirt and shorts, Juliette was instantly likeable and quick with the tea and digestives.

'Doctor Flint! I read your book.'

'Which one?'

'Economy and thingammy.'

'Economy and Society in Third-Century Britain?'

'Yes, I found your approach, rather...' Juliette seemed to be hunting for a polite way to disapprove.

'Radical?'

'Yes.'

Radical was a term of deprecation in some circles. Flint dropped Juliette into the 'Old Imperialist' pigeonhole.

Lisa and Flint were seated on a dusty sofa beside a potted palm, allowing their eyes to run around the room which was mainly full of pottery in various stages of classification or assembly.

'Does your house look like this?' Lisa whispered, as Juliette fussed with a kettle.

'I hate pottery,' Flint muttered, 'and I live on a houseboat.'

'Is there a Mrs Flint?' Lisa probed.

'Don't believe in marriage.'

'Live-in-lover?'

'Sugar?' asked Juliette.

Lisa took her tea and was gradually excluded from conversation, except to say 'Yes,' or 'Really?' at the correct point, whilst otherwise meaningless archaeological gossip was exchanged.

'. . . but don't quote me!' Juliette grimaced, 'I do go on a bit. Yes, poor Sebastian. Dear Emma was so cruelly upset, she still hasn't forgotten him. You do know Emma Woodfine?'

'And her sister. We all keep in touch.' Gosh, that was a whopper Jeffrey Flint.

'She was *so* devoted to Sebastian.' Juliette was an old hand at the game of tittle-tattle and puckered her cheeks with an impish, yet apologetic smile.

'They were lovers, Emma told me all about it after his death.' Flint expanded on the lie. If nothing else, it would replenish Juliette's gossip stockpile.

'Did she? That was rather brazen, she never told me! We all knew, of course. Sebastian would never admit to anything improper; he was very faithful to his wife's memory. Didn't you know? She died about six years before he did; cancer, it was very traumatic for poor Sebastian . . .'

The ramble continued, with Flint trying to regain his grip on the knack of investigation. 'Emma and Sebastian fell out just before he was killed.' He inserted a pause. 'Emma went off in a huff and had dinner with Doctor Dracolopoulos. Do you know him?'

'Do *you* know Christos Dracolopoulos?' Juliette gave a bemused, partly disapproving shake of her unkempt hair. 'Greek men have a reputation for being hot-blooded, but Christos and a pretty face! Oh!'

Could one equate Emma with a pretty face? It was perverse but possible.

'He's not a well man,' Flint said.

'No, his gigolo days are over. His wife's mad, don't you know? She has schizophrenia, always has.'

Juliette drifted off-tack with another classicist-on-heat story. Flint listened politely, smiling to Lisa when he could, then dived in with a last question. 'Sebastian was in some sort of trouble; do you know anything about that?'

The narrator seemed unhappy to break off mid-saga. After a pause, Juliette began to talk more slowly. 'We come here in alternate years, so it must have been my second season when it all happened. It's funny, but I remember it as clear as if it were last week. Sebastian came flying up here in his yellow bus, he wanted to see Neil – that's Dr Neil Ennismore. He's at the British School now.'

'You've no idea what he was worried about?'

'Work permits, I believe, or perhaps the licence to excavate, or some such bureaucratic nonsense. Ever since the socialists took over, they have been making excavation so much more difficult. Do you know, we can't even dig this season? They say we must write up what we've already excavated. I ask you!'

Perfectly reasonable, thought Flint, feigning sympathy.

'There was much less red tape under The Colonels, though I dread to say it.'

'Shoot first, fill in the forms later,' quipped Flint.

Juliette frowned.

'Sorry, I was being subversive.'

'Yes. You have that reputation.' Juliette changed the subject and talked for another forty minutes before the couple politely extricated themselves.

'Emma was having it off with Doctor D.,' Lisa announced, settling herself in the car seat.

'Never.'

'Everyone else is at it with everyone else's other half. All your people have complex love lives.'

'Yes, but not Emma.'

'Just because you don't like her you think she's incapable of forming a relationship with a man.'

'Sorry, I'm being sexist. Doctor D. hardly struck me as being a sex machine either, even seven years ago.'

'Female priorities differ from those of men.'

'So what does your female intuition tell you?'

'Emma and Sebastian were hot-and-cold, trying to pretend nothing was going on between them. They have a tiff, she goes off to see Doctor D. He drives her home, hand on knee, they hop in the back, you can imagine the rest. It explains why Emma is so shitty to you: she's simply crushed by guilt. It explains why Doctor D. told a lie. Would you be proud of bonking Emma?'

By way of an answer, Flint grimaced, finding the scenario too unsavoury to contemplate. He started the car. 'Sorry. Nice theory, but I don't believe it.'

'Super, what a waste of a morning, why am I doing this?'

'Don't snap, I'm very grateful . . .'

'Sound grateful,' she said.

Flint ground the Datsun around in a tight reverse turn. 'I'm grateful, I need you Lisa, I'm a foreigner here.'

'I'm the foreigner – you two were talking in your own special language. What was all that about a licence to dig? It sounded very technical and very boring.'

Flint explained the rules governing the supervision of foreign excavations, but as he talked, an idea broke through. It had been naive to limit his suspicions to Emma.

'And I thought he just meant me,' Flint said with a touch of awe in his voice.

'What?'

'Long, long ago, when we were having a barney up in the olive grove, Embury said he was tired of people interfering and telling him where to dig.'

'Someone interfered,' Lisa said, 'and they made sure he never dug anywhere, anymore. If I were you, Jeff, I'd find yourself another suspect.'

There had, of course, only ever been one suspect. When Flint parked beside Taverna Mikos, the rest of the earthen space was filled by a blue and white police car. Through the plate glass window he could see a navy blue figure lounging against the bar, capturing the attention of the taverna owner.

Scarface turned and gave a wry smile as Flint walked inside.

'Mister Jeffrey Stanley Flint,' he said.

'Doctor Flint now, but friends call me Jeff.'

'So, Doctor Flint,' Scarface said pointedly. 'You are back in Nauplion.'

Mikos suddenly found pressing business in the kitchen.

'Yes, I'm looking up old friends . . .'

Scarface had learned to speak English in the intervening years and his uniform had changed. Both indicated he had been promoted.

'You should have stayed in England.'

'We're all Europeans now.'

The policeman collected his hat from the counter, as if to leave. 'I hate paperwork, Doctor Flint. That is what you are – paperwork. I have to open my files again. You were too expensive to extradite, but now you are here. Don't run away this time.'

Chapter Eleven

The holiday was over. He remembered Scarface as humourless and vindictive and seniority had obviously compounded his flaws. To distract himself, Flint telephoned Vikki, but he found little to say that did not involve Lisa. Next he rang his research student Tyrone Drake on site in Hertfordshire. Flint winced at the idea of a field archaeologist with a mobile phone; what was the world coming to?

Tyrone was OTT, as expected. The final season at the Burke's Warren villa was already yielding the buckets of evidence missed in the previous years. It was predictable that Tyrone would be the one to scoop up the goodies and Flint was left with the feeling he had made the wrong decision in returning to Greece.

Over one of Mikos' questionable Souvlaki – the cooking had not improved with practice – Flint talked over the old times with the perpetrator of the meal. Mikos looked through the seventeen photographs which Flint had taken during that first excavation. He paused at each face and tried to guess the owner's name.

'Did Sebastian have any enemies?' Flint asked.

Mikos turned down a lip as he shook his head.

'Did he used to argue with anyone – apart from me?'

'What is argument?' Mikos asked awkwardly. 'My neighbours come here and we argue politics or some boy will forget to pay for his drinks. Okay, Sebastian would argue, but so what? He was a man, he had his honour.'

For the Greeks, arguing was part of life. For the English, it was a painful experience to be avoided at all costs. Mikos seemed unaware of the subtle difference, so the line of enquiry was abandoned in favour of an early night.

Flint lay in bed well beyond ten the next morning. He was out of ideas, the trail was cold and Lisa little more than lukewarm. Amid bleak philosophising that would have been more at home in one of those turgid Scandinavian films he abhorred, Flint walked across the site, eating a peach for breakfast. He took the New Road, as Mikos called it, passed the olive grove and the breezeblock building, crossed the gully on an embankment, then climbed to the neck of the valley towards Anatoliko. A quarter of a mile beyond the olive grove he turned aside to visit one of the outlying farmsteads he had once surveyed.

A flash of red and white revealed a two-metre ranging pole lying neglected in a patch of coarse weeds, and further down the hillside he came across a survey line, still partly pegged in position: the archaeology of archaeology. Unseemly haste had typified his last departure from Greece. He picked up the ranging rod, then found a boulder and sat against it, disturbing a lizard who scuttled into a crack.

The sun was hovering over the distant hills, turning them into shimmering haze as Flint brooded. Some might find literary murder fascinating, but real corpses oozing real blood were repulsive to civilised thought. Investigating the lives of dead people was fine when they had been in the ground over a thousand years. Toying with the loose facts of Sebastian Embury's death verged on bad taste.

One figure came around the bend in the valley, then another, both dressed in blue and wearing peaked caps. Both policemen were lower down the slope, moving crosswise, stepping with care amongst the stones and brambles, pointing and searching for something: him.

The human brain is the product of five million years of evolution for survival. On instinct, Flint pulled in his legs, then rolled around the boulder into its shadow, mimicking the lizard. Why had he done that? His pulse rate was up, adrenalin had forced a reflex action upon him. His heart pounding, Flint allowed himself a few minutes, then glanced around the rock to see the two figures were much further off, hands on hips, obviously lost or confused or apathetic. Finally, they moved off with purpose, back towards Palaeokastro.

Flint felt vaguely guilty in his evasion, but Amnesty campaigning days came back to reinforce his resolve. If Scarface wanted to cause trouble, he was willing to stand up to him this time; but only with a lawyer present. He would hang around for an hour, then speak to Vassilis Boukaris.

*   *   *

Outside the Taverna, Mikos was seated at one of four tables, playing dominoes against two aged, overdressed men. Flint strode up in t-shirt, shorts and sandals, bearing the ranging pole like a spear.

'The police came here,' Mikos said. 'They went upstairs.'

'Oh shit.' Flint lobbed the ranging pole violently at the rubbish-strewn terrace beside the taverna. It bit into the earth and stood quivering.

Mikos' expression made plain that he disapproved of such petulance. 'They will come back. Where were you?'

Flint deigned to reply, making straight for his room. It had been searched, messily and obviously. His passport had gone, his return air ticket had vanished as had his chequebook, wallet and credit cards. Even the back pocket of his jeans had been relieved of its burden of money. He always hid his travellers cheques, but they would be useless without identification. Seven or eight clinical obscenities were chosen at random.

He hurtled downstairs, past where Mikos was nonchalantly laying down a double five, around to where the Datsun was parked. Had been parked.

'Mikos! Where's my car?'

'The man from the rentals, he came.'

'But I hired it for the week!'

Mikos gave a groan, then apologised to his fellow players and gesticulated to Flint. 'Come, telephone.'

'I want you to find Vassilis Boukaris,' Flint panted. 'He defended me last time – I want to know my rights.'

'I hope you have a lot of money.'

Actually no, thought Flint, I don't.

Finding the lawyer took time. Flint sweated by the bar, growing restless as the Greek grew more impatient with the voice at the other end of the line. Mikos suddenly turned and winked, a finger inclined towards the drinks cabinet. The archaeologist took out a cloudy bottle of lemonade with thanks. The bottle had been drained by the time Mikos waggled the receiver at him.

'Mr Boukaris for you.'

'Jeffrey Flint here,' Flint explained what had happened, the other saying little. Boukaris had always been economical with words.

'I will see what I can do,' the voice said, terminating the phonecall.

Flint tried to ring Lisa, but her receptionist informed him she had gone to Argos. Ringing Vikki would be futile – it was one of her days chasing Eurocrats in Brussels. College was on vacation, with both colleagues and students scattered across the world's archaeological sites. Tyrone would be halfway down a third-century rubbish pit in Hertfordshire. Jules Torpevitch, his sometime flatmate, was working on a bone assemblage somewhere north of Marathon, but for the moment he may as well have been on the moon. Temporarily, Flint was out of allies.

He went back to his room and re-checked his possessions. The photographs were still there, as was his notepad and that irrelevant golden trinket. He lay back on his bed, passing his trowel from hand to hand as he waited. He had carved 'JSF' onto its handle to prevent trowel-rustling by rookie excavators who had not yet learned that an archaeologist and his trusted trowel are seldom parted.

'Jeff! Telephone!'

Flint sprinted down the stair to hear what he hoped would be Vassilis Boukaris' soothing voice.

'Doctor Flint,' said the lawyer, 'You should have remained in England.'

He objected to paying for duplicate advice. 'Why?'

'When this unfortunate murder took place, nobody wanted the publicity. Nauplion is a quiet town, these things do not happen. It was easy for me to persuade the Prosecutor to drop the case. Now, things are different, we have a new Prosecutor, a very determined woman. I will give you the same advice I gave you all those years ago. Leave Greece.'

'I can't, not this time. They've taken my passport.'

'You don't need a passport, not any more. Simply leave, that is my advice, I make no charge for it.'

'I need your help. I need legal advice to stop the police harassing me.'

'I have spoken with the police. They have re-opened your case, they have evidence they failed to use before.'

'What evidence?'

'They have a witness to the killing. Go home Doctor Flint. I cannot save you this time.'

Chapter Twelve

Mikos would take no payment for the lemonade, which was fortunate. Flint remained leaning on the thin formica counter, unable to find a logical way out of the mire into which he had slipped. He was a thousand miles from home and suddenly way, way out of his depth. Unless he could quickly understand what had transpired, he would be sucked under.

'Bad, Jeff?' Mikos smiled for a tenth of a second.

'Worse.'

His mind was playing on all the unusual, unexplained events, past and present, trying to tie them into a pattern. 'Do you remember the night Lisa came around for dinner?' Flint asked. 'We ate moussaka and listened to Bob Dylan. Someone called for Sebastian and he went outside. When he came back, we had a row over something stupid.'

'Was it the biro-stylo you found?'

'That's right. Have you any idea who was outside? Sebastian came in steaming, just looking for a fight. Whoever he met really wound him up.'

Mikos shook his head. 'It was two men in a car. They were not from around here, I never saw them again.'

Two men. Emma had been inside and uninvolved. Flint glanced along the bar, regretting that it gave only a slight view of the main street. Unpleasant thoughts were stalking around his mind. Fear was slowly taking its hold, he found he was watching for the inevitable police car without ever having planned it. He would go back upstairs, lie on the bed and analyse his predicament.

Once upstairs, muddled thoughts replaced neat schemes of intellectual analysis. Flint paused before pushing open the door of his room. The last English archaeologist to sleep there had been beaten to death. He hoped the Gods on Olympus were not plotting an ironic, symmetrical end to the drama.

Too many coincidences were troubling him. Embury had turned irrational just before the picture began to take on a sinister tinge. Who were the mystery men? Who stole the minibus? When did Embury learn the minibus had been found? What had been the purpose of that drive into Nauplion? Did Dracopoulos deliberately lie about Emma walking home? Where had this mystery witness suddenly sprung from and who had prompted Scarface into resurrecting the moribund case?

Embury always seemed to be going somewhere, meeting someone, telephoning someone. Flint thought around names dropped by the director and recalled faces of Greek and foreign vistors to the site, trying to identify others who could be involved in whatever-it-was. Conspiracy theories started to form in his mind. If this had been Italy, he would have said 'Mafia' and become terrified. As it was, this was Greece, but he was still terrified.

Tyres on loose chippings and a motor rattling in the narrow streets drew him to the window. All his paranoid delusions blossomed into reality. Chequerboard blue and white, the Datsun police car was pulling up outside the taverna. In a fraction of a second, Flint had dived for his rucksack and the spare pair of socks stuffed deep in the left side pocket. Precious moments slipped by until a satisfying, paper-rich crunch rewarded the risk. He dumped his dirty laundry from a carrier bag, then swept his pile of odds-and-ends into the bag in one motion. Next, he hung his camera around his neck. A few seconds were wasted debating what else he could take before panic drove him from the room.

At the rear was a claustrophobic box-room where Emma had once slept. It had one small window which overhung the flat roof of the rearward toilet block. As Flint skipped across the landing, he could hear Mikos greeting the policemen once again. If relaxed, the police might gossip for a few minutes, otherwise, they would pound straight up the stairs and slap on the handcuffs. Flint pulled himself onto the window ledge, then slid out, feet first. Then he lay still on the sticky tarred felt, listening for the feet on the stairs. When none came, he doubted his own fears, then self-preservation overcame self-doubt and he wormed to the back of the toilet block. Feet first, he scraped over the edge and landed badly on the slope below.

Flinching from a grazed knee, he moved swiftly across the back of the building, past an alleyway and behind a low wall. What next? His heart pounded hard. He remembered seeing a black bicycle propped in a passageway close to the petrol station and suddenly he had an objective.

Palaeokastro lay stunned by the noon heat, so not a soul observed the Englishman dodge from the shadow of an alley, cross the street and disappear into the dark of another. Gearless, black and rusting, the bike offered an environmentally sound means of salvation. He slipped the carrier bag on the handle bars, mounted whilst still in the alley, made four quick strokes of the creaking pedals and was into the sunlight once more.

At the top of the hill, the police car was still stationary and unoccupied. Flint cast himself down the pothole-cratered road with reckless speed and was soon able to freewheel. No brake levers graced the handlebars, a fact Flint noticed whilst already passing twenty miles per hour. In four minutes he had made a mile, his arms shaking with the strain of holding a steady course over endless ruts and stones. The village faded into an off-white blur on the hillside, and the road levelled out amongst a bland valley bottom of scattered fruit trees and goats. He began to guess how long the police would stay in the taverna, how wide their search would be.

The bike slewed violently as it came out of a pothole, the handlebar fought to escape his grip. The worn seat bit deep into his buttocks, but Flint remained upright. Far ahead, the road began to climb through orange groves before meeting the highway. A flash of sun on windshield told Flint that a car had turned onto the Palaeokastro road. Two hundred yards away, Flint could see a ramshackle hut some way back from the road. He began to weave to lose speed, then discovered the bike braked by backpedalling. With no margin to spare he managed to bump and coax the bike through the lines of citrus trees and behind the wall of the shed. A black car swept past in a cloud of dust and shower of gravel. Flint played with possibilities then decided to wait, recover his thoughts and see if the police car retreated to Nauplion.

Half an hour ticked by on his scarred wristwatch. The shade of the shed was cool, a nearby herd of goats stood nonplussed, but only wasps and red-tailed hornets threatened his safety. The police car remained in Palaeokastro and after twenty minutes was joined by a second, plus a van; the hunt was afoot. With limbs recovered from the first frantic bout of pedalling, Flint dared to resume his ride. One of a myriad of plans had gained prominence.

Rough and in places ill-defined, the track which began just beyond the goat shed was a perfect escape route. He knew this path, or had done in what seemed another life, for the most part it was level or sloped gently downhill. Flint coasted down buttock-battering inclines and cycled along flatter sections where ruts and stands of dry vegetation permitted. He was alone amongst the dusty fields and sweet-smelling groves of fruit trees and only a pair of donkeys bore witness to his passing.

After an hour, he came to the coast road and timed his sprint across. His head swam and he feared heat-stroke; where had he left his hat? The bike became a burden, heavy and squeaking as he pushed it up the last stony track to his sanctuary. Blue and cooling, the Gulf of Argos sparkled below the deserted chapel; objective attained.

Flint ran the bicycle deep into a conifer-choked gulley, then fell into the shade and lay inert for fifteen or twenty minutes. Rushing was unnecessary; where could he go, wearing just one pair of shorts, one grubby college t-shirt, one pair of Jesus sandles, his watch and his glasses? With deep pessimism, he investigated the contents of his carrier bag, which contained his notepad, the old photographs, a roll of toilet tissue, his trowel, two biro's and one pair of blue Y-fronts. He took out his red socks and unrolled them, allowing fresh Greek notes to spill onto the pine needles. One by one he picked them up, counting twelve thousand drachmae, something under fifty pounds. Digging deep into the bag he hoped for more, and from the bottom drew the treasure of Palaeokastro; a zip-lock bag containing a glittering but crushed pen.

The hours between four and dusk drew themselves into a featureless haze. As evening settled, only bats and insects disturbed him. His stomach regarded the breakfast peach as a dim memory; tea had been forgotten and supper was out of the question. He wished he had grabbed one of Mikos' attempts at a sandwich whilst he'd sipped that lemonade. He wished dark to come so that he could sleep and when it did, sleep was almost impossible. Surprised at the cold and unable to find a comfortable spot to lie, he crouched, bored and seriously regretting the impulse that had brought him to Greece.

The first light of dawn awoke him, with the miserable realisation that after no breakfast, he had no lunch to look forward to. As the sea rinsed the toes of the Argolid, Jeffrey Flint knew thirst he had never known before. So far, he had remained free, but the crucial element of his only plan relied on one friend knowing him better than did the Greek police.

Chapter Thirteen

A metallic blue Opel bounced to a halt beside the ruined Chapel and Lisa emerged, throwing furtive glances in all directions. Flint rushed at her, delivering a hug and a whoop of delight. He took her hand and pulled her within the ruin.

'My God, you look a mess. But then, you always did.'

After just one night in the chapel, Jeffrey Flint carried the look of a Biblical hermit.

'Hotel Flint is short on facilities. Hot and cold running lizards, but no shower.'

She studied him with a mix of curiosity and admiration.

'I hoped you'd guess where I was.'

'You're pretty lucky I remembered that twaddle about this being your sanctuary.'

'Lisa...' He took a step closer, but she side-stepped the motion.

'Jeff, the police know that we've been seeing each other. They know we went snooping round the Dracopoulos place, so they came round first thing this morning, demanding I tell them where you were.'

'And?'

She deepened her voice and adopted the hand-on-hips stance of a macho policeman. '"Lisa Canelopoulos, where were you last night?" . . . "being groped by one of your randy sergeants, Sir" . . . "Oh thank you" . . . They were gone in five minutes.'

Flint let his mouth hang open.

'He's called Spyro, he's married and he's eight years younger than I am. It's a relationship made in heaven.'

'Great.'

Lisa narrowed her eyes. 'You're the last person I'd expect to discover Victorian morality.'

'It's just old fashioned jealousy.'

'You'll get over it. For that matter, so will Spyro, one day. I don't think he'll like being my alibi.'

A liquid gurgling interrupted her and Flint grasped his stomach. Lisa went to collect a bag of groceries from the car and deposited it amongst the broken tiles. The hermit thanked her as he grabbed the offerings.

'I must look like Patrick Troughton in "Jason and the Argonauts"' he said, 'but no Harpies!'

Flint pushed a piece of bread into his mouth, then realised it was too large. It was no way to impress a lady. She watched him eat, her face stern and wary.

'I don't understand what you're playing at, my boy.'

Oh no, she was onto the 'my boy' tack again. Once he'd chewed the salty chunk of bread into submission, he managed to reply. 'There's something deeply spooky happening. I came to Greece with the idea I might clear up a few nagging questions, but basically I wanted to see you and have a good time.'

'See me? You're bullshitting again.'

'No bullshit. I have these fond romantic memories of moonlit tavernas and sun-drenched beaches. Greece seemed quite appealing on a rainy London afternoon.'

'I thought that time was your business. Times change, people change.'

'Are you familiar with the concept of the Reality Bubble?'

She shook her head. 'My education must be lacking.'

'It's as if Paleaokastro has hung in a time warp since I left; the investigation froze whilst I was away. The moment I came back, the spell broke and things started stirring.'

The bemused look on Lisa's face was appealing, it took years off her, reminding Flint of how he had once been entranced. Lisa took her time to respond to his fanciful analogy.

'Spyro told me a witness has come forward, a waiter from Hotel Daedelus who remembers seeing you on the night of the murder. He described you perfectly: glasses, beard, t-shirt, everything. It was you.'

'That's ludicrous, after all these years? I'm being framed Lisa, you must know I'm innocent!'

'Running away doesn't make you look innocent, quite the opposite. How are you planning to get out of Greece?'

'I'm not, there's no point. If I escape to England, and

their evidence is genuine they'll have me extradited. If their evidence is phony, I may as well stay here.'

'If they catch you, you'll be archaeology before you're free. Half the police in the Argolid are after you, you don't stand a chance hiding here.'

Flint was unbowed. 'The police won't expect me to have got so far so quickly. They will hunt around the village until the bike is reported missing. Then they'll realise their mistake and start checking the train stations, ferry ports and truck drivers. I'll stay here, keep out of the sun until the hunt dies down, then I'll find out who killed Sebastian Embury.'

This statement left her incredulous. Lisa looked at him, long and hard, then simply said, 'How?'

'I may need a little charity to keep me going,' he admitted.

'Mine, presumably. Be realistic Jeff, if a whole police force can't get the right killer in seven years, how can you hope to succeed?'

'Intellectual arrogance. The police suffer a big disadvantage: they have me as the one and only suspect: case closed, no need to search for anyone else.'

A roller-coaster of logic had been triggered and Lisa had one chance to block its momentum. 'Look, we all know you're brilliant. If this was some academic problem and you were in your college library, I'm sure you could solve it. But this is the real world, and you don't live in the real world, you never have. You need clues . . .'

He drew a battered green notepad from his carrier bag. 'We've found clues, I have a theory.'

'I've heard your theory, it was a *crime passionelle . . .*'

'No, no. New theory.' He waved a hand to rub out past thoughts. 'Theory of the day is that Embury was into something dodgy and I'll bet that Emma and the good Doctor D. were into it too. Embury was lured to that place and told to come alone; hence, I had to stay in the car. Naturally, he would tell me nothing about it. So, he meets his mysterious contact, gets beaten up and dies. Perhaps his death was deliberate, perhaps incidental, but I end up in the frame. By the time the police realised they couldn't make the charges stick, the trail was cold.'

He took a long swig of mineral water. 'I figure on hunting out a motive first; if I can discover whydunnit, I can then postulate whodunnit.' He paused, trying to read her mind. 'Don't feel obliged to help me. I'll understand, I mean, I'm in it up to my ears. The person who discovers the body is always a suspect, so the cops were only doing their job in arresting me first time around, but this time it seems to be personal. There's an officer whose name is unpronounceable – I call him Scarface. He gave me a heavy hint that I should pack my bags and run. Next day, a witness with perfect twenty-twenty night vision suddenly remembers he saw me do the killing ten years ago. Not the usual vague five foot ten man in his mid-twenties, but me, right down to my birthmarks. I smell a rat, a great big rat. In fact, in the words of the guru, it's rats all the way down. Someone doesn't want me digging up the past.'

'You're paranoid, dear boy.'

'I'm not a boy, and I'm not paranoid. I need help; I've no money, no transport, nothing.'

Lisa sucked in her cheeks.

'We're talking justice, Lisa. Justice for me and justice for the killers of an old man.'

'Who you hated.'

'Not enough to enjoy seeing him die.'

'Alright, cut the preaching, I am helping you, I'm here. I went through all the conscience searching last night after Spyro told me what happened. Now you have to move; tourists come up here all the time, they show me the photographs, they all think this is their private sanctuary too.'

He nodded vigorously. 'I need to be somehere where there are lots of other people, so I can move about. Che Guevara wrote that a fish needs a sea in which to swim. Preferably one full of other fishes.'

'I can find somewhere in Tolon to hide you.' She tugged at the end of his beard. 'But first, Che Guevara, this beard needs to come off: I put a razor somewhere in that bag, it's the one I use for my armpits, I hope you won't mind?'

Flint fondled the beard, 'No.'

'I also brought you some hair dye, I'm sure tawny is your colour.'

He was amazed at the depth her planning had already reached.

'On Thursdays, my grocks go to a fisherman's beach barbecue with cheap red wine and bouzouki music.' She stuck a thumb towards the crescent beach. 'That beach will do for a change: their rep. is just a kid, she'll believe any lie I tell her. Wait here for a day and I'll bribe the boatman to move the barbie down here. Once the grockles are all pissed, you just slip down and join them. You can do the Zorba dance, can't you?'

Chapter Fourteen

The blade slipped across his throat and a speck of blood dripped onto his t-shirt. Forgotten territory glistened white in the falling light of day. Flint wriggled his features in the mirror to familiarise himself with the weak chin and pale cheeks.

His hair fell next, all those long straggling trails he had cultivated so well tumbled onto the pine needles. Snipping, hacking, mutilating; visions of a police photo board featuring a Jesus look-alike spurred the scissors in their work. He cropped back the mop to no more than one inch all round, paused and looked at the shapeless shambles in the mirror. Professional hairdressers had won his undying admiration and envy. With a series of grunted curses, he worked around his head once more, trying to even out the rougher patches, producing a spiky punk effect. He checked the mirror and winced. He would forget the dye.

A motor launch spewed tourists onto the beach below. Tiny figures fanned out like badly organised marines and claimed their spots on the sand. From cover amongst mimosa bushes, Flint watched the barbecue being set up and the fun gradually organised. He waited for an hour, then, with dry mouth, sauntered into the party unnoticed. He took his rough red wine and plate of overgrilled fish, and tried to relax in the company of fellow Britons.

'Hello, you're new?'

Flint took fright, then cursed the polite games the English play. A couple of red-faced fish-eaters were trying to kick-start conversation. Patricia and Patrick from Dudley introduced themselves as the 'Two Pats', then launched into beach-party small talk. Flint forced a smile and began to lie. He stole the name and background of a former schoolmate, then proceeded to invent a life story as he talked. Recycled truth was more convincing than sheer lies. Dull anecdotes were repeated in a carefully flat, non-intellectual, accent. Both Pats nodded, whinged a little about the food, the heat and the shower in their hotel. It was a long, inordinately hot afternoon.

The launch motored sedately back along the coast to Nauplion, from where the tourists were redistributed to their various hotels by road. His new hideaway was within a rambling compound of pastel chalets on the high ground behind Tolon. He loitered until Lisa arrived.

'I escaped.'

'Your hair looks awful.'

'Thanks. I look like a British National Party candidate.'

'But, the important thing is, you look nothing like an archaeologist.'

At the farthest end of the complex, a pink box stood unloved, overlooking a field of rank weeds. Beyond this, a farm had been partly demolished and an apartment block partly constructed in its stead.

Lisa quickly unlocked the chalet. 'The owner fancies his chances – I can wind him round my little finger.'

She apologised for the state of the plumbing and then made him sit down whilst she tried to tidy up his hair. 'I like you better without the beard, you look more like a real person, less nineteen-sixties.'

Lisa breezed off after asking his size, so she could hunt out some clothing, and reciting a list of instructions to stay quiet and keep the lights turned off. Flint listened, nodded and allowed himself to be dominated. Once alone, he enjoyed an erratic shower, then took his choice of beds and collapsed into it.

Hide in plain sight was the immediate strategy. Jeffrey Flint lounged on the beach, narrow and well populated, and mingled discreetly with the tourists when necessary. Red-rimmed glasses had been his only fashion statement and had to be left in the chalet. Without them, he could read and recognise faces within ten feet. Beyond that, the world became pleasantly blurred. The glasses featured prominently in the 'wanted' posters, so Flint was condemned to blunder around in semi-blindness in the hope that nothing evil saw him before he saw it.

Fuzzy green islands lying just offshore were perfect

travel-brochure stuff and he supposed the white shape was a church. The water-skier could be heard but not seen and the rippling sea breeze carried the taint of toasting flesh, lightly basted with sun-tan oil.

His eyes were down, reading a dog-eared copy of 'Who Pays the Ferryman', found in the camp library, when a crunch of shingle and an accented voice startled him.

'Monseiur!'.

He rolled, to see two dark smudges turn into uniformed policemen silhouetted against the sun.

'Sir? Are you English?'

His pulse rate shot up to a hundred and fifty. He shook his head, lacking the moisture to speak.

'Have you seen this man?'

Someone did not believe his denial. 'Nein, Deutsche,' he stammered. Goddamit, blue eyed and blonde, he could be a fresh SS recruit!

Concentration was needed to stop his hands shaking as he took the picture offered by the policeman. Grief, how ghastly passport photographs were: did *anyone* look like that?

The men in blue towered over him as he sat up, trying not to meet their eyes.

'Nein,' he repeated, praying they did not demand a passport.

One of the policemen knew a spattering of German and pressed the question. Flint frowned and looked again, trying to seem sincere, but planning four sentences of flawless, fast, colloquial German. Outclassed, bluff called, the policeman nodded and

114

showed disinterest, accepting the photograph back. The pair moved onto the next couple; corpulent, roasting and also German.

Flint was left trembling and nauseous. He should have seen them coming, it had been so close! So close, yet he had survived! The trembling turned to the thrill of success, even power. The police would finish scouring the resort that day and turn their attention elsewhere, leaving him the freedom to move.

Back in the semi-dark of the chalet, Lisa lay on a bed and read aloud a Greek newspaper account of his escape; he had been seen in Corfu and Athens and a port called Killini. She then moved on to a Daily Mirror, but Flint grabbed it first.

'You're quite famous,' Lisa said.

He saw the name at the head of the article: Vikki Corbett. Flint spread the paper across his own bed and flicked through the text. Never had he read a Corbett masterpiece which tried so hard to be fair.

'Ring her,' he said, reaching for a biro.

'Who is she?'

'Friend and confidante.'

'Oh yes?'

'Not *that* confidante,' Flint added. 'Ring her to say I'm safe, but don't give her your name and don't tell her what I'm up to.'

Lisa frowned.

'Vikki would sell out her grandma for a good story. Don't tell her anything you wouldn't want pasting across page one.'

115

'What nice friends you have. Do you know anyone at the Express?'

He took the Express from her and turned to page four, immediately groaning with annoyance. 'This is fantasy. Look at this, "communist activist", what a load of bollocks.'

'Reporters don't just make things up, Jeff.'

'Yes they do, all the time.'

He was known to Special Branch (but isn't everyone in CND?). He wrote radical articles (in the *Journal of Roman Archaeology*, for goodness sake?). He had been arrested for arson (with a good barrister he could win a few grand for that whopper).

'Do you have a police record in Britain?' Lisa asked.

Flint allowed himself to betray irritation, 'I got arrested on an anti-racist demo when I was a student. The police started chasing a group of us, this girl tripped and fell, I tripped over her and we both got nicked because we were the easiest to catch. I got fined ten quid, I think.'

'Is that all? You're not a real radical revolutionary, I'm disappointed,' Lisa had a broad smile. 'All that Chairman Mao and Che Guevara . . .'

'You're teasing, Lisa,' Flint growled.

'Am I?' She took the paper from him again. 'Sorry. Don't you like women who tease?'

'No, and you don't seem to like academics.'

Her eyes fell on the paper, 'I do sometimes. I did actually spend two and a half years reading English at Exeter University you know. I'm not just a dumb blonde.'

'You're not a true blonde and I never said you were dumb.'

'I'm mixed up in all this – that makes me dumb.' Lisa glanced at her large, numberless watch and guessed at the hour. 'I must go, before you trick me into that life story nonsense. Is there anything else you want?'

'Paper, pens, index cards, paperclips, sellotape, a universal diary, a map of Nauplion and one of Greece generally . . . I wrote a list.'

Idle hours were spent pacing around the tiny chalet, stopping on impulse and scribbling down notes. As the weekend crawled by, Flint began to compile a chart of dates, times, events, persons and places, lists of motives, lists of possible alternative actions. Sheets of paper sellotaped together held criss-crossing lines of logical connections and boxes of free-floating facts.

Step by step, Flint wrote a diary of the excavation, starting with the first meeting with Sebastian Embury, back at the Society of Antiquaries in Piccadilly. Relations had been tepid after that meeting, becoming awkward on the journey to Greece and difficult thereafter. Only in the week before the murder had the personality clash become intolerable.

'Problems begin about time we start work in olive grove', he wrote.

Had there been a sudden crisis? Flint's amateur psychology had diagnosed that the director had been under pressure, but from whom? Embury had always boasted of his connections – he knew everybody who was anybody in classical archaeology. Discounting half his claimed familiars as mere dropped names, Flint was still left with the impression that Sebastian Embury had built up considerable influence in academic circles. If he had been hassled by mysterious men in a car, he would have called on his contacts at the various archaeological schools or the University of Athens and had them pull strings, as he always claimed he did. Unless of course, he was mixed up in something where academics carried no weight.

'Embury out of his depth,' he wrote.

'Did not tell Emma (so said Emma)'

'Did not tell Dr D. (so said Dr D.)'

'Always on the telephone (to who?)'

'DID see Neil Ennismore (so said Juliette Howe)'

Embury could have used the phone, but had gone to see the academic in person. Flint should do the same, but he had been told Ennismore was now in Athens. He took out his map of Greece, laid it on the bed and began to plan his escape from the Argolid.

Chapter Fifteen

She'd left Jeff hiding on the beach, where everyone could see him. It was a neat idea, that one, it amused her. How she'd engineer his escape to Athens was another matter. Lisa was winding her tongue around a tune she had picked up on the radio as she pushed open the door into the cool, dark, hotel interior.

'Mrs Lisa Canelopoulos?'

She stopped singing as the two uniformed men advanced from the lounge. She stopped smiling as they explained why they were there. With a solidly locked jaw, she allowed herself to be escorted to the police car waiting in a side street.

Nothing was said by either policeman as they drove her the ten miles to Argos. Lisa nibbled a fingernail and stared out of the window. The mountains receded, the sea was replaced by marshland and orchards. Steadily, she acquired composure. The police had to be grasping at straws, they might suspect, but could have no proof she had helped Jeff. Breathing deeply and slowly she prepared her position. Polite indignation, plus empty co-operation, was the mood to adopt and keep.

Interrogation proceeded in English and Greek. Greek when she felt she was winning and wanted to enhance goodwill, English when she felt threatened and hedged by the questions.

Yes she knew Jeffrey Flint.

No, they were not lovers.

No, she had not seen him.

Bright light streamed from a window high above the head of the police inspector with the scarred face and bad breath. Lisa hated the man instantly, and hated the light even more. Deceit needed darkness.

No, she had not helped him.

Alibis were required and produced, all convincing, most fraudulent, all impossible to check in their triviality. Solidly she resisted intimidation, all suggestion she was keeping information back. She could lie, she could stonewall and still smile. She could recognise when the police felt confident in their questioning and when they were simply hoping to trick her into confession.

No, she did not know where Flint had gone.

No, she saw no need for a lawyer.

Why did she visit Doctor Dracopoulos?

Now she knew who had tipped off the police. She played the innocent, smiled at the rude and aggressive detective and bottled up the anger for later. Internally, she weakened as the pressure built up. Externally, she maintained her charade. Four hours passed, with the time measured in fractions of seconds. Scarface rolled his eyes towards his young colleague and grunted. He folded up his file and left the room. The other policeman sighed, then smiled at Lisa.

'Okay. I can drive you back to your hotel now.'

*   *   *

Lisa was not singing as she again pushed her way into the hotel lobby, which now seemed cold and dingy. The young hotel clerk with the quiff and the nervous smile flourished an envelope. Her mind was elsewhere and she slit open the letter and read half of it before she realised what it was.

'Bastards,' she muttered.

All sunhat and floral smock, Pat Abbotts from Dudley sidled up to her and began to whinge. Lisa hardly heard, re-reading the letter, cursing her late husband, the police, God, and most of all, Jeffrey Flint.

'But Mrs Cannypullos,' Pat from Dudley was becoming insistent, 'you said you'd see about the shower, room seventeen.'

So many of her hate figures were safe, but Mrs Abbots was in range. Lisa spun around and allowed her emotions to explode.

'Why don't you just fuck off!'

The abuse echoed around the lobby. Mrs Abbot's mouth fell open. Lisa pushed past the tourist, hearing the clerk expressing concern. She turned and glared at him.

'And you're out of a job.'

Chapter Sixteen

Flint had wandered in the security of a soft focus fantasy garden. Nymphs in wispy veils picked flowers and danced to Dylan tracks. A crashing door jolted him awake. He sprang out of bed on reflex as the door opened and the light snapped on.

'Hi.'

No mob of burly blue-clad men poured inwards. A woman stood with her back to the door. Familiar, yet totally unknown. She had bobbed, ear length black hair and was completely without make-up.

'Elena Kyriacou,' she introduced herself.

Flint's eyes had adjusted to the light, he felt for his glasses and slipped them on. 'Lisa?'

She gave a grunt. 'Did I frighten you? Sorry.'

'What's the game?' He realised he was naked and sat back on the bed, glancing at his watch. 'It's two am.'

'We have to get out of here quick. I spent all afternoon at Argos police station, they know what you're up to and know I'm helping.'

He blinked, trying to disassociate dream from reality.

'Plus, I had a letter. Dear George's friends who

loaned him the money for the hotel have suddenly decided they need it back.'

Flint had found one sandal and reached under the bed for the other, feeling like Jonah for swamping Lisa's dreams.

'Don't apologise or anything,' she said. 'I've only lost my hotel, my home . . .'

'I'm sorry . . .'

'Don't be sorry!', she snapped. 'I was stupid getting mixed up with you again. I should have told you to piss off when you walked into my hotel, but I can't change that now. Let's just get those bastards, Jeffrey.' Lisa almost sobbed the last words and she fell against him.

Flint held her tightly, knowing that whoever stopped Embury excavating was determined that nobody else would start ferreting around in the facts. The bad guys were queuing up to stop him and with no way back, the only escape route was forward.

'We have to go,' she pulled herself away from him. 'We have to run, or someone is going to kill us.'

'Athens?'

'If you like.'

Lisa had packed a few clothes into a rucksack belonging to a client and requisitioned an 'Argus Rentals' 125cc motorbike from the Hotel forecourt. Flint had never been happy on motorbikes. In the dark, on the mountain road to Epidauros, he rode pillion, wearing the rucksack for added instability. Slowly, haphazardly, they wound through the Ahraneo mountains, past Epidauros, and down towards the glowing eastern sky. Telegraph poles and roadside rubbish grew in the feeble headlight beam, then faded into the dark. An occasional car charged them from behind, or blinded from ahead, but the police seemed to be slumbering.

As the sky brightened, Lisa pulled to the side of the road. Cold and stiff-legged, Flint scrambled to the top of the road bank, peering between pine trees which cascaded towards the sea.

'"The rosy pink fingers of dawn are rising above the wine-dark sea"', he mis-quoted.

'What?'

'Poetry.'

'Oh, yes, that's Byron isn't it?'

'Homer, "Odyssey".'

'Of course, how thick of me not to know. I would have failed Eng. Lit. if I'd stuck it out.' She yawned, dancing a tight circle at the road margins to pump life into her legs. 'I could murder a coffee, couldn't you?'

'Bad taste joke of the day.'

'Sorry, I don't function in the morning without coffee.'

Without coffee, they followed the twisting route overlooking the Saronic Gulf. An hour found them in a small, unwashed taverna, breakfasting with a chunk of bread and two coffees each.

The sun was high and blazing when they emerged once more. A bare right leg and bare right arm felt the prickle of heat as Flint clung to Lisa's back. Lead on, the breeze told them, the Corinth-Athens highway was ahead, rumbling with traffic. Brain-numbing noon saw Megara approaching, where the petrol tank ran dry and they coasted into a filling station to buy just enough fuel to see them to Athens. Back on the highway, buttocks ached, arms ached and lungs rebelled against the choking petrol fumes. No romantic odyssey led them from ancient Eleusis to Athens, where the dual carriageway churned through an industrial jungle of refineries and scrapyards. Oil tankers and private cars hurtled towards the capital with no knowledge of a highway code, leaving Lisa to battle in their slipstream, braking, swerving, accelerating and cursing. Flint simply hung on, as close to death as he ever hoped to be, hating the modern world with more conviction than ever. Tourist-laden jets whined low overhead and the heat-haze of summer smog throbbed with their passage. Scrapyards gave way to building sites and a jumble of concrete-coated hills: Athens.

A random left turn carried them into the backstreets of Peristeri, where they dismounted, groggy as poor sailors after an ocean crossing. Flint took out a ten drachma coin and unscrewed the bike's single number plate, which slipped neatly down a drain. The bike was abandoned in an alley, with key left irresistibly in place, for some local hooligan to steal as soon as it fell dark.

On foot, then by bus, Flint was introduced to Athens anew; bewildering, chaotic and thoroughly modern. The single day he had spent killing time at the Acropolis before his last flight from Greece years before had not prepared him for the confusion at street level. He needed to meet people, unearth facts, but first they must hide. Lisa would nod at his suggestions, read street signs aloud, looking for a location which matched his ideal; somewhere undistinguished, crowded and cheap.

Regular hotels were beyond question, all would require a passport, which had to be registered with the police. So the anabasis ended at an apartment block to the east of Omonia Square. A word in a kafenon led them to Mrs Kondyaki, a black-swathed widow who on occasion, took guests.

Mrs Kondyaki may have been in her late forties, but seemed older, with a practised stoop and heavily weathered features. She seized Lisa's attention and extolled the virtues of the room. With its view of grey high-rise blocks framed by the wooded peak of Lykavettos, it fell yards short of a Michelin entry. As a refuge from unknown enemies, it was heaven at a discount rate.

Flint dropped the rucksack in one corner as Lisa translated odd lines of monologue. Mrs Kondyaki lived in daily expectation that her son would find a wife and bring her back, so they would have to be ready to move out at a day's notice. Even the bed was ready, the widow's old wedding bed given to the son, awaiting the arrival of the wish-bride. Lisa flaunted her Greek lineage and waved away the inadequacies of the place. Embarrassed by poverty, the woman fussed over the guests, as custom dictated she should. A plate of olives and herbs was served in her kitchen, whilst Lisa concocted an impressive and completely fake life story.

Only when Lisa yawned did the widow take pity on the travellers and usher them to the bedroom. Flint flopped onto the bed, Lisa flopped by his side, arm held over sweating brow.

'She's friendly enough,' he said.

'Too friendly,' came the exhausted reply.

Flint let his eyes and his mind wander. Above him, on the wall above his bed was a fading print of a blue Madonna and traditionally swaddled Child. Not quite in the centre of the ceiling was an off-yellow lampshade suspended by a thin grey cord plus several spider's webs. He rolled his head to look out through the open shutters to the balcony-window. Someone in the flat opposite could watch him as he lay there, watch everything he did.

'We're married, by the way,' Lisa said.

'Oh. Always saw myself as a perpetual bachelor.'

'Will Vikki mind?'

Visions of a fist wielding an afro hair comb came into his thoughts, overridden by the memory of a recent one-night liaison with a stunning Canadian student, in turn erased by one particular weekend of lust which had embedded itself in his psyche.

'Vikki and I have an open relationship,' he said.

Lisa guffawed. 'The sixties will never die whilst Jeffrey Flint lives.'

An evening walk took them towards Exarha square; perversely triangular and lined with music bars and kafenons aimed at the student pocket. The wall of years had been broken down and Flint saw Lisa relax and regress towards the warmer, less bitter woman of younger days. For an hour they could have been back at Andreas' in Nauplion, in the carefree week before the murder. In that distant past, seducing Lisa Morgan had been his principal objective in life, but priorities had changed somewhat. Or so he managed to convince himself.

Back within the apartment, Flint chased away a pair of moths who assumed vampire bat proportions inside the lamp shade, whilst Lisa undressed and slipped into the bed. He turned the light off at the wall, then followed her.

She rolled over to touch him, with one hand on his chest, naked and sticky sweet. For a long time they said nothing until Lisa broke the silence.

'Do you know what I fancy?' she said.

'Tell me.'

'A damn good Open Relationship.'

Chapter Seventeen

Dawn clawed its sticky fingers into the Athenian sky. Car horns sounded reveille for the pair lying back-to back amongst the ruin of bedclothes. Flint awoke first, listening to the soft breathing behind him, watching the sunlight stream around the inadequate curtains.

He groaned inwardly; Flint, you're a rabbit. One day he'd wake up and not be surprised to learn the identity of his bedmate. One day, his libido would be brought into line by his political conscience, but perhaps not today; Lisa was beginning to stir.

A rack-and-pinion railway leads idle pilgrims to the church atop Lykavettos. From the mountain top, amongst a sprinkling of camera-clicking tourists, the heart of ancient and modern Athens lay before them. In the pleasing heat of late afternoon, the city smelt of concrete and traffic, but the city was an out-of-focus jumble of grey and white. Flint blinked, then took out the glasses which had nestled in the black trousers he had bought from a street vendor in Eoulou.

Lisa clicked her fingers in front of his eyes. 'Captivated?'

'Saddened,' he said. 'Athens, Rome, Naples, Cairo, London, you name the classical city, and the modern world has fouled it up.' Flint pointed to the sprawl of flats and offices which marched towards the horizon. 'Junk architecture, cars, and tourists.'

'Oh, ignore all that. Look at all the archaeology sparkling up at you.'

He looked again, ignoring the tower blocks and letting his eyes rest on the monuments one by one. There was a certain magic luminescence in the marble and he saw how captivation would be so easy.

Lisa took his arm and pointed out landmarks. High on the sanctuary, they mapped out their next moves, like gods on Olympus plotting the fate of men. Flint unfolded a map of the city and indicated the goals of his research; the National Library and the University lay back towards their apartment, with the Archaeological Museum beyond that. In the more select district at the base of the mountain lay The British School of Archaeology, sharing its grounds with the American Institute. Nearby was the Gennadeion Library and around the base of the hill, the French School of Archaeology. As the bases of itinerant scholars working in Greece, the foreign schools were at the hub of the world around which Sebastian Embury had moved. His friends, and his enemies, would know them well.

Flint occupied a telephone box for half an hour. His mum needed to be reassured (don't believe what you read in the papers). Next, Vikki needed to be found.

132

'Jeff, what's going on?' she enthused down the telephone.

'I stirred up a rat's nest in Nauplion.'

'Terrific; my editor says I can fly out this afternoon.'

Flint let his eyes rest on Lisa, leaning on a wall, distress etched on her suntanned features. 'I don't think that's a bright idea, love.' To put both Lisa and Vikki in close proximity would be like dropping two ferrets into a sack. One murder was enough to occupy his mind.

'Are you with that Lisa?' Vikki stiffened.

'I met her,' he said after just a fractional pause.

'Well, I don't care what you're up to so long as there's a story in it for me. Get it?'

He couldn't tell her where he was, or what he was doing. Vikki was a tenacious reporter, but she had the subtlety of the massed band of the Grenadier Guards. Facts were released in carefully rationed amounts; sufficient to correct the wild nonsense appearing in some of the papers, insufficient to be of any use to the opposition.

'In return for all that, my sweetheart, I need money – say five hundred quid. I'll pay you back. Give me a name in Athens, someone with nous, who can pass it on.'

Vikki muttered something inaudible – probably abusive. She rustled pages of a fil-o-fax then said, 'Hugh Owlett' and passed over his number.

'Thanks Vik, you're a heroine.'

When shops re-opened in the late afternoon, they strolled through a maze of streets opening off Ermou;

shops spilled onto pavements and what they did not offer could be bought from men with handcarts or baskets of second-hand goods. He borrowed money from Lisa, bought a battered typewriter and more clothes to suit the new personality he was designing. A carrier bag of assorted stationery turned Mrs Kondyaki's scratched and aged dressing-table into a work station for Flint's research. In the evening, all those hours spent learning the art of draughtsmanship finally found its pay-off. With a fine black pen, a rectangle of card and a much-hunted pack of Letraset, Flint gingerly faked a new identity. The University of London crest was far simpler to forge than that of Central College and after only one failed attempt he created a convincing library card. A high quality photocopier was needed to produce the correct effect, but suitably crumpled and artificially aged, his forgery should pass the eyes of bored librarians around the city. He showed Lisa and she was impressed. The test was whether it would impress anyone else.

The following morning, Lisa dressed him in a very cheap, ill-fitting black cotton jacket. The plain shirt looked good, but she warned it would probably wash badly.

'You look the part of a sad little academic now Mr Adams,' she began, pecked him on the cheek and laid on a gently Americanised accent. 'Have a nice day at the office, honey.'

Paul Adams, no longer a bank clerk, had rapidly graduated from Cardiff University, and was even now preparing a doctoral research project at the London

Institute. Flint had used their library hundreds of times, he knew plenty of names and faces. His only gamble was that he'd avoid meeting inquisitive Cardiff alumni.

Flint held ambiguous views about the British School at Athens. He resented its colonial overtones, yet empathised with its deep roots in Greek archaeology. Many great names had passed through its doors and it was one of those calm, yet intense havens of academia which entranced him.

The white-walled building sits amongst neatly tended gardens. Flint braved the blue doors, armed with a pack of fabricated credentials and thoroughly rehearsed lies. A pair of startled professors in London had been telephoned and persuaded to perjure themselves as Paul Adams' referees. Flint breezed inside, put on his most serious, elevated facial expression and spent twenty minutes moulding a case for admittance. Prim but earnest, a Mrs Edith Hopkins frowned as he waffled and fibbed within the sheltered, echoing calm of the vestibule.

The administrators had not received his letter, he was not expected. Oh dear. He waved fake cards, fake documents, fake copies of fake letters. He needed to register in order to stay at the School. There was a procedure, there were forms, he needed a referee. But he knew enough names and managed to con-nect Mrs Hopkins with the perjured professors in London and this credible fiction led to his eventual admittance.

Mixing charm with evasion he muddled through the

formalities, paid his fee and let his hand hover over a document stating that he would not become involved in Greek internal affairs, politics or publish articles which could cause offence to the Greek state. He thought of Vikki and headlines incorporating the words UNJUST or CORRUPT or FRAMED, then the innocuous Paul Adams signed the form.

Flint had stayed in Athens overnight with Embury all those years ago, but had kept in the background whilst the director glad-handed old acquaintances and there was no-one whom he still recognised. Paul Adams took the librarian's hand in a firm shake and smiled a deep, broad smile. Loose amongst shelves of books and racks of catalogues, Flint was at home. Within days he would be able to use his new-found credibility to gain access to a dozen other institutions in the city. A little subtle small talk and he might worm his way into academic lunches, tea parties and soirées. Information was the key: he would hunt the motive, leaving Lisa to pursue the suspects.

Emma had hinted that Sebastian Embury may have been on the brink of that lifetime discovery at Palaeo-kastro. A discovery that could have made his name, or his fortune, but had brought only death. Flint doubted that any mysterious ancient wonder lay buried at Palaeokastro, but these things happened, it was what even the most puritan archaeologists privately dreamed of. If the site held a secret, someone had obviously found evidence as to what it was. All Flint had to do was repeat the feat.

*   *   *

Tame PhD students have their uses, even if the student is an unreformed Thatcherite like Tyrone Drake. Tyrone was ambitious and had a good sense of where his best interests lay.

'Tyrone?' Flint was using the telephone in the vestibule of the British School. His student was using his infernal Vodaphone.

'Hi Doc, I read about your latest adventures.'

'Safest thing to do. Meanwhile, ditch Burkes Warren and get back to London PDQ.'

'But, we've found the late bath-house!'

'It's been there for sixteen hundred years, one more won't make any difference. Excavate me out of a hole. I want you to read three papers: two by Sebastian Embury on Palaeokastro, plus the original German excavation report. Next, work back through the references, checking what Embury said about the site.'

'What am I looking for?'

'Something he deliberately missed out of his last paper. Something worth dying for. Send a telemessage to the British School, addressed to Paul Adams.'

'Who he?'

'A sad little academic. Keep it brief and be discreet.'

Tyrone seemed to be clicking his tongue. 'I can't read Greek.'

'Drag Anna Georgiou out of the library; tell her that if she helps you, I'll re-mark her last essay.'

'That's corrupt!'

'It's a sad, sick world, Tyrone.'

*   *   *

Pamela Shrivenhurst had been Sebastian Embury's niece and the subject of many monologues concerning Estate Agencies in the Cotswolds. She'd never been to Greece, knew little about archaeology, so even a doubtful Lisa could impersonate her without risk. She cautiously followed Flint into the British School that same morning, carrying a list of the names Embury had dropped, in descending order of frequency. Dr Neil Ennismore was tall, dark (if one discounted greying strands) and had the weathered good looks of a footballer, or square-jawed ocean yachtsman. He also knew a family restaurant high in the Plaka, where the service was polite and the bill could be contained.

'No,' he declared, shaking his head. Ennismore held his wine badly.

Lisa held hers rather better, trying not to enjoy the balmy night air, the bouyant bustle of the narrow street and the obvious advances of the academic. Role playing was difficult when sober, but she continued the act. 'I spoke to Juliette Howe at that little bungalow in Epidauros. She said my uncle had lost his work permit.'

'Ooh dear, let me see, yes. He rang me, it must have been a day or two before he died . . .'

'Day, or two?' Lisa pressed, hoping to God she'd remember all this.

'I can't remember, honest scout, he'd gone to the Bungalow . . .' Ennismore rambled slightly, '. . . he had a problem with his terms of reference for his excavation; some dispute with the site guardian. He asked me to put a word in at the Ministry of Culture. I knew this woman there – professionally, of course.'

138

'Of course.'

'There was no problem, the Min. of C. were happy as birds. Dear old Embers could carry on excavating for all they cared.'

Lisa took a paper napkin and a pen and scribbled a few notes.

'You must have been close.' Ennismore slurred.

'Mmm,' Lisa said, 'But someone wanted him to stop digging?'

'Most definitely, but Zeus knows who.'

'Doctor Dracopoulos?'

'Old Christos? He's a queer bird, is he still alive? I never had much time for collectors, too shady for my likes, smuggling of portable antiquities, underhand deals in brown paper parcels . . .'

'But wasn't he the one trusted to look after the site at Palaeokastro?'

Ennismore nodded, then scowled at an empty Achaia bottle. 'He was site guardian, the one who keeps an eye on we foreigners, makes sure we don't march off with any treasures.'

'And he was the one Seb . . . my uncle, complained about?'

'Indirectly, I suppose, yes.'

Why was this prat talking backwards? 'What do you know about Emma Woodfine?' she asked, knowing the wine was going to win.

'Dreadful woman. Sorry, do you know her?'

'Awful. I don't understand what my uncle saw in her.'

One eyebrow flicked upwards, indicating this was

news, perhaps Ennismore absorbed gossip badly. 'I say Pam, can I call you Pam? This wine has evaporated, it must be the heat. Shall I order more? No? How about a raki or an ouzo?'

What the hell, she wasn't paying.

Chapter Eighteen

Jules Torpevitch had chosen a golden yellow college sweatshirt that day: its innumerable creases betrayed the fact that he was missing his wife. The tall, dark-skinned, round-cheeked Bostonian looked at himself in the mirror within the gent's lavatory of the American School. Using the crack between door and toilet cubicle, Flint watched as Jules smoothed a hand across his bald pate. Jules followed the instructions on the cryptic message to the letter, indeed to the note. Sounding foolish, he whistled the opening bars of the 'Star Trek' signature tune.

'We come in peace!' Flint stepped out of the door.

'Fuck me!'

'No thanks, kind offer Jules.'

'Jeff, kid, what are you on?'

'I'm Paul Adams – did you read the papers?'

'Yeah, you made the Athens Times, but . . . what's with the U.S. Marine haircut?'

'I'm in disguise, I'm in hiding.' Flint gave a brief resumé of his newly adopted persona.

'Brilliant ruse, kid. An English academic wants to hide, so he disguises himself as an English academic.'

Flint grabbed both elbows of Jules' sweatshirt. 'No fooling: I need to be able to mingle.'

'Hey, they'll think we're perverts.' Jules broke free.

'Homophobe!'

'Cross-dresser!' Jules slapped Flint on the shoulder. 'Sink a beer?'

'Tonight?'

'Sure thing . . . Paul.'

Paint flaked from the walls, tablecloths were fixed by clothes pegs and the flies seemed to dine well. Whilst Lisa was being charmed by Dr Neil Ennismore at some chic joint in the Plaka, Flint skipped down the menu of one of the cheapest downtown tavernas. It was no longer as cheap as the night Sebastian Embury had brought him here: a supposed big-hearted gesture from the old Hellenophile. Greece was in the EC now, no longer a poor relation, but sitting at the rich man's table. Prices were beginning to rise towards London levels; impoverished Englishmen would not be able to play the wealthy colonial forever.

His anarchic thoughts were interrupted by a group of blatantly American students joking and jostling their way into the bar. Jules was towards the rear of the group, searching the taverna with nervous glances.

'Paul! fancy meeting you here,' Jules forced the rehearsed line from his lips.

'Jules, long time no see.'

The dozen polyglot Americans tumbled into seats with a barrage of jokes. Flint caught the eye of the one who seemed to be the self-appointed Organiser. Max

Halleck, star of the group, was stocky, broad-handed, with a bushy red moustache to match his unwieldy hairstyle and co-ordinated sunburnt nose. He seized upon Jules' long-lost friend, made the introductions, ordered the wine, forced menu choices on the doubters and finally led the others in song. Paul Adams lifted into the mood. They were archaeologists, the taverna owner accepted their eccentricities; laissez-faire was the rule and the students let rip. Jules sat at the opposite end of the table, saying little, drinking rather more, seeming to find it hard to play the lie.

'We've got a little Bronze Age site over near Marathon. You know the battle of Marathon?' Max's lips hovered on the brink of a guffaw at the end of each sentence, as though he had just retold a risqué joke.

'Marathon? Greeks one, Persians nil: Athens through to the next round.'

Max burst into an unreasonable belly laugh. 'Soccer, right?'

Before Flint began to regret the football analogy, Max switched back to archaeology. 'We're about half way done now, finishing up by the end of August. And what's your field Paul?'

Paul Adams was not the sort to push himself too far. 'I'm re-assessing Kevin Andrew's work on fortifications in the Peloponesse.' He suddenly sensed danger, 'Or I intend to,' he added. 'I've just started the background reading.'

The qualifier allowed him to be ignorant if someone in the group happened to be a fortification fanatic.

'Basically I'm going to do a photo-mosaic of a dozen fortress walls.'

'Walls, he had us weeding walls,' Angie, the Afro-American drawled, pointing a knife at Max, 'and Lincoln thought he'd abolished slavery.'

Max suddenly noticed Jules playing with a left-over chicken bone. 'Put it down, Jules, it ain't dead yet!'

Jules waggled the leg-bone, 'There is more bone here,' he slurred, 'there is more bone in this sad, sorry meal than on our whole sad, sorry site. Honestly, Jeffrey, its pathetic . . .'

'Bones, bones, bones: why did he marry a veg-etarian?' Flint launched in a panicked flurry, glaring at Jules.

Jules closed his eyes very tightly, then blinked.

'Have you met Sasha? Gorgeous, too gorgeous . . .' Max crooned.

No-one was sober enough, or alert enough to have spotted Jules' gaffe, Flint tried to relax once more. Diggers' tales flowed around him and Paul Adams was forced to respond with stories belonging to Jeffrey Flint. Max lectured the Englishman on his great brain-child: earth-searching radar. His father's company was experimenting with it to search out utilities beneath city streets.

'Will it improve on a resistivity meter?' Flint asked.

'That's yesterday's technology, this is the future. Resistivity is dead, digging will be for losers. We're talking direct linkage to computers, which draw three-dimensional plans without human participation. One day, this kind of gizmo is going to put you shovel-and-pick merchants out of business.'

'I'd like to see it.'

'Come on out to Marathon.'

'I may do so.'

Flint thought back to his own resistivity survey in the olive grove at Palaeokastro, then of another shovel-and-pick merchant who had been put permanently out of business. What an irrelevance that survey had been! A notebook had been filled with completely useless data. The hubbub of the room faded as a perverse thought came into his head. If Embury's great discovery had been at the bottom of the site, why had he not taken the equipment down there?

Chapter Nineteen

'That Neil Ennismore was a real character, I mean a real character.'

Morning-after hangovers had been dispersed by more street-corner coffees and Lisa walked beside Flint, nibbling the long *koulouri* that dangled from her wrist and trading good-time-tales.

'I think he fancied his chances, you academics are desperately oversexed.'

'It's what keeps us sane.'

'Or drives you insane. Honest, we got through two bottles of wine plus the ouzos and raki. He was pissed as a newt when I loaded him into the taxi.'

'And you?'

'Oh I'm immune.' She rolled her head slightly. 'My head just hurts from too much thinking. The last thing I want to do is go back to that stinking room and start shuffling your cards again.'

Back in the room, below the fading (and disapproving) Madonna, she stripped down to panties and T-shirt and lolled face-down on the bed. Grabbing at her notepad, Lisa frowned at what she had scrawled the night before. Flint sat in the chair, cards at the ready, cool and clinical.

Lisa propped herself on her elbows and summarised her evening. 'Embury went to see Ennismore a day or two before the murder.'

'It was the day before,' Flint said, 'We wanted the minibus to go to the pictures.'

'Shall I tell the story, or shall you?'

He waved his hand with good grace and listened to her news, ignoring the litany of good food and flowing wine, jotting down the key points.

'So we can forget anything relating to work permits, *synergasia*, permission to excavate or whatever. The survey had the backing of the authorities or it would never have begun. So, whoever was pressurising Embury was unable to influence the Ministry of Culture.'

'Or didn't have the time,' Lisa said. 'Everyone knows civil servants take forever to do anything. Greek civil servants take twice as long.'

'True. So let's say the problem came up quickly; too late to stop Embury getting his permission renewed, probably after we actually started on site. You know, we were chatting about resistivity surveys last night . . .'

'What? Remember, I'm a bear of little brain.'

'It's a way of looking beneath the soil for hidden features. It saves a hell of a lot of digging. I ran this excruciatingly futile survey of the olive grove at Palaeokastro, when by all the laws of logic, Embury should have deployed the equipment at the bottom of the site, where he was directing his main effort. It's just one more irrational fact that doesn't tally.'

Lisa stared at him, a creeping expression of disquiet invading her face. 'Jeff, is all this my fault?'

'What do you mean?'

'If you remember, everyone in town had heard you found gold in your olive grove. When we were in Andreas' place in Nauplion and I showed everyone your crunched up old pen, they all wanted to know about the treasure from Palaeokastro.'

'No, it can't be.' He dismissed her with a wave and a shake of the head.

She become animated, raising her voice. 'But why not? We're looking for a motive. Have you thought about a local gang of crooks getting to hear about your gold and trying to get your Prof. to share it with them?'

'Which of course he couldn't, because I never told him about the pen.' Flint looked back out of the window, obviously troubled by her suggestion. Slowly he added, 'That is, not until the night he died.'

Flint picked the pen out of the pile of belongings on the floor and tossed it to her.

'What does it tell you?' he asked.

She read the name Byron F. Nichols, commenting on the antique styling and the heavy feel.

'Artefacts are text,' he mumbled, 'they can be read, each object tells a story.'

'What?'

'Hermeneutics – the assignment of meaning to objects. Forget it, you'll accuse me of bullshitting again.'

'You are – and you're going to ignore my idea.'

'I like the idea, it's just a little . . .' he thought around for a polite putdown, 'it's too ironic. My theory is as follows: Embury discovered something important.'

'Like what?' came a bleary voice.

'Dunno, but he shunted me out of the way so he would get all the glory. Someone else heard about it and for whatever reason, they told him to stop. If this had been some routine bureaucratic cock-up, he would have grumbled to Emma, then to Doctor D., the site guardian, but both of them denied knowing anything . . .'

'But Ennismore said Dr D. knew about it.'

'So the pair of them are telling porky pies. They might have had a hand in trying to warn Embury off, but he simply turned manic. He telephoned everyone he could think of, but gave away no detail. This was his discovery, the only one he has ever made, and he was keeping it to himself.

'Next, someone nicked the minibus just to show they were serious, and he agreed to a secret meeting. There was an argument, the bad guys roughed him up, he died, and I got framed in order to terminate the excavation. As a final twist, someone paid for the best lawyer in town to get me off the hook to avoid a trial.

'Now, Embury, an Old School Imperialist, thought the English had God's right to excavate anywhere they choose. He'd have taken his complaints to the top. He could write pretty fierce letters when he got angry. I bet someone in the Ministry received a letter, or at least holds notes on a phonecall from him. He'd make a fuss, name names if he was being pressured.'

'A fierce, fussy archaeologist?' Lisa asked, 'Convinced he's right, listening to no-one else, going straight to the top, even if it kills him.'

'That's right: that was Embury.'

'I was talking about you.'

'Touché, Lisa.'

She smiled and nodded at the compliment.

'So, my brilliant, witty, surrogate wife, I'm afraid you're going to have to get into the Ministry and see if you can find that woman Ennismore mentioned.'

'Nope.'

'Come on Lisa.'

'Not me.'

'It's the only way.'

'To get caught. I know the system here, I will need to write for an appointment, they will want to write back. It will take time, we'll need a postal address which will lead the police here. Or, they might check up on this Pamela woman I'm supposed to be playing. It's not a good cover story Jeff, I didn't know the old boy well enough to play his niece.'

'Okay, say you're a reporter.'

'And then they will pass me on to the Press Secretary who probably drinks with all the reporters in Athens. I'm not Vikki, remember?'

Ooh, out came the claws and in they sank! Flint edged around his opponent, trying to find a vulnerable flank. 'Don't be negative.'

'I'm being practical and trying to save your lily-white skin.' She tossed her notebook onto the pile of paperwork. 'You've marked my homework, one out of ten, failed again.'

Lisa lowered herself back into the face-down posture with her hands supporting her chin and looked away from him, into the dim, unswept corners of the room. Both were silent for several minutes whilst the passion dispersed and became something else.

'I think we're just playing games,' she said quietly.

The bed creaked as he sat beside her.

'We don't stand a chance of finding any real clues.'

He lay a hand on the seat of her pants.

'We're going to sit in this room every night, drowning in our own sweat and every day we're going to run around Athens like idiots asking idiotic questions, until my money runs out or we get caught. We find out nothing, you go to jail and I go to jail, all for some stupid old git who you never liked anyway. And if the police don't get us, someone else will.'

'Eight out of ten – with a little note in red biro saying "see me".'

'Go away. Go away, damn you! I wish you were guilty, so I could turn you in for a reward.' She rolled to face him. 'You're an old ghost come back to haunt me.'

'I thought we had something going.'

'That's a line from one of your damned movies – I never thought we had anything going.'

'I thought, perhaps, you and I could see the world. You always wanted to see the world.'

'Not like this,' she said. 'Not sleeping in sleazy fleapits and eating in the cheapest caffs in town. Young, exciting men are good for one thing, Jeffrey Flint. I need a fat old man with pots of money.'

'You tried that.'

'So I did, but you and your friendly lawyer screwed that up for me.'

'My lawyer?'

'Boukaris, the big-shot. He's one of the directors of a company called Korifi; they own a whole load of hotels and bars. George borrowed his money from them. Your man doesn't offer charity any more.'

'He's been got at,' Flint stated. 'That's why he wouldn't defend me this time. Who's the money in Korifi?'

She frowned deeply, 'Someone Charamboulos: he's the banker. There's a developer among them too, I think he's called Scarlatos.'

Flint the anarchist almost smiled; bankers and developers were tribes he would enjoy taking on.

Chapter Twenty

Korifi Corporation (1975). Land (agricultural), Hotels, Restaurants.

Directors: V. Boukaris, D. Charamboulos, A. Scarlatos.

Within the library of the Chamber of Commerce, Lisa translated the information and Flint filled in his index card.

'There's no mention of Doctor D. there?'

'No.'

'That would have been convenient, but we don't know which part of the food chain he occupies – is he a shark or a minnow? Where did the orders come from?'

When Lisa smiled, arrows of age pointed the way to her wide brown eyes. 'Korifi own three hotels in Nauplion and Tolon,' she said, tantalising him with the details. 'Pentelikon, Niki, guess the name of the third.'

He knew instantly, 'Daedelus.'

Where the waiter worked, the one with the perfect night vision and the delayed memory. Linking the property company to the case opened up a wide new field of motives for Embury's death. It was time to meet Hugh Owlett, vulture of the press, and throw some morsels his way.

Seeing the white bones of the Parthenon a dozen times a day had gnawed at his dedication. All he needed was one excuse and he would be climbing the Acropolis and touching the vanishing stonework.

Hugh Owlett had been lured to the Acropolis by a deliberately mysterious phonecall. Flint wanted crowds, lots of foreigners and a hint of drama to excite the journalist's imagination. Confused by Athenian topography, unable to read street signs, he also wanted a place he could find. In the sultry late afternoon, he pushed his way up the worn steps of the sanctuary, remembering too late that he would be charged entry and regretting every drachma spent.

Owlett was leaning over a parapet below the Erecthion, sun on his back, adding more smoke to the smog which was dissolving the monument. He carried a black umbrella as a signal and beneath the Panama hat, a light safari suit sat uncomfortably on his frame. Flint tagged behind a group of Dutch, looking for alert tourist police or suspicious men lurking in shadows. Satisfied that the man with the brolly was Owlett, and that Owlett was alone, he detached from the tourists and dropped alongside.

'Hi.'

The reporter frowned, leaned to look under the brim of the cheap white sun hat, checked the short hair, then said, 'So who are you?'

'Jeffrey Flint; I'm the communist revolutionary you may have read about in the Express.' Flint pulled himself onto the ancient wall and sat facing the crowds.

Owlett was a red-faced, pugnacious man whose waistline advertised too much good living at trade lunches. He pushed out a hand. 'You know Vikki Corbett?'

'Fairly well.'

'Nice girl, Vikki. So what can I do for you?'

'Is there a brown envelope?'

'It's white.' Owlett passed the money under his palm, as if paying off a crack dealer, then also turned to face inwards.

Despite long-standing contact with Vikki, journalists ranked just above developers, bankers and policemen in Flint's personal bestiary.

'Vikki tells me you were accused of murder seven years ago and let off on a technicality?'

'I was framed and the cops were too embarrassed to admit it.'

'Fine. Then you come back and they frame you again?'

'Precisely.'

'Forgive me, Doctor Flint, I hate to sound the cynical old hack, but it sounds to me like the police have a case this time.' Owlett rumbled, in his north Kentish accent.

'I'm innocent.'

'The gaols are full of innocent men. Why don't you bugger off back to England and let the law sort it out?'

'Ever read Sun Tzu, or Mao? There were thirty-six basic stratagems known to the Ancient Chinese. Stratagem thirty-six is 'Run away'; I've tried that. This time, I'm going on the offensive, asking questions and picking up facts, but I need to stay undercover until I have enough data to prove who was behind Embury's death. If the cops catch me before I've amassed my evidence, I won't stand a chance of clearing my name in court.'

'You'd be surprised. Greece has changed. It's not like it was under the Colonels, this isn't the third world. If you're innocent, what's the problem?'

'If you were a murderer, would you mind doubling your score?'

Owlett had a wary, even cunning look in his eyes. 'Do you smoke?' Owlett clearly did and groped for an inner pocket.

'No, it pollutes the soul.'

The smoker frowned and tried to smile at the off-beat comment. Owlett slid his hand into a different pocket and withdrew a leather-bound notepad. 'So who did it?'

'I don't know, I hoped you could help.'

Any flicker of enthusiasm in Owlett's expression promptly died. 'Vikki told me there was a story in this, but you want me to go out and find my own story?'

'I'll find the scoop for you, if you'll perform a few services in return.' Flint stopped. A pair of tourist police had appeared, walking slowly through the multitude.

'Shall we walk?' Owlett suggested nervously.

Flint slipped off the wall and walked in the shadow of the journalist.

'You were saying, services? Remember, I'm free-lance, I need a story at the end of the day.' Owlett watched where he was walking to give the impression of disinterest.

'Do you have contacts at the Ministry of Culture?'

A noncomittal movement of the head acknowledged that he might. Flint related the series of messages he suspected had passed through the Ministry. Owlett stopped walking, dropped his indifferent expression and jotted down a few notes.

'How much more of this do you have?'

'Heaps. It's like I'm doing a thousand piece jigsaw puzzle. I've got a dozen pieces from somewhere down the bottom left and a few chunks of sky, but I can only guess what the picture is.'

'Very poetic, sure you can handle it?'

'Of course I can handle it! It's my job, piecing together the past is what I do. Last week, or last millenium, it's all the same.'

The pen suddenly launched into a fury of short-hand.

'What's that you're writing?'

'I'm quoting you, kiddo.'

Flint laid a hand on the pen. 'Don't write anything about meeting me.'

Owlett spread his hands. 'Where's the story if I don't?'

Out came a sheet of paper, two sides crammed with close printing. 'I sent you a letter: it's all in here, just

159

don't mention that I'm in Athens and don't say I'm doing my own investigating. I don't want a demarcation dispute with the Union of Private Detectives.'

The reporter took the letter and read it. 'Nauplion . . . Dracopoulos, Korifi who are they? . . . what's this say? Byron who? . . .'

'Forget him, not all the detail is relevant, I just wrote everything down, hoping something would click.'

Half closing one eye, Owlett glanced up at Flint, then around himself at another archaeological jigsaw-puzzle. He was weighing up risk and gain. 'The Greeks are going to have my arse on a kebab if they find out I've helped you. Secrecy works two ways.'

'Officially I'm in hiding, waiting for a chance to get out of the country. If the police catch me, I never saw you.'

'Huh.' Owlett snorted and closed his notebook. 'Will you be around the next few days?'

'I can be.'

'Here's my card.' He gave Flint a crisp business card. 'Call me, say the beginning of next week, after I've had time to check these details.'

'Next week?'

'You don't get instant answers from civil servants. This will take time.'

Owlett tipped the point of his hat and walked away. The archaeologist quickly dodged into a large group of Britons gawping at the Parthenon, half hearing tales of gunpowder stores and lightning strikes. He was safe, no-one was tailing him, no-one was watching him. A glance at his watch confirmed it was still early.

160

His eyes were drawn upward by Periclean marble, then across to be seduced by Caryatids in silhouette. Lisa would understand, he reasoned, it was time for a treat.

Chapter Twenty-One

The week passed in which the days saw continuous charades and the nights ran together as a blurr of lust; less inventive, less energetic than a decade before, but age blunts inclination just as time embellishes memory. Only in the dark were Flint and Lisa truly together. In the mornings they parted, he to a library, she to another rendezvous. All her enquiries were throwing up blanks, uncovering nothing beyond the usual bitching and polite backstabbing endemic in the rarefied world of academia. None of Embury's cronies knew of any vices, any debts, or any dark personal secrets. His world had been archaeology and nothing outside seemed to affect or interest him.

Flint took great delight in continuing to evade the police and his confidence increased with each day he remained free. A telegram was waiting for Paul Adams at the British School. Tyrone had been instructed to be discreet and succinct. Both criteria had been taken to extreme:

ZILCH.

It was signed D. Duck. Very funny, thought Flint.

He could see little further use for Tyrone. Inviting a 'known associate' to Athens might attract attention: contacting Jules had been a mistake that had won no profit. Flint had always believed that the optimum size for any organisation is one.

His philosophy had been slightly compromised: one-man bands were fine if they could speak the language. Within the panelled, period gloom of the National Library of Greece, Flint found a new task for his partner.

'I've done as much research as I can into modern Nauplion and my student has drawn a blank in London. Next I'm going to work through the approved reading Embury gave me before I was appointed: there were only twenty or so references. I'm going to look for ancient texts, classical allusions, archaeological reports, things which Embury might have found since he wrote his last paper. Do you follow the logic of all this?'

Lisa looked bemused, even patronised, but nodded quietly.

'So, I want you to search out any Greek reference to Nauplion or Palaeokastro: maps, newspapers, history books, folklore, anything. Any mention of Korifi, or Messrs Charamboulos, Boukaris, Scarlatos or Doctor D.'

She cast her eyes around. A very large number of books stared back at her. 'So where do I start?'

'You look at the modern stuff and work backwards: I'll meet you in the twelfth century. Anything in English I've probably read by now.'

164

'But what am I looking for?' she said between her teeth.

'When you find it, it will bite you.'

'Your wish is my command,' Lisa bowed slightly in mock submission.

Flint walked to the German School of Archaeology on Fidou Street, with Lisa on his mind, hoping she could keep her head above water. Already a week had been expended since the flight to Athens and he had found no likely motive for Embury's death. Perhaps he had been over-optimistic, or perhaps he needed to work harder or perhaps there was value in Lisa's love triangle and it was the archaeological theory that was romantic illusion.

Smiles, fibs, letters of introduction, a pleasant German student named Katrina and anecdotes about his time spent working in the Romisch-Germanisch Museum, Koln, bought his way into the German School. He began to assault the tedious pile of references, skimming through, ignoring any line that seemed irrelevant, aiming at completing a dozen works that day. At three, his head fell onto the centre of a copy of *Bonner Jahrbuch*. He had read these books before, he had read them all twice. Palaeokastro was not a well-known site, its bibliography short and dull. What little was known about the Roman and Greek town was published. There were no tantalising suggestions of hidden wonders, no partly revealed secrets, only total blank spaces where no work had been done. If Athens was the cradle of Democracy, Palaeokastro was where they had thrown the dirty nappies. His energy and enthusiasm were beginning to wear thin, the whole exercise seeming gratuitously irrelevant.

He would work all day Saturday, and drive Lisa to work too: who knew how long their game could continue? Sunday could be the day of rest, they could explore Strefi Hill and lie in the sun, distracting each other for a few hours. The age gap seemed to matter less now, intimacy was pulling them together. Flint opened his eyes, *Bonner Jahrbuch* 1931.

Strefi Hill gives a view back over Exarhia and towards the Archaeological Museum. Idiosyncratic landscaping has created woodland grottos and mock castles rambling around the prominence. Lounging in wooded shade was a welcome escape from the maze of anonymous apartment blocks, hard streets and dark libraries below.

Flint was thinking about Palaeokastro in the Middle Ages, something he'd awarded little attention.

'Athens feels like home after a week, don't you think?' Lisa broke into his thoughts.

'Home? No, I love travelling, but I'm never at home and I'm totally immune to that Hellenophile bug which seems to bite the English. Greece is a great place, but I feel like an alien. I don't belong here, I could never even pretend to belong here.'

'The Greek half of me would stay here forever,' she said in a languid, dreamy voice. 'The Greeks have a special way of doing things. Their attitude to life is simply wonderful.'

Flint groaned, 'Sorry, I don't believe that twaddle about Greek lifestyle you travel people are always pushing.'

Lisa came back sharply. 'You sound as if you don't like the Greeks.'

'Oh, the people are wonderful when they're not trying to arrest you. I just find that romantic Zorba-the-Greek-aren't-the-peasants-wonderful notion terribly ethnocentric.'

'God, you're on form this morning, that was a mouthful, even for you. You've no romance,' Lisa asserted. 'Well, I love Greece. I don't miss Real Ale and fish and chip shops and Test Match Special.'

'Neither do I.'

'Fibber, I saw you reading the cricket scores yesterday.' Lisa grimaced. 'Hey, we've only been married for a week and we're already squabbling.'

He hugged her close to squeeze home his opinions. 'Intellectual discourse is not squabbling. You win: Athens is marvellously, splendidly, extravagantly grand! Tomorrow, I'm going to to the British School to look at local saints and martyrs.'

Lisa let out a long moan and dropped onto her back. 'Bloody Palaeokastro. Why didn't someone just build an airport on top of it, or a leisure centre?'

'Perhaps someone wants to,' Flint suggested.

'I'll drive the bulldozer,' Lisa said.

He could see how total obliteration of the site would be appealing. 'Okay, fantasies apart, I'll stock up on references tomorrow, so you can hit the Gennadeion on Tuesday.'

'So I get a day off tomorrow?'

'No, no, I want you to hunt for maps. Start in the Blegen library at the American Institute, I can talk you in. My friend Jules is good buddies with the student on the desk.'

'You academics all stick together don't you?'

'Yes,' he snapped, then softened his tone. 'That is, when we're not sticking the knives into each other's backs. Chin up, Lisa. We're building up masses of information, the pieces will start falling together soon, we're getting closer.'

'What about the other people?' she asked. 'You're not the only one who can do research. Are they getting closer too?'

So another week began, with Flint slouched back in a library chair, eyes barely seeing the text resting on the edge of the desk. Pottery? Were there any books devoted to pottery in the Argolid? No, too trivial. Metalworking? Goldsmith's hoards? Any evidence that Greek settlers buried their wealth to keep it out of the hands of the Romans? With a heavy sigh he scribbled down his latest wild ideas, with no facts to support them. He had skimmed virtually every volume of *The Greek and Byzantine Journal.* There was nothing new, nothing left to say about Palaeokastro. Grotty, insignificant little dump.

Thymios K. Angelos sat within his white Citroën, parked in one of the expensive side-streets at the foot of Lykavettos. Lunch on expenses was always a pleasure.

He folded the *Daily Express* neatly and thoughtfully. Tourist resort death case shock re-opening! British communist activist framed for murder. Greek government cover-up. Greek police corruption. Greek provincials in sinister conspiracy. He tapped the dashboard of his car in rhythm to the music then snapped off the radio. Straightening his suit he left the car and walked around the block to the British School.

Angelos slipped inside with practiced coolness, hardly glancing at the undistinguished academic in a second-hand jacket who passed him in the doorway. The two photographs he produced brought only frowns from Mrs Hopkins, but within his sophisticated English vocabulary, the word 'no' had an elastic, negotiable meaning. He talked his way into the library, with teeth so white, grooming so immaculate, and his enquiry surrounded one word: Palaeokastro.

Chapter Twenty-Two

Mrs Kodyaki fed them breakfast each day for a modest price, which included listening to her constant chatter. She soaked up the lies Lisa was forced to invent to spin out conversation. Flint would sit with eyes glazing as the Greek passed to and fro. Afterwards, in the intimacy of their room, Lisa would relate annoying snippets of news; 'She wants us to meet her neighbour,' or, 'She's been telling all her relatives about us,' or 'She hopes her son will be coming home next weekend.' Flint had no doubt that he would shortly hear Mrs Kondyaki on local radio, informing all of Athens about her lodgers.

Lisa had bought a bottle of turpentine-grade retsina and drank most of it in an hour. Adopting the Christine Keeler pose astride the chair, she watched her lover as he sat cross-legged on the bed, reading. Wearing only boxer shorts, with the faded virgin and child just above his head, Flint could have been a guru selling sex and instant enlightenment.

She had followed her instructions and obtained more information for Flint. Palaeokastro had featured on a map of American forces' road building programme of

1949 and Lisa had been thrilled with her discovery; to find any mention of the place seemed a miracle.

'I thought it was a funny place to build a road.' Lisa seemed to crave conversation.

He'd read a little about the Greek Civil War; a war fought between rival factions of abbreviations: EOK, EKKA, EAM, ELAS and even a group known as X. The communist 'Democratic Army' had resorted to the customary democratic techniques of murder, kidnapping and intimidation to bludgeon the mountain villages into co-operation and the nationalist government had been equally subtle. The communist defeat was achieved only after a horrific loss of life.

'I said, it's a funny place to build a road,' she repeated.

'That's the military for you,' Flint said, without looking up. 'The Romans were the same, pushing roads into areas they wanted to control. The Americans were helping mop up in 1949, they might have needed a road into the hills so that the Government troops could move quickly inland and shoot a few communists when they needed to.'

'So you already know all about my road,' she said, making her disappointment obvious.

'Well, yes, it was on our site map. The Americans built that embankment to carry the road over the gully; the one that Embury had me scrabbling about in.'

'So what the hell are we looking for? Buried treasure?'

Flint spoke with a tired and strained voice. 'A chance in a million says Embury had stumbled on the lost

172

civilisation of the Argolid, but it's far more likely he caused some local offence. Theory of the day was that he accidently desecrated a holy shrine or a saint's last resting place, but I'm crossing that one out.'

Frustration suddenly burst from within her. 'Jeff! I'm pissed off with wasting time finding out nothing.'

'It's not wasting time, collecting negative evidence is important.'

'What crap you talk sometimes. Negative evidence! What is that supposed to be?'

'We're eliminating explanations, daftest first. We're discovering reasons why Embury wasn't killed.'

'Oh brilliant. He wasn't killed because he had bad breath. He wasn't killed because he wore a string vest . . .'

'Lisa . . .'

'It will take forever, I think your brilliant brain is going soft; it must be too much sex. It won't take much imagination for the police to guess where we are or what we were doing.'

'Police forces don't have any imagination,' Flint asserted.

'God, I wish I had your confidence!'

He began to read again, wishing Lisa would stop undermining his resolve.

'Take me out on the town, treat me like a lady,' Lisa purred.

Flint had to ignore her. 'If Palaeokastro was an English village, we'd ask 'what happened there'? The Vikings founded it, the Normans burnt it, it was for Parliament in the Civil War, the Nazis dropped a bomb

173

on the cricket pitch . . . maybe we've been looking too far into the past.'

'You have – I've written a pile of notes an inch thick about modern times and you've hardly looked at them.'

He nodded. 'Second World War, Nazi gold, stolen art treasures, icons concealed by priests . . .'

'Flying saucers, the last hiding place of the abominable snowman . . .'

'Lisa!'

'Take me for a walk in the moonlight. We could go up to the Plaka and sniff at restaurant doorways. We could watch people in the real world having fun. You can seduce me on the steps of the Acropolis if you like, but get me out of this stinking box, please!'

He nodded thoughtfully, 'We haven't tried travel writing.'

'Jeff,' she implored, 'There is going to be another murder, in this room, in five minutes. Victim: you. Culprit: me. Motive: boredom.'

'You go if you want, I'll just finish this book.'

She muttered the words 'stupid kid' under her breath as his eyes fell back on the pages. 'Fine, I will,' she said aloud, taking up her jacket in an effort to draw attention. Flint heard the door slam and felt the mood lift. He quickly finished the book on the history of Greece he had picked up in a cheap bookstore. Nauplion featured in the War of Independence, when it had become the capital of Greece, but Palaeokastro rated all the attention it deserved: none.

After jotting down a few notes, he took up a paperback account of the Second World War in Greece and began to skim through its pages. Thirty minutes later his eyes came to rest on one passage:

'One of the earliest successes of the British Mission to Greece was the destruction of a chain of railway bridges linking the Peloponesse with Corinth. The noted guerilla leader Stylanos Boukaris played a key role in covering for the demolition team. It was in fact the only major success for this nationalist grouping, who were soon driven into the Arcadian mountains by the Germans and virtually destroyed by rival communist bands. Boukaris was to lose his leg later in the war.[12]'

It had to be *the* Stylanos Boukaris, father of Vassilis, model for an imposing bronze statue opposite Doctor Dracopoulos' house. The world just kept on growing smaller.

Lisa had been gone a long time, he noticed. At first he missed company, then he began to miss Lisa, now he fretted over her safety. When two hours had elapsed, he started to contemplate a sudden exit of his own. Outside, Omonia was lit by the last glow of evening; backstreet bars, pimps and pickpockets would be starting their nightly trade. Flint looked under the bed, but found only a disturbed patch of dust where Lisa's canvas handbag had lain. She had taken the money. Her distant apathy had been a warning he had ignored. Without her, his investigation was hamstrung.

Flint fell back on the bed and let his eyes rest on a spider beside the lampshade.

Work, work and keep working, it was the only way to keep sane. If he was on his own, so be it. He could bring Vikki over, Tyrone too if necessary, Lisa was not indispensable; Hugh Owlett must speak Greek. To convince himself that he could maintain momentum, Flint sat upright and checked note 12 at the end of the chapter. In an instant, he felt an icy chill and his skin turned to goose flesh:

[12] *Arcadian Commando. B.F. Nichols. 1947.*

The crushed golden pen lay on the dressing table, a McGuffin without a plot. The coincidence was uncanny, too uncanny. Flint could hear voices above the television set in the adjoining room, but Mrs Kondyaki never received visitors.

It was a sell-out. Lisa, how could you? Flint rolled off the bed and made three steps towards the balcony before the door shot open. Lisa bounced inward, a glow on her full cheeks.

'Hello inspector, solved the case yet?'

'God, Lisa, I was worried.'

Her chin twitched as she confessed, 'So was I.'

'How far did you get?'

'Three stops on the underground: I walked back.'

'Why? Is it my sex appeal or the justice of my cause?'

'Egotist!' Lisa was on the point of laughing, or weeping. 'You're a self-centred, self-satisfied egotist, but you wouldn't run out on me would you? You fight racism and sexism and all those other -isms and you'd fight for me, if I were in a corner.'

'Guess so.'

She tossed aside her handbag, kicked away her sandals, then flopped on the bed. He immediately sat beside her.

'I need you, Lisa.'

Arms linked around his back, looking up at him. 'Don't ask me why, but right now, I need you.'

'First,' he said, I want to show you something. You're not going to believe this . . .'

Chapter Twenty-Three

Angelos enjoyed his work. He had a softness for northern blondes, so Katrina from the German School naturally attracted him. Athens in midsummer could be claustrophobic, he had told her, too many tourists, too little air. He knew a little place – smooth talkers always know a little place – above the city, above the rush.

Over rice and lamb, they chatted in German, in Greek and in English, switching language as the mood took them. Yes, she knew the academic he was talking about. She half-closed her nordic blue eyes as she tried to describe Paul Adams. Yes, that was his name, he carried a pass from the British School. His spoken German was imperfect, but he would read books extremely quickly, perhaps ten or twenty in a day. He would arrive when the library opened and stay until she closed the doors. Angelos refilled her glass and ordered coffee. He enjoyed his work.

Travel writers, military anecdotes, recent biographies. Lisa was within the American Institute, hunting Byron Nichols and Stylanos Boukaris. Flint had gone on the same mission to the American Library at the

Chamber of Commerce. They would meet at noon to compare notes.

Over to her left, by the desk, the student librarian caught her eye. He looked away, almost guiltily turning his head down towards a catalogue. A frisson of fear ran through her; she was being watched. She opened another subject index drawer, aware of her pulse rising, trying to remain calm. A glance towards the desk confirmed it; the youth with the spots and the Jehovah's Witness haircut was staring at her. His eyes shot back to the catalogue.

Lisa controlled the trembling of her hands as she flicked the cards before her.

Military biography/Travel/History (Second World War)
Nichols, Byron F.
Arcadian Commando: memories of a mountain war
Atlanta, 1947.
154pp

She read the card again, blinking, then made a hurried note of the class mark. The drawer squeaked closed. Five minutes of searching amongst the shelves brought her to a slim, grey, hardbacked book kept almost at floor level, in a corner, near a radiator. The name had almost faded from the spine and the cover was blank. Lisa was on her knees as she withdrew it and opened the dedication page.

'To Stylanos Boukaris and his family'

Excitement overcame nerves. After a moment absorbing the thrill, she allowed herself to slump to a sitting position and began to flick from page to page, having learned Flint's knack of assessing the worth of books. After twenty minutes, the last page passed her eyes and she looked around. No-one seemed interested in military biographies, or that corner of the library. *Arcadian Commando* was a small book, smaller than the canvas handbag. It slid very neatly inside.

Humming quietly she breezed towards the spotty student librarian, who gave her a transparent smile. She responded with a hotelier's practised insincerity.

'See you this afternoon.'

A thunderstorm had rolled overhead and soaked Flint as he had walked to the rendezvous with Lisa. Dripping below a shop awning, he felt once more vulnerable and conspicuous. No other tourists were in the street. All that was required was one policeman to take a dislike to the dishevelled figure, ask his identity, and it would be a long time before he felt rain on his face again.

He wrung out the sunhat and spread it on a low wall to dry, then sat beside it, staring at the traffic. A well-dressed Greek couple walked sedately along the pavement; he holding the umbrella, she taking his arm. The white-suited man nodded towards Flint, then stopped and felt in his pocket. Before the archaeologist could react, a bronze coin bounced into the hat.

Flint was still looking aghast at the hundred drachma piece when Lisa appeared, smug and happy, walking crisply across the steaming road. A hooting taxi missed her by inches, but Lisa seemed hardly to notice.

'Find a caf., I need a coffee.'

He showed her the coin and told the story. She guffawed and pulled him to his feet.

'Do I look like a tramp?' he asked.

'Habitually. I remember you telling me you'd get by on charity.'

'That was a manner of speech.'

The kafenon was totally deserted, even its owner could barely raise the enthusiasm to serve, and a blaring television recaptured his attention immediately afterwards. A pair of plywood chairs and an aluminium-topped table filled the corner by the window, where Lisa waited for Flint to bring the coffees.

'Prez.' Lisa pulled the slim book from her handbag as he sat down.

Flint took the small offering, reading the title and the author's name three times before it sank in.

'I stole it,' Lisa added casually.

'Knowing my luck, they'll add an extra year to my sentence for handling stolen library books.'

'I can't go back there in any case; a spotty kid kept giving me strange looks.'

Flint raised one eye from the book.

'I didn't ask him about it, I didn't want to. There was something about him, he suspects something.' She turned her head to see which part of the book Flint was looking at. 'Byron Nichols was some sort of commando, helping the Greeks fight the Germans during the war.'

Flint turned to the fly leaf. '*Et in Arcadia Ego*', he read, 'I was born in Arcadia.'

'That title from a better man I stole.' Lisa quoted, 'Evelyn Waugh used the same motto for the first part of *Brideshead Revisited*. The two books must have come out about the same time.'

'You did learn something at college, after all.'

Flint cast his eyes over the introduction, written by an American journalist who had met Nichols during the war, then arranged for his journal to be published.

'He really fancies himself, this Byron Nichols,' Lisa continued, 'talk about purple prose; glowing sunsets, glittering marble columns and wine-dark sea on every second page.'

'Is there anything about Palaeokastro?'

'Not that I saw.'

'Damn.'

'But look at the dedication. Remember the statue in Anatoliko? Right on Doctor D.'s doorstep? You said something would bite me, and this bites me.'

'Brilliant, Lisa, well done.'

'Patronising chauvanist. Can you pay for these coffees?'

A hundred drachma coin slid across the table towards her, 'Here's my contribution.'

The room smelt of trapped air and damp washing. Lisa allowed herself an 'early night' whilst Flint lay propped up in bed, devouring the book. *Arcadian Commando* was a heartfelt work, full of classical allusions and clumsy prose. Too few jokes and too many bearded sheep-herders dispensing mountain philosophy. Flint was reminded of *Seven Pillars of Wisdom*, the product of another Oxford scholar turned soldier.

Byron Nichols had been a Classics Don recruited for the British Mission to Greece. His own wartime exploits were mentioned in passing but it was upon the life and character of the mountain people that the author concentrated his effort. Hemmingway might have turned it into a classic, but Nichols probably saw no more than a few dozen copies of his book in print. Flint grappled with the myriad of abbreviations (ELAS, EAM, EDES etcetera) made brief notes on names, dates and places, but there was no Palaeokastro. Nauplion featured twice, Argos rather more, but the action was firmly set in the Arcadian mountains.

The Italians and Germans had invaded Greece in 1940, but it wasn't until 1943 that Nichols parachuted into the Peloponesse. He had blown up a series of bridges with the aid of Stylanos Boukaris and a rabble of nationalist EDES partisans, then spent a year being hunted in the hills until 'Operation Noah's Ark' chased the Germans from the country. Stylanos had apparently had his shin shattered by a German bullet during the retreat; a captured Italian medical team had performed an amputation without anaesthetic. For much of the time Nichols seemed to be sorting out squabbles between the rival guerrilla factions who expended more of their ammunition on fellow Greeks than they did on the Germans.

The book closed with Nichols' reflective entry into liberated Athens in 1944. In the past week Flint had skimmed through three such accounts of the mountain war and other than its author's name, this offered nothing more than the others. As ever he was impressed by the strength of the common people and depressed by the stupidity of politicians.

He looked hard at the faded grey cover, knowing the American Institute was now barred to them. When he had received strange looks at The British School, he had explained it by his increasingly dishevelled appearance and increasingly obscure requests. Lisa was more streetwise and had her full wardrobe available; she had not been imagining things. He wondered about the pleasant student who worked on the desk at the German School – what was her name? Katrina? She had seemed inquisitive that last afternoon; too inquisitive.

He glanced at Lisa, half-covered by a sheet, naked and dozing in the bed. It was a quarter to one, he noticed, but his brain was too over-stimulated for sleep. Stepping out of bed, he put down *Arcadian Commando* and grabbed at his bulging file of offbeat ideas, flicking through it with edgy impatience.

Flint went back to the book, searching for a point around page eighty. Captain Nichols and his EDES men were playing cat-and-mouse with supposedly allied communist guerrillas of ELAS. Young Vassilis, son of the guerilla leader, was hit in the head by shrapnel from a mortar explosion.

'At first we gave him up for dead and despaired, but then a pulse was found. Although nearly scalped, Vassilis was alive and could be evacuated to the cave where I had endeavoured to establish our doctor. Thus I was saved the trauma of informing my greatest friend of the death of his son.'

Vassilis had survived the war and clearly thrived on his father's status as local hero. Indiscriminate shrapnel had clearly left his sharp lawyer's mind intact; Vassilis Boukaris would be the one to ask about Byron Nichols – if he truly was his father's 'greatest friend'.

No, he was unsure how close Vassilis was to Doctor Dracopoulos.

'Doctor!' he exclaimed.

Lisa stirred, 'What?'

He bounced onto the bed beside her and kissed the upturned cheek.

'If Vassilis was old enough to fight for Stylanos, Doctor D. is old enough to have been their medic. I don't know where this is leading, but I'm convinced we're getting somewhere.'

'Super. Wake me when we arrive.'

Chapter Twenty-Four

Lisa hummed to herself as she worked around the shelves of the Gennadeion Library. She had walked out on Flint, then walked straight back. A romantic aura carried her along like a newlywed. She had a home (a rented bedroom) a gentle lover (Flint) and an aim in life (keeping him out of jail). For the moment, she was the complete woman.

Helena the librarian was a sweetie. Always smiling, always keen to help with the obscure request. She would hold back the fringe of her hair as she talked in whispers.

'You wanted books on Christian martyrs?' Helena asked.

'No, the Second World War and the Civil War.'

'That's a little late for us; we have a great deal about the War of Independence and Lord Byron.'

Wrong Byron, thought Lisa. 'I'll see anything you have about Palaeokastro, east of Nauplion.'

'I would never have guessed so many people would be interested in such a small place.'

That frisson came back to her. 'So many?'

'You, your English colleague.'

'And?'

Helena pushed back her hair on the left hand side and grimaced. 'Oh, another man was here yesterday asking about Palaeokastro. He asked me out to dinner,' a smile replaced the grimace. 'I told him my husband would shoot us both.'

'What man? What was he called?'

The librarian sensed the sudden angst. 'He didn't tell me his name.'

'Was he old, was he young?'

'Young, or so.' Helena waved her hands, 'Perhaps thirty-five, very handsome, very well educated. He wears the latest fashion, all very expensive. He has a white Citroën, one of those long, new ones.'

He could not be a policeman, but was he a reporter? Lisa hated the other possibilities. 'What did he want to know?'

Helena sighed. 'I knew I shouldn't at the time, I'm sorry. I told him you were here looking for things connected with Palaeokastro. He was very persuasive, he wouldn't take no for an answer, he kept twisting his words around, asking the same thing in different ways.'

'Oh.' It was time for some lies. Splendid, technicolour lies. 'Please,' Lisa said, 'Please don't mention us again. I can't explain, it's all to do with family, legal claims, inheritance, you know, it goes back a long way.'

That was an awfully disjointed piece of rubbish; Lisa tried to clear her thoughts. 'If he comes back, just don't mention we've been here. We're going back to England in a day or two and he could spoil things.'

'I knew,' Helena shook her head, 'I knew there was something odd about him. He reminded me of one of those American gangsters, he gave me the creeps.'

'That's him,' Lisa said mechanically, wanting desperately to be elsewhere.

She found a dark corner to read through her books, which proved a worthless occupation. The man had been a reporter, she convinced herself. He was following up the story from the inside pages of the English press. The walls seemed very close that afternoon, the bookshelves very high. Claustrophobia began to crowd her world again and she lost her newlywed's glow.

Innoculation against the Greek bug was fading away and Athens was beginning to feel like home. It was clear he would soon be forced to leave, yet Flint fought against it. He walked the familiar streets around Omonia Square and nodded to faces who were becoming acquaintances, even neighbours. One or two would call out polite greetings and he responded with the odd phrases Lisa was teaching him. He could put 'fifty words of Greek' on his next CV.

Crumpled, but wily, the man at his barrow-stall pushed a Greek war medal into Flint's hand, as he did every morning. Without embarrassment, the Englishman was able to decline the bargain with a smile. A smell of strong Greek coffee and just a hint of sewage drifted through the air of the narrow alleyway between two of the monotonous high-rise blocks. Above him, washing hung over the balconies and female voices called across from one building to the next. The noise of traffic faded to a background hum as he infused the detail of life around him.

At the intersection of Gladstone and Kanigas Street is a diminutive square, free of cars and well explored for entrances, exits and sight-lines. Owlett was already sitting on a bench by the tiny fountain, pretending to read *The Athens Times*, but glancing about himself every few seconds. Flint slipped on his hat and glasses and scraped a knuckle across the new growth of stubble. The journalist seemed to notice him and stood to his feet.

A bunch of Australians were devouring *souvlaki* outside a corner stall. Flint waited until they moved on, clearing his view along the street, then began to stroll up Kanigas Street with practised aimlessness.

Owlett caught him up. 'So you're still a free man.'

'I am that. I saw your piece in the paper.'

'Ah, yes. It came out rather too heavily edited for my liking, but they pays the money, they makes the choice. What have you got for me this time?'

'It's more the other way around.'

Owlett groaned, 'Another bloody wild-goose chase.'

'I'm sorry about your sodding story, it's hard for us you know.'

'Us?' Owlett stopped walking.

Flint had to think fast. 'Northern turn of phrase; like "buy us a pint".'

'Aha.'

'Did you get any further with the Ministry people?' Flint started to stroll once more.

'Well, I must say, I didn't believe a word of your story the other day, I thought you were spinning me a yarn.'

'You've found evidence?' Flint stopped walking outside a kafenon doorway.

'Not exactly, but I found a sort of absence of evidence, know what I mean?'

'We call it negative evidence in the trade.'

'I found your woman at the Ministry of Culture and she confirmed that your professor telephoned her, as did a couple of his friends. Do Doctors Ennismore and Dracopoulos mean anything to you?'

Flint nodded, keeping his excitement hidden. Doctor D. had denied knowing about Embury's problem. The tag 'culprit' stuck to him firmer than ever.

'Next, I called on a few friends, you know, in law, in business, in government. I had my own theory, you see; land speculation. There's a lot of it going on and your Korifi company are the sort that are making the big Drachmas. Archaeologists and speculators never get along, do they?'

'Like bootleggers and revenue men.'

'Well, I found out that there are no planning disputes near your site: it's the middle of nowhere, it's not the kind of place anyone would want to build anything, is it?'

Not apart from Lisa, thought Flint.

Owlett had an odd, conspiratorial look. 'The day after I spoke with the Culture woman, an old friend called and asked me out to dinner. It was a nice restaurant, he paid, which was even better. You'll never guess what we talked about? You. He knew more about you than I did.'

The day was going to be hot. Flint's armpits stuck to his unwashed shirt, but now a creeping tingle tip-toed its way up his spine and took hold in a crown around his scalp.

'Do you know who he works for? The Ministry of the Interior. You've touched a nerve, I don't think they like what the editors in London did to my article. The Greeks are very sensitive about scandals, they're still shaking off the image of being corrupt and repressive they gained in the seventies.'

'So we're getting close to something?'

'You're getting close, kiddo.'

'What do you mean?'

'I mean this is too hot for me, they know I met you. I'm out on my ears if I start airing dirty laundry the natives want hidden. Reading between the lines, that article nearly cost me my press card. Don't be ungrateful. I've done what I can.'

'Shit!' Flint kicked an abandoned Coke can viciously and sent it rattling into the gutter, then gazed around the square, angry and even frightened.

Owlett took out his cigarette packet and pretended to ignore the burst of temper.

'Okay, Hugh, bow out if you must, but you might receive the odd phonecall.' A piece of paper changed hands. 'I put this small ad. in all the newspapers I could think of.'

Owlett read the appeal for information. 'Byron Nichols? You told me he was irrelevant.'

'I was wrong. He was here during the war and he's a real Hellenophile, so might still be living here.'

'That's my phone number!' Owlett had noticed the bottom line.

'I don't have a phone – and you want a story.'

'Bloody liberty!'

'I rang the Consulate too – they will be getting back to you. Oh, and a couple of friends from the Oxford Institute are grubbing around, so expect a call in a day or so. Nichols was an Oxford Don; they tend to return to roost.'

Owlett took a long, lung-scouring drag on his cigarette, turning slightly green at the news. From under his arm, he produced an A5 padded envelope marked for J.S. Flint, care of Hugh Owlett. 'This is for you. It came in the post this morning. Vikki said I should stand back when you open it.'

Flint looked at the parcel. At one time, people had adopted a habit of sending him unwelcome parts of animals – and worse – by first class mail. He sniffed the envelope, detecting no offal, excrement or naptha. A fingernail slit it open, and he withdrew a familiar burgundy passport.

'Someone is giving you a hint.'

So that was why he had escaped so easily. He was supposed to run, as he had seven years before. He gripped the passport tightly and for a moment he was tempted to go home, take stock and address the problem anew. Then he realised that the police might be relying on him taking the hint; the hunt had been called off in the hope he would simply melt away.

Owlett's eyes flicked away for just an instant. On impulse, Flint looked towards the figure who had captured the journalist's attention. To say the man was smoking was as unnecessary as to say he was Greek. He loitered some sixty feet or so away and behind, but was too casual, too nonchalant and too interested to ignore.

'Were you followed?' Flint hissed.

'No-one knew where I was going.' Owlett retorted, not sounding sure of his ground.

Dark and welcoming, the kafenon door beckoned. 'In here, you can buy me lunch.' Flint darted towards the door.

'I haven't got time!' Owlett was left on the pavement, taking a few seconds to react and follow Flint.

The place was small and packed. The figure had not yet followed them to the door.

'Toilets!' Flint implored of a youthful waiter, trying to remember the Greek words and making flushing motions with one hand. Owlett chimed in with a line of Greek and a nod of the head pointed the way. Flint darted towards the rear, pulling Owlett in his wake. Passing the open kitchen door, he spotted what he wanted; a back exit.

'It's okay, this is a speciality of mine,' he said to Owlett, 'Go in the loo and close two doors!'

Owlett vanished into the noisome washroom. 'There's only one . . .' came a muffled voice, but Flint was no longer there. He had dodged into the kitchen, smiling toothily at the man chopping peppers and slipped into the back yard with a strong sense of déjà vu. An eight

194

foot wall stood before him, with a padlocked back gate, but a pile of crushed cardboard boxes could serve as a springboard. Running towards the wall he bounced up, grabbing at the crest with both hands, scraping both arms. One leg was up, then the next and he was down into the shadowed alley that ran between two cliffs of concrete. He covered the hundred yards to its end at Olympic qualifying speed, almost falling into a taxi ordered by his protecting deity. He was still free; free to discover the enormity of the task facing him.

Chapter Twenty-Five

Athenian taxis are cheap, but driving half way out of town snapped a hole in the modest sum remaining from Vikki's five hundred pounds. There would be no more escapes, Flint was certain. Memories of the odd looks he had received in past days haunted his journey. The hands of a conspiracy could be seen grasping at him, closing in. His new appearance and his alias would now be known; Athens was no longer safe.

When the taxi driver stopped to pick up a second passenger, Flint stepped out, parting with the fare as if money were blood. Aware of watching eyes, wondering where the hell he was, Flint loitered until the taxi moved away, then hailed another. This delivered him directly into the compound of the British School, where he asked it to wait. He bolted inside to be rebuked by a stern female voice stabbing him from behind.

'Mister Adams!'

'Sorry, I'm in a hurry.' He slid to a halt on the polished floor and turned to face Mrs Hopkins.

'One could walk when one is inside the School.'

'Has anyone asked about me?' he panted

The woman's glacier expression thawed slightly.

'Why yes, a Greek gentleman has called once or twice.'

'Did he leave his name?'

'No, but he said he'd call back.'

'You couldn't describe him?'

She creased her brow, making the horn-rimmed spectacles slip half an inch down her nose. She pushed them back into place. 'He was tall, a little taller than you, as I said, with one of those bristle moustaches, very well dressed.'

Flint was shaking his head slowly, deeply worried.

'He was rather handsome, debonair, his English was impeccable, but . . .' she paused, 'Is he a friend?'

What did that 'but' conceal? Flint could not probe deeper and made up another impromptu lie, 'It could be Toni, he's an accountant now, but I haven't seen him for years . . .'

'Accountant?' The woman seemed unconvinced, 'I thought he was another reporter; we had one here two days ago, asking questions about that sordid tragedy. You must have heard all about Sebastian Embury?'

'Yes, yes.' Flint cursed Owlett, and began to twitch with nerves and impatience. He was tormented by several minutes' recapitulation of the crime and its aftermath.

'Things are becoming quite hectic; did you know there was a girl sneaking around here pretending to be one of his relatives, I'd bet pounds that she was a reporter too.'

Flint squirmed a little more, 'I'm very sorry, but I have a lot of research to complete today.'

The tabloid horror story had been terminated mid-flow. 'Very well.'

Flint went straight for the library and collared the junior archivist, a few years his own junior. Within moments he had established that the shadow in the slick suit had asked about Palaeokastro, even consulting the archive.

'Don't ever let him do that again!' Flint burst out.

'I'm sorry?' The library seldom heard verbal passion.

'He's a crook: the whole lot is likely to be stolen.'

'It's hardly worth stealing,' the young man said, unconvinced of his own voracity.

'I'd better check – I have an inventory; could you bring everything into one of the study carrels?'

The junior archivist was quickly bullied into compliance, delivered the heavy box of notebooks and the two tubes of rolled plans, then went for lunch, ignorant that a prophecy was about to come true.

The taxi returned Flint, plus stolen Palaeokastro archive, back to Mrs Kondyaki's flat. All information should be in the public domain, reasoned Flint. He was a member of the public, the information was therefore his.

He walked to a kafenon, waited for a telephone to be free, then spent an agonising half-hour chasing Vikki around her various offices. She, too, had acquired a mobile phone and he found her on an Inter-City train bound for Peterborough. Vikki was relaxed and chatty.

'There's a really gruesome double sex killing here, it's terrific copy.'

'Wonderful, hope you enjoy it.'

'Jeff?' The rumble of the train could be heard in the background.

'As soon as you get back to London, I want you to nobble Emma Woodfine, she's Emma Yarm now.' Flint dictated Emma's phone number from memory. 'Tell her everything – no, I don't trust her, but I've reached the point when I need to gamble on hunches. I'm going to ring Emma tonight and I need straight answers. Bully her, bribe her, blackmail her if you have to, but tell her I need answers.'

Vikki agreed with enthusiasm. She probably relished the 'blackmail' aspect. 'How is Lisa?' she asked.

'I don't know.'

'Liar.'

'Okay, she's very depressed. Her husband died and left her childless, the bank repossessed her hotel and I've put her on the "most wanted" list.'

'Glad to see you're giving her a good time.'

'Have a nice murder, sweetheart. Give the people what they want.'

'I will. Keep digging, professor.'

A quiet street corner phonebooth and a handful of coins was what Flint required. Cars and taxis still streamed past, voices called in the night, holidaymakers bumbled their way from street-light to street-light and Athenian youths, as youths the world over, made idiots of themselves at every opportunity. Flint waved away a lady who sidled towards him making curious coo-coo advances, then went to find himself another phonebox.

'Emma.'

'What . . . Jeffrey Flint?' She sounded incoherent, it was possible her husband was out and she had found the key to the sherry cabinet.

'Emma! Listen!'

'You're crazy Flint! What are you doing in Greece? The police will get you in the end.'

'I thought you were brighter than that, Emma.'

'What do you want?'

'I want to find out who killed Sebastian. It wasn't me, and you know it.'

'Prove it' she hissed.

'I've got my passport back. Shall I fax you a copy of it? The Police wouldn't have returned my passport if I were guilty. Sebastian's killer is still out there, and he's going to get away with it, unless we do something.'

'I talked to your girlfriend.'

'Vikki?'

'How many girlfriends have you got?'

In round numbers? 'Emma, if Sebastian's killer gets away, it will be your fault for not telling me the whole truth.'

Suddenly, unexpectedly, the voice at the end of the line turned into a mixture of sobs and snuffles. The hard edge of Emma Woodfine-Yarm dissolved in tears. 'I'm sorry, I'm sorry, I let him down, we all let him down.'

'How did you let him down? With Doctor Draco-poulos?'

Sobs poured down the phone with even greater conviction.

'Emma, the police won't find the killer, because

they've wasted their time chasing me. I'm very, very close to proving who did it, but I need to squash the red herrings.'

'That's a bad metaphor.'

Emma had always been a pedant, but Flint was determined to bear any insult she flung his way. 'Right, red herring number one. Where did the minibus turn up?'

'Out on the coast road,' Emma said after some thought.

'To the north of Nauplion?'

'I think so.'

Is that how Embury was taken for a ride? The bus still had all its wheels, it was clearly no regular car theft. Flint tried to think fast, get his information before Emma suffered a reversal of mood. 'Okay, red herring two; what was the real reason Sebastian sent me over to the olive grove?'

'I thought that was obvious. You were a bloody pain, his words, not mine. He wanted you out of his hair. Then when you started finding things, he decided to keep you up there.'

'What things? We found sod all. Adam said the action was all down the centre of the site.'

'What did Adam know? He was an artist, not an archaeologist.' Emma said sharply. She would rattle out the truth rather than be thought ignorant. 'Sebastian told me there was something of significance on the site, he had evidence. I'm a professional, Flint, I may not like you, but I know what you can do. So I said, if he wanted the survey doing properly, we needed you back with us. And he winked at me.'

'Winked?'

'Yes, he winked. Then he said "wait and see".'

'Did he tell Doctor Dracopoulos?'

'I don't know.'

'Did you?'

She moaned slightly. 'I'm very tired, can this wait? Can you ring again tomorrow?'

The prostitute was back, coo-cooing through the glass of the phonebooth, offering a "nice time" in three languages. Flint gesticulated strongly. She was onto a loser: he needed less sex and more cash. The painted face gave a careless smile and wandered back into the darkness.

'One more thing, Emma,' Flint said, watching the mini-skirt vanish, 'Where are the finds?'

'At one of the museum stores, I can't remember which.'

Flint formed a plan immediately. 'Okay Emma, big favour time, not for me, for Sebastian. I want you to pull all the strings you can tomorrow. Get Hubert to help, he's a big gun out here isn't he? I need to get at those finds, say I'm Professor Grant on a flying visit, make up any lie you like. I'll ring you at twelve sharp: I'll want to get into the store at two.'

'Yes, yes,' she said in her tired voice.

'Cheers, Emma, sleep well.'

Her reply was quiet and soulful. 'Get him.'

Flint returned to Mrs Kondyaki's apartment for the last time. The light was still on, but Lisa was almost asleep. He touched the black hair as it curled around her ear, then he eased himself into the creaking chair by the dressing table. He hunted for his chronological chart.

'Problems began about time we started work in the olive grove,' he read under his breath.

He picked up the composite site map drawn from all the old excavation reports. Empty spaces yawned wide, even after filling in the evidence from the last, ill-fated survey. The olive grove stood bare, right up against the Americans' road embankment, where logically the construction of the road would have ruined the archaeology. He, Jeffrey Flint, had argued the point, but Embury had been insistent; survey the olive grove and the approaches to the watercourse. Then the party had begun. Casually he shaded in the small square now covered by concrete and bricks.

Emma was innocent, he was certain. She had let slip one vital piece of information that any conspirator worth her cut would have kept concealed: Embury had been working to a plan. Flint had assumed that Embury had placed himself in the area most likely to yield the grand discovery, but a devious game had been underway and the old archaeologist may have been more cunning than he seemed. Had the activity in the olive grove been a smokescreen to hide the real work in the valley, or vice-versa? It was difficult to accept, but just possibly, Embury had spotted significance in the survey results that a younger, impatient Flint had overlooked.

Chapter Twenty-Six

His heartbeat quickened. Flint could see the rented VW minibus from the window of the museum store. Getting inside had been difficult, it had taken a hefty tug on all the strings that Emma had within reach, and all his tenacity to gain access within the day. A curatorial assistant had hovered over his shoulder as he ticked off box numbers on a list. She was in her late twenties, overweight, spoke no English and hid dumbly behind her huge black glasses as 'Professor Grant' manoeuvred around the building using hand-signals.

The building was one of the outlying annexes of the Archaeological Museum, tucked into one of the cheaper side-streets on the northern slopes of the city. It was little more than a warehouse for artefacts too dull to be exhibited, but too precious to be thrown away. Wooden racks twenty feet high filled most of the space; each rack was piled high with boxes, crates and loose artefacts. Flint was reminded of the closing sequence of *Raiders of the Lost Ark*. The raider of the lost motive could feel the presence of the attendant just behind him as he found the boxes he sought.

It had been a day of risks: Lisa risking the use of her

Greek identity card to rent the minibus for the day. Flint making a supreme act of will in trusting Emma not to suddenly double-cross him. The site finds were in strong cardboard 'skelly boxes', as wide as a shoe box, but deep enough and long enough (in theory) to contain a disarticulated human skeleton. Box numbers fifty to fifty-five drew his attention. These were the finds from the olive grove.

Down came the boxes from the racking, out onto a long bench beneath the window. Flint fussed over them but could not risk unpacking anything, so pretended to scan his list, then loitered before the racking in a pose of intellectual indecision. He had to kill another seven minutes, with the girl sitting on his shoulder like a pirate's parrot. A modern Lord Elgin would hardly be able to sail out of Greece carrying a potsherd, let alone several tons of marble.

A long, impatient buzz came from the main door. And again. The assistant gave a nasal grunt and disappeared from view. Six boxes at four kilogrammes each. Flint quickly formed a pile. The boxes had sagged under pressure and the pile wobbled as he lifted it. Waddling like a penguin he shuffled across the concrete floor to an emergency exit he'd noticed at the side. Spinning around he hit the crash bar with his buttocks and the door came open. Immediately, an alarm sounded.

He hurried, as well as penguins can, back creaking, arms stretching. Lisa came running into sight, urging him onwards, a look of sheer panic on her face. From behind her, something was shouted in Greek. Flint heaved the boxes into the back of the minibus,

Lisa slammed the doors and he ran around to the passenger seat.

Only this was Greece, and the passenger seat was on the far side, where Lisa was pulling open the door.

'I thought I was driving?' she shouted.

'So did I.'

Flint turned the key in the ignition and wound the engine. It failed to catch. He tried again, trembling, it worked! His feet fumbled the clutch and the van stalled.

A fist thumped the vehicle side and stirred him into renewed effort, letting off the handbrake, allowing the minibus to roll away down the inclined street. He tried the ignition again, then again, his face burning red. The engine awoke to roaring life, the gallant museum assistant gave one last thump on the side of the van and was left standing in the road.

'I hate you Jeffrey Flint!' Lisa shrieked, but a smile returned to her lips.

Flint simply laughed, a deep, pantomime sorcerer laugh. 'Did it, did it! Emma Woodfine-Yarm, I take it all back!'

'You're lucky she fell for your charm,' Lisa said.

'I like to think she fell for my logic.'

He reached the end of the side-street and faced a new terror: Athens in the rush hour. 'Guide me out, please!' he implored. 'I hate driving, even on the left-hand side of the road, even when the signs are in English.'

Even when he could find the right gear. He crunched the gearstick across and veered into lane on Lisa's instruction.

'I should be driving. You don't belong in the modern world,' she taunted. 'You'd be happier in a chariot.'

'Much.'

'You need to be over there!' She jabbed her finger, 'Ignore that bastard, hoot back!'

'We're going to die and I'm not insured!'

Flint blundered his way through the traffic, constantly in the wrong lane, with Lisa shouting directions over the engine roar and the habitual hooting of other drivers. Sweat-laden, the wheel slid between his fingers as he found National Road 1 and headed north. He was free, in his own version of a Road Movie, the fugitive with a woman at his side, and a hired minibus instead of a Pontiac.

The confusion of junctions gradually eased as the city of Pericles was lost behind the encircling hills. The driving was still manic, but most cars were heading in the same direction, with the VW minibus simply part of the stream. To the north and east lay Marathon, and beyond it, the eponymous battlefield.

Well after dark, they were still driving around, stopping at small tavernas, asking if their clientele had been swelled by a dozen hard-drinking excavators.

The Americans were found encamped just beyond their site, some quarter of a mile from the sea. The Bronze Age settlement mingled with more modern drystone walls enclosing tiny vegetable plots, and was dotted with the inevitable olive trees. On a gentle knoll, a beehive 'Tholos' tomb formed a backdrop to the scene, with an orchestra of cicadas on all sides.

Max was effusive in his welcome for 'Paul Adams', giving 'Elena Kyriacou' a bear hug when introduced.

'Is this your bus, Paul?'

'No, it's Elena's.'

Lisa glanced sharply at Flint.

'So what are you into Elena?'

'I'm helping her sort out her post-excavation,' Flint said.

'Where are you digging?'

Flint groaned inwardly, but Lisa was as sassy as ever. 'Oh I don't dig, I'm just the dogsbody. The prof's gone home, leaving me the van and the paperwork.'

'Ah.' Max seemed partly convinced, partly put down by her bouncy response.

'Look Max, we're just about out of funds, we need to stay somewhere for a couple of days until Elena can sort out her papers.'

Max spread out both arms to indicate the vastness of his campsite. 'Choose your pitch.'

'We're a little short of camping gear too. No sleeping bags, no tent.'

Max said 'no problem', then strode off to talk to 'his people'.

Flint turned his attention to the minibus. The heap of finds boxes had fallen over, but the lids were still in place.

'I like your friend.' Lisa said, 'Will he help?'

'We're in a foreign land, foreigners stick together against the locals.'

'Well I'm half local; I have to live here when your games are over, don't forget that.'

When Max came striding back, Jules was at his side and they had found one sleeping bag and a solution. 'Elena can bunk up with Angie. You can crush in with me and Jules.'

'No, three's a crowd. If you can find Elena a couple of blankets, I'll take the sleeping bag down to the shore and sleep there.'

'Great – we do that sometimes.'

'It will take me back to my student days.'

'I thought you were a student!'

Damn, nearly caught again! 'My foolish student days.'

Max wandered away, leaving Jules looking uncomfortable in the gentle glow of the minibus' interior light. 'One day, you're going to end up in shit so deep you're going to drown.'

'Loosen up, Jules, we've cracked it.'

'We've cracked it,' Lisa echoed, without sincerity.

Flint introduced Lisa under her pseudonym. 'This is my drinking partner, Jules. He's into bones, hates to see anything with its skin on.'

She extended her hand. 'I'm Lisa in real life, but don't tell Vikki.'

Jules glanced at Flint, who gritted his teeth.

'Deeper and deeper,' Jules said with a shake of his head.

Flint and Lisa slipped back into their real personas as the Americans made for their beds. He closed the door of the minibus and they were plunged into the total, moonless, night of the campsite. Lisa stood with her back against the minibus, looking towards Orion. The air was thick with the musty smell of dune grass mingling with sounds of surf on shingle and the ever-present cicadas.

'This is not real,' she stated quietly. 'Here we are, grown up people, running around, stealing pottery, making up names for ourselves . . .'

'It's a bit like "Bonnie and Clyde" without the hillbilly music and gunfire.'

'But what am I doing here with you?' she laughed, 'This life suits you; you're an adventurer and a revolutionary, you'll always be twenty-five, you'll always be a hippy. But I've grown up and all this terrifies me, it isn't a game. The police are going to get us.' Her tone had suddenly become sober.

'Don't be daft, I've got my passport back. Someone thinks I'm innocent.'

'Sending you that passport could just be a trick to try to lure you to the airport.'

'I know, but I didn't go: plan foiled. Tomorrow I'm going to introduce you to post-ex.'

'Huh.'

He thumped the side of the van. 'The answer is in here.'

'You're so terribly full of yourself . . .'

Flint was tired and his morale was sagging, 'I've got no choice. It's me and you versus the rest of the world, with a little help from our friends. If I don't believe in myself, what chance do I have?'

'Sorry,' she said, stroking his arm, 'I'm always pulling

you down and I shouldn't. It's because I'm tired. Would you mind if I went and found that girl's tent?'

He laid his hands on her waist and kissed her. 'Go on, I can't handle you tonight, I don't have the energy.'

She ruffled his hair. 'That will be the day.'

Flint awoke with glorious dawn. Viewed over the rim of his sleeping bag, the experience outweighed the stiffness induced by the sand. At first he missed the close proximity of Lisa, then allowed himself to sink back and appreciate the scene and the sounds. Water breaking on the shoreline eased him awake as it had eased him asleep. Across the straits, a sliver of burning gold shimmered above the mountains of Euoboea, a sight which once must have greeted twenty-five thousand Persians encamped on that same shore. None of them knew that sunset would see their army in bloody chaos and the invasion plans of their king in ruins. Flint took a handful of sand and reflected on the past, his home ground, the place he knew best, but a place he could never go. The sand dribbled through his grasp, one grain for each Persian slain by Athenian bronze, each man forgotten. No glory awaited the loser.

Excavation began with the air still cool and the sun still rehearsing for midday. The Americans dug from seven till eleven, took a four-hour break, then worked from three until six. Flint and Lisa joined the Americans for second breakfast, taken at nine, sharing bread and cheese. Elena Kyriacou said little to expose her charade, whilst Paul Adams tried hard to be the subdued character he had already created. Once his team were working again, Max commandeered two trestle tables and set them beside the Avis minibus (now technically stolen) which was drawn up in concealment beside a wall. He helped the pair unload the boxes and site notes.

'So what are you guys up to?' Max asked Lisa.

'He's the expert,' Lisa said, 'I just hope he can help me sort out this mess.'

'Is this the stuff from Corinth you were talking about, Paul?'

Flint made an ambiguous grunt. He hated lying to someone as open as Max.

'Just checking her data. This lot is going home next week and we just need some space.'

Again Max seemed to sense the brush-off. 'Swell. Okay, just holler if you need me. I can't jaw all day, we need to be off site by next Saturday and and there's a billion chores to do.'

'Where do we start?' Lisa asked quietly, once Max had gone.

Flint checked a list of plan numbers and box numbers which corresponded to his work in the olive grove. 'Box 52 is the junk from the gully and 55 is from fieldwalking under the olives. We'll start with those.'

Each box was tightly packed with brown paper bags marked in Emma's distinctive italic hand, already fading with age. Flint grabbed the first bag.

'I hate these paper bags, they're a pig to use and they rot after a few years. I asked Embury to buy

polygrips, but would he listen? No. Story of his life –
and his death.'

Scrubbed artefacts of several eras were tipped into a
pile. Lisa watched every action he made.

'So what are you doing?'

He was rummaging through the pile with a finger,
flicking objects to one side or another. 'The jargon for
this is "finds processing".'

'Shouldn't you be careful with those things?' Lisa
asked, almost alarmed.

'Only if anyone's watching.' He picked up a sherd
of pottery. 'To you this is a valuable piece of a
two-thousand year old pot. To me, it's just very old
junk.' He tossed it aside. 'Seen one, seen 'em all and
it's not what we're looking for.'

Finds from box fifty-two rattled onto the table top.
This was the rubbish he remembered, but each piece
was examined, checked against the record book, then
shunted into a pile. Sherds of modern bottles, a button,
a few bones, a couple of hunters' cartridge cases and
other, even less stimulating material.

Lisa picked up the button. 'More gold,' she said
with irony.

'Brass.' Flint took it off her, wondering about the
style of design on the green corroded object. Then he
picked up the brass cartridge cases.

'Do you notice something about the patina?'

'The what?'

'The corrosion. Both this cartridge case and the
button show the same level of corrosion.'

'Does that mean they're the same age?'

'Have a degree in archaeology.'

Lisa grinned broadly, 'Thank you. So what's this then?'

She prodded a small, furry piece of lead.

'We have the cartridge cases, so I guess that was a bullet. See how it's flattened? Some defenceless rabbit probably copped it.'

'But these are never rabbit bones, are they?'

'No.' Flint ran his index finger through the pile of bones, making wild, unspoken guesses. After a few moments, he arose.

'Time to see Uncle Jules.'

Within the tent which served as the Americans' site hut, Flint talked over the problem with Jules, with Max leaning on the table, uncomfortably interested in what was said. Roles still had to be played and Jules was obviously uneasy.

'Jules just loves bones, don't you Jules?' Max crooned.

'Yeah, so why did I come here?' Jules said with a hint of nerves.

'He says our soil is all wrong,' Max said.

All the bones on Jules' own work table were in tiny, barely identifiable fragments. 'If you guys got bones, show me, give me a treat.'

The expert left his own work and came over to the sister project. Jules sat on a box and sorted through the thirty bones spread on the table. Twenty immediately went into a pile as he recited, 'Sheep, goat, sheep or goat, goat or sheep.'

Coming to a trio of small knucklebones, Jules paused and pushed them into another pile.

'What are those?' asked Lisa.

'Those, my dear, are human.'

Flint met her alarmed glance with an enthusiastic nod.

Jules seemed to be thinking deeply, 'What's your soil type?'

'The usual; arid, alkaline. This context is adjacent to a water channel, so you could expect periodic inundations.'

The expert nodded. 'You know, none of these are very old,' Jules concluded, consigning some rib cage fragments to a 'rabbit' pile. 'These knuckles still have ligaments, they were probably articulated until you disturbed them. What sort of site are you digging? A graveyard?'

Chapter Twenty-Seven

A graveyard, not old. It was something which could have caused offence and Christos Dracopoulos, site guardian or Vassilis Boukaris, son of local hero, were both well placed to take up the cause. Sebastian Embury was a man who might ignore warnings, even misread them to assume he was about to stumble on something spectacular. That was theory of the day.

The American excavation had seven days to run, one week for Flint to kill before he could act. Each day, he would walk a mile to a grey concrete petrol station cum coffee shop and vegetable stall which stood back from the coast road. He would spend an hour, or two, wrestling with the telephone system, keeping Vikki at bay and making a dozen attempts to find Owlett.

Vikki had begun to agitate; where was her story? When was he coming home? How much was all this costing? Lisa, too, was becoming restless, less passionate and more introverted each day that crawled by. Flint grew nervous, fearing his investigation had hit stalemate, fearing the situation was slipping away from his grasp.

He would watch Max dragging his radar cart across the stony terrain, cursing and playing with the electrics. He watched as Angie struggled with the software which translated the signals from the machine into printed read-out. Max would bring 'Paul' over to witness his results, then have to explain later why so many readings turned out to be electronic wishful thinking.

'Back home, my pa can find sewer pipes under concrete highways, but sewer pipes are easy. Archaeology gives it a headache, some features are simply too subtle.'

Flint's technophobia was justified yet again; the shovel-and-pick merchants still had a good few years' work ahead of them, it seemed. He left Max to his gadgetry and made the long walk to the petrol station again.

Vikki's voice seemed strained and irritated.

'Vikki; has Owlett rung you?'

'No, I can't find him, what have you done with him?'

'Nothing: the last time I saw him, he was being followed into a gent's loo.'

'Who by?'

'I don't know; some goon. I skipped out the back, over a wall.'

'You left poor Hugh? If something happens to him, I'll never forgive you.'

'I'm sure he can handle himself, he's been around.' Flint sounded more certain than he felt.

'He covers Trade Shows mostly,' Vikki said, 'He doesn't do murders.'

Flint pushed all the air from his lungs into a long,

demoralised groan. 'Vikki, I thought you'd sent me a pro!'

'He's the only person I know in Greece. You'd better find him!'

Vikki slammed down the receiver – or whatever one does to a mobile phone.

Had Hugh Owlett eaten his last trade lunch? Had he been arrested, or deported, or chased into hiding, or was a crumpled body lying undiscovered down an Athenian alleyway? Flint wandered back to the site in hopeless dejection, wanting to retrace his steps and wind back time. He couldn't say anything to Lisa, he'd play boring old Paul Adams to the letter and try again tomorrow.

On Monday, he left his walk to the petrol station until late in the day, allowing Fate time to bring Owlett back to life. Flint leaned heavily against the metallic phonebooth, watching a mechanic and a marooned driver argue over the bonnet of a rust-red van. Suddenly, he was through, at last.

'Ah, Rodger,' Owlett said after Flint had spoken.

'Where . . .' Flint began.

'Rodger, good to hear from you. Hang on to your hat, I've found your friend.'

Flint stiffened. Something was badly wrong. 'Who?'

'The late Captain,' Owlett said, after a pause.

Captain, captain? It could only be Byron Nichols.

'Where is he?'

'Leoferas Poseidonis – the war cemetary. He's been dead over thirty years.'

Nichols was dead and Flint's rising optimism plummeted back to earth. What was wrong with Owlett? Who else was listening?

'But,' Owlett continued, 'someone who tends his grave is going to meet you. It will be a day later than when we first met, but otherwise, same time, same place.'

This code took some deciphering, it must mean the Acropolis, Wednesday, 2pm, in front of the Erechtheum.

'But who?'

'Well, we can't chatter all day, can we?' Owlett said.

'No, cheers.'

Numbed by indecision, Flint stood in the telephone box until the mechanic tapped on the glass. He allowed the man to take his place, then walked to barter for a melon. Owlett had been a changed man; talking in cypher as if he had company, or as if his telephone were bugged. Without doubt he had been followed, approached, threatened, even arrested. Lisa was demoralised, Max seemed suspicious, Jules was reluctant to become entwined, now another ally had fallen out of the battle; the struggle began to feel less like the triumphant victory of Marathon, more like the gallant last stand at Thermopylae.

Early the following day, Jules drove Flint to Aghios Stephanos to board a local train with the clanking third-class comfort of a cattle truck. He buried his face in his notes concerning the Civil War, spread in three stages from 1944 to 1950. Added to the death toll of Hitler's war, over half a million Greeks had died in a decade of savagery. The story of international volunteers fighting fascism in Spain was well known, but few in Britain knew that hundreds of their countrymen had died fighting communism in Greece. The British Government had slowly grown wise to the rule of twentieth century warfare: don't send troops to the Balkans. Once the British had withdrawn their soldiers, American aid took their place and dollars battered the communists into exile. It was an episode strangely absent from those pithy histories of Greece found in the front of travel brochures.

Athens seemed like home. Dodging the cars, dodging the eyes of the policemen, Flint felt oddly secure in the streets he had begun to know. He walked a mile from the station and made the hike up the Acropolis in good time. He wanted to gain a feel of the people around him, spot the latecomers and the one, mysterious person who Owlett would not describe.

Tourists, in bulk; Tourist Police, bored and disinterested; workmen battling to save the past for the benefit of the future; a couple swinging their legs over the edge of the parapet. A tall, possibly American man walked slowly across the scene in his loose shirt and tartan trousers. Flint started to move towards him, but the man drew out a camera and pointed it towards the hazy city below.

Just a chance said that Owlett had betrayed him to the police, or worse, used the tantalising story as bait. But Owlett was an old hand; Vikki gave him less credit than he merited. Fretting, watching, fidgeting, Flint's eyes fell on a delicately dressed woman, somewhere in late middle-age, stepping uncertainly over the rough rock below her high heels. The light knee-length skirt flared at the waist and ruffled as it caught the wind. Its colour was white, with just a suggestion of pink. She held onto her wide-brimmed co-ordinated hat and looked around herself through totally black sunglasses. In her other hand she clutched a thick hardbacked book, a biography, with its hero shown in Suliote dress.

'Byron' read the flowing gold script.

'Byron Nichols?' Flint whispered, approaching from behind.

The woman gave a sharp intake of breath and spun around, still holding her hat.

'You frightened me. I'm not used to this.' Her voice was educated, she spoke English with a transatlantic accent and only a trace of Greek flattening her vowels.

'I'm sorry, I don't know who you are,' she continued. 'My name is Sofia Kionghis. Mister Owlett said he could not come, in case the police were watching him. I didn't want to come, my husband would be so angry, you would not believe how angry he would be, but I wanted to tell someone about Byron.'

She indicated the biography of the poet. 'Not Lord Byron, but my Byron.'

Flint suggested they walk away from the crowds, into the shade of one of the lesser, pre-classical monuments beyond the temple of Athena. This was no trap, he was certain. Sofia removed her sunglasses, checked her seat, then sat upon the base of a fallen column. Her age was perhaps close to sixty, yet she looked a decade younger. She was one of the blue-eyed Greeks, with skin finely stretched over her strong cheekbones and age held at bay by the best of cosmetics. She moved and talked with the elegance of the moneyed middle class. Flint was instantly entranced; had he been a poet he could have rushed back to his garret and turned out pages of prose in her praise.

'Do you know about the Civil War?' Sofia asked.

Flint nodded, he had become a minor expert in the subject.

'This is a difficult story and it all happened a long time ago. My family is wealthy and my father was in politics before the Germans invaded our country.' Sofia spoke hurriedly, as if wanting to tell and run. 'We spent the war waiting in Alexandria, and when it was over, we returned. I was seventeen when I saw Athens again, and soon afterwards I met a young man called Stephanos Sarris.' She gave a distant, wistful smile. 'He wrote poems about love, and freedom, and justice and my maid smuggled them to me.'

The smiled faded. 'When the Civil War started again, I hated my father, because he was wealthy and he was a politician and I blamed him for the suffering. People were starving, but my father and his friends ate well. Students of my own age were being locked up in an island prison, some of them were being tortured and killed and the men who signed these orders would come for dinner and my father would tell me how it was all for the good of Greece.

'Stephanos came to me on my birthday, eighteenth

December 1946. He asked me to run away with him. He said we would have adventures, hide in caves, live on wine and goats 'cheese.'

She grimaced. 'I was just seventeen and a silly girl, don't you think?'

'I was pretty silly at seventeen.'

'So my father asked the British to send Captain Byron Nichols to fetch me back.'

'He was a commando, wasn't he?'

'Byron wanted to be a teacher, and there he was, come to rescue the little truant. He was an incredible man; dark as a Greek, speaking the language of the mountain men, yet so educated.'

She described the Oxford classicist, his love of Greece, its people, its history and of his habit of reciting long stretches of Homer during the dark mountain nights. Nichols had been an enigma: quiet and thoughtful but concealing a capacity for action and violence. Not the sort of man Flint would invite to a party.

'I know he killed people,' she said quietly. 'The Greek men who came with him were all afraid of him. But that was not the real Byron Nichols. Byron wanted to write, he wanted to remember the beautiful face of Greece, not the war. He told me all this whilst we were alone. We talked and we talked. He was the gentlest man I ever met.'

Sofia continued to extol the virtues of Nichols, elevating him to the status of demi-god, then suddenly she stopped. 'You don't want to hear this, do you? You want to hear my story?'

'I'm not going anywhere; tell me whatever you like.'

'Okay, so Stephanos took me away to his village: it was somewhere in the Argolid, but it had been burned by the fascist terrorists, organisation Chi. There was the letter Chi – X – painted on every door. So Stephanos said we would join the communists and I could be an *Andartina* in the Democratic Army.'

'I can't imagine you firing a machine gun.'

'It all seems very crazy now, I was not even a communist.'

'I used to be a communist,' Flint admitted. 'But I grew out of it.'

The woman managed to smile once more. 'We never found the Democratic Army. The first time we stopped at a village to ask for water, men from Chi took us. Their leader was a huge murdering animal, he did not care about politics, he just wanted to rob and kill. He killed Stephanos, he took out a knife and...'

She made a throat-slitting motion. 'Poor Stephanos did not deserve that.'

'So when did Byron Nichols enter the story?'

'Byron and his men found us and tried to strike a bargain with the bandits. A boy arranged it, but something went wrong. The fascists killed Stephanos, then took the boy away to shoot him. So Byron and myself were left alone, locked in a little room at the back of a house for four days. We had nothing to do but talk, we talked and we talked about everything.'

A trance seemed to fall upon Sofia. Flint broke it by asking more questions.

'Byron said we had been betrayed and that the fascists

had learned who I was and who my father was. He said we might be killed or that Chi would blackmail my father, but that never happened. On the fifth night, there was a storm. Byron snapped the leg of a stool and used it to break a hole in the roof; it seemed so easy. I took his hand and we ran into a storm of snow; I was thinking an ancient hero had come to life to carry me away from danger. We met his other two men, we hid in caves and we ate goats cheese. I had my adventure.'

Sofia gave an embarrassed laugh, then stopped it short. 'That is all. Byron took me to Athens, and my father sent me to America.'

'How did he die?'

'I don't know. He left me in Athens on St Valentine's Day, 1947; there was something he felt honour-bound to do. I tried to write to Byron from America, but my letters were sent back. I lived in America for six years before I returned to marry. Then it was I learned that Byron was dead and I saw his . . .' she clicked her fingers.

'. . . grave?'

'. . . memorial.'

Tourist Acropolis had been forgotten, Flint had been carried back to the winter of 1947 and was fighting the war in his own mind. 'Did Byron ever mention Stylanos Boukaris?'

'I think the boy's father was called Stylanos. Byron was very heavy-hearted about losing the boy. He knew he would have to break the news to his friend, after he said goodbye to me.'

'Was the boy called Vassilis?'

'No, he had another name, a made-up name for the war.'

'A nom de guerre? What did he look like?'

'I can't remember, it was forty years ago. He was short, very thin, and he had a great red scar, on his forehead, shaped like the letter gamma. Byron said it once nearly killed him.'

Flint was puzzled and might have questioned Sofia's memory if he had been sure of his facts; he would read *Arcadian Commando* again.

'You never tried to find out what happened to him?'

She shook her head. 'I was married – it would have caused a scandal. Decent girls did not have adventures. Then, so many of my friends had died, I had run out of tears.'

Flint took the pen from his pocket and passed it to Sofia. She read the inscription and ran a fingernail along it, her mouth falling open, her hands visibly trembling.

'His mother gave him this, she named him after the poet, she always wanted him to write. My Byron said he would write about the liberation of Greece, like the great Lord Byron. I always had a soft place in my heart for poets.'

Chapter Twenty-Eight

Lisa and Flint sat in the dappled shade of olive trees, close to the beehive-shaped 'Tholos' tomb, watching the Americans clearing up for the midday break. Another olive grove was on Flint's mind.

'Dead poets make the best poets,' said Flint, as he concluded the retelling of Sofia's story. 'And dead heroes make the best heroes. If Stylanos Boukaris had lived into his dotage, he'd have been forgotten. For a while I thought the clues were pointing towards events during the Civil War, but I'm no longer sure. Sofia's story was full of death and despair, but there's still no motive for Embury's killing.'

'What about the bones?'

'If they're Civil War bones, no-one can be convicted of anything, no matter how heinous the crime. All the ex-guerillas are dead, or have returned home. They have a thirty-year Statute of Limitations, it's all in the past and the Greeks want to forget about it.'

'So?'

'We know Byron Nichols was a trained killer, we know Stylanos Boukaris made his name that way and his son – or sons – probably learned at their father's knee. Any or all of them could have dumped a body at Palaeokastro and it wouldn't matter any more.'

'It might matter to someone. Murder is murder – your Sofia still sounds cut up about poor romantic Byron Nichols.'

The shadow of Byron Nichols stretched towards him, inexplicably confusing the facts.

'Nichols is long dead. Stylanos was abducted and murdered by communists and this boy with the scar was executed by fascists.'

'It's a lovely world, don't you think?' Lisa cut across his argument.

'But there we have the conundrum,' Flint continued. 'Sofia says the son of Stylanos is dead, but we know that Vassilis Boukaris is still alive. I checked *Arcadian Commando* and Stylanos *did* have a second son, but he died in 1942. Vassilis was the one wounded in the head, but Sofia said the boy had a Y-shaped scar on his forehead, like the mark of Cain. Perhaps there was a third son . . .'

'You're worrying over nothing. That old woman is probably confused.'

Calling Sofia an 'old woman' was a little like calling the Erechtheum a condemned building, but her story could not be made to fit the facts unless *Arcadian Commando* was as innaccurate as it was turgid.

'I spy a shoal of red herrings swimming past,' Flint said. 'There's a book, a classic, by Mortimer Wheeler, called *Testimony of the Spade*. What we should do, is return to Palaeokastro and dig a dirty great trench right through the middle of the olive grove.'

'Whilst the police stand around and watch you do it? You could take some extra spades, get them to help.'

He overrode her cynicism. 'I might – in the end, if we have prepared our case first. We need to talk to Doctor D. again. He knew Embury, he lives in the same village as Stylanos, he may have been the doctor who saved Vassilis Boukaris, and he's at least old enough to remember Byron Nichols.'

She looked at the ground and tossed a piece of gravel into a group of ants, 'I don't want to come.'

'We've already agreed we need to go back.'

'You've agreed.' Lisa sank her head onto her knees. 'Oh God, save me from brilliant men with brilliant ideas.'

Flint ran a hand through her hair. 'Trust me.'

'The last people who trusted you saw a van drive away full of their archaeology.'

He stood up, left her alone and jogged onto the site. Windmilling his arms, he yelled, 'MAX!'

The American stood up from where he'd been adjusting his radar sledge, shielded his eyes to identify the caller, then walked to meet Flint halfway.

'What can I do for you, *Sir*?'

Flint held out an arm and touched Max on the shoulder. 'Come for a walk.'

Leaving Lisa and the diggers behind, the men walked uphill, towards the Tholos tomb. Distance was needed to establish camaraderie and male conspiracy. At the crest of the hillock, Flint found an uneven stone projecting from the grey dome and sat down. Max already seemed wary, primed by smalltalk of buddies and allies

231

sticking together. He remained standing, with his hands on his hips. 'So what's up, Doc?'

'I've got an apology to make, Max. I've been spinning a yarn since the day we met in Athens. Everything I've told you is . . .' he ran into difficulty.

'A lie?'

Flint breathed heavily to let the confession spill out. 'I'm not Paul Adams.'

Max rolled his tongue around in his mouth, making his moustache twitch.

'Paul Adams works in a bank in Bradford, he's never been near Cardiff University, or the London Institute. I borrowed his name.'

'And yours is?'

'Jeffrey Flint, you might have seen me in the news-papers.'

Slowly Max nodded, 'You're the one all the Brits are talking about? You don't look much like your picture.'

'That's the idea, I'm incognito, working undercover.'

'And is Elena, Elena?'

'No, she's called Lisa, you'll find her in the papers too.'

Max drew a finger like a six-gun. 'But Jules said he knew you!'

'I was best man at his wedding. We go back a long way.'

'Don't they say you killed a guy?'

'I was framed.'

'Sure.' He looked far from sure.

'I need your help Max. I need your team, and your radar gear.'

'What for?'

'I want your people to get into your bus and drive down to a little village called Palaeokastro and do some digging.'

'Digging? But you're wanted by the cops, we could all get into really heavy trouble.'

'Yes.'

'So give me one reason why we should do it?'

'Truth, justice and the American way.'

'Bull!' Max looked out to sea and said nothing for a while. 'Whose fingers are in the artefact bag?'

'That's what I need you people to help me find out. Someone in Nauplion rubbed out my boss. If I can find out why, I can find out who.'

A random selection of evidence was quoted to looks of doubt, wonder and amusement. The moustache twitched up into a smile. 'You're serious?'

'Dead serious. I've been playing bloody cops-and-robbers for the best part of a month and I'm telling you, it kills your sense of humour.'

Max pushed his hands into his pocket and squinted back towards his dozen diggers. 'We're excavating until Saturday, then we have to clean up the site, fill the holes and get our gear back to Athens. I could ask for volunteers and leave the rest to complete the chores. But, if just one of them says no, you know you're through?'

'That's up to them. We'll go back first, there are things we have to do. Tell your team tomorrow, then

233

if someone sings to the police, we've already gone. If all goes well, when could we see you?'

Max thought hard, lips silently counting days. 'Tuesday.'

'No sooner?'

'Monday? I can't push it earlier; there's a squad of big names driving out here on Saturday, the people who put up the bucks and vet the books.'

'Whenever.'

'You're going to owe me a lot of beers after this, Doctor Jeffrey Flint.'

Flint selected out what he called his 'exhibits' and asked Jules to take care of them. After lunch on the Friday, he drove the minibus to the ferry port of Raffina and abandoned it on the quayside. Max followed in his Toyota Land Cruiser and brought the Englishman back to site. Flint hoped he had offered the Greek police an amusing diversion; taking a ferry to the Aegean islands would be a bizarre route for an escaping fugitive. The double-bluff might also confuse other, more efficient, pursuers.

As on every Friday, the Americans held a beach party. It was the usual crowd, the usual food and the usual booze, but the tag 'party' and the end of the excavation altered the mood. Lisa sat bemused below the dunes, whilst the introverted Paul Adams suddenly developed a love of Bob Dylan, took turns on the guitar and led half the songs. The night was extended into a dreamy, alcohol-soaked celebration of reckless youth. Events were adopting a neat symmetry.

Flames of a driftwood bonfire were settling to a restrained glow and the American ranks grew thinner.

'Come for a stroll,' Flint whispered into Lisa's ear. 'You could sleep down here tonight.'

'Isn't it cold?'

'No, it's idyllic. If I were Byron F. Nichols, I'd write a whole page about it in deathless prose. "To slumber on the beach at Marathon, hearing echoes of the centuries, sleeping in the nest of history . . ."'

Lisa stood up, 'Come on, drunkard,' she slurred.

They hugged each other tightly for support and comfort and walked away from the light, until the fire became a distant crimson dot, about to disappear over a dune.

'Fancy a swim?' he asked, 'skinny dip?'

'You're a big kid, Jeffrey Flint.'

'That's what makes me so loveable.' He kicked off his sandals.

'Is it? Is that what it is?' She gave an exclamation of mock despair. 'Oh God why do I do this?' Lisa bent down and slipped off her sandals. 'I should have grown out of this, you know? Beach parties, sing-songs and midnight dips. I should be living in a semi in Barnstaple, with three kids and a Labrador, not frolicking on the sand.'

'Middle class senility is not compulsory.' Flint had reached skin first.

'You're bloody impossible Jeff, that's why . . .' She stopped.

'Why?'

She failed to complete the sentence and instead,

kicked off her panties and sprinted for the sea. Not to be beaten, he raced after her, hitting the water a second later. The sea damped the alcohol and raised the pulse rate. Splashing and yelling like teenagers, shrieking at cold patches, falling over each other in the dark they let out their tension and erased mental exhaustion. Reaching a high, Flint grabbed at Lisa's hand and brought her running back to the beach. She tripped and they tumbled giggling onto the sand. Lisa first, Flint second.

Before intimate contact came a pause. Both were panting wildly after the run, both had drunk to excess, both held back stresses compressed by the claustrophobia of the Athens flat. In moments, the containment snapped and out came the frustration, the muted passions, and all control was gone. Athens had seen the undress rehearsal, but on the Marathon beach, the violence of lust found two victims. Sand and salt on their skins, each fought the sexual enemy who had to be tamed. Time was an unknown constant until Flint came back to his senses, fearing the depth of physicality, shivering against the unexpected cold, exhausted by the frenzy. He hugged her tight to his chest, controlling his own breathing.

'God I love you sometimes,' she said.

'That's good,' he murmured.

'I'm cold.' Lisa suddenly rolled away as if bitten. 'Where did my clothes go?'

'Lisa?'

'Forget it Jeff, I never said it.' She found and immediately pulled on her t-shirt.

'Okay.'

The combatants said nothing else as they dressed, then hurried back to camp. Lisa mumbled a quick goodnight and vanished towards her tent. Flint collected his sleeping bag and returned, cold and aching, to the beach. It had been a reprise of that first weekend, another lifetime in the past. This could not be repeated, his relationship with Lisa had to stabilise, or it would sublime. Byron Nichols would never have taken advantage of Sofia, would he? Not the saintly, heroic, Captain Nichols, the gentleman who put death before dishonour.

Chapter Twenty-Nine

Raised on grainy black and white war movies, Jeffrey Flint found it hard to settle on the train. Images of leather-clad Gestapo men demanding 'papers' came to mind as he sat on hard seats at the back of the open compartment, but this was not Nazi Hollywood and he was still one jump ahead of whoever was in pursuit. Dropped at Aghios Stephanos and travelling by slow, cheap trains, heading south defied logic. They changed trains in Athens and would change again in Argos, from where the track to Nauplion passed within yards of the site of the murder. Adventure was bringing them full circle.

Flint touched the huge, tender bruise on his neck; love hurts. Lisa appeared sunk into a trance, so he suggested, 'Snuggle up.'

'No.' Her voice was tired and strained, more than simply hung-over.

Nothing was said for a few more minutes. He watched her staring straight ahead, with a blank and inexplicable expression on her face.

'Drachma for your thoughts.'

Her mouth gave half an acknowledgement, a stereo-type Lisa half-smile which said, 'I refuse to become involved'.

To their right, the green-and-brown hills of the Isthmus of Corinth slid by. To the left, the brilliant blue of the Saronic Gulf. Even through a dusty train window, Greece glowed in the sunlight. He had caught that bug, he had become entranced, and long ago he had fallen in love.

'Lisa,' Flint drew his eyes away from the scenery. 'Sorry about last night.'

'It takes two. Don't let it worry you. You're getting a complex. It's Freudian guilt, you can't have good sex without guilt.'

'You said you loved me.'

'But I didn't mean it. Sorry.' The Greek woman in the headscarf was knitting furiously and obviously spoke no English. Two more locals at the far end of the car had their interest fixed firmly on monstrous hunks of bread.

'Once, perhaps,' she added.

'Embury's death rather cut us off short.'

'It would have ended, believe me. You were young and impulsive; it was a holiday romance.'

She was right, of course. As a couple, they were unsuited and always had been. Jeffrey Flint picked up his notepad and doodled away the hours.

A white Citroën was parked outside the most expensive hotel in Marathon, a spare jacket dangling from a coat hanger behind the driver's seat. Within the hotel bar, the man in the light suit could have been mistaken for an executive as he opened his briefcase and took out a file of notes. Angelos re-checked the ferry timetable and his map. Raffina, why Raffina? Another minibus had been stolen, and this too had been found intact. Events were striking an odd parallel with those of a decade before. As for the boxes stolen from the museum, they obviously contained – had contained – something of value to Flint, otherwise the risk would have been preposterous.

Of course, Raffina could simply be a multi-layered bluff within a bluff. Back to the ferry timetable: where could one travel from Raffina? Euboea? Andros? Tinos or Mikonos? None of these options made sense, unless Dr Jules Torpevitch had somehow involved his Turkish wife. The Americans had come to the attention of Angelos just a little late: the irritant would have to be neutralised.

Angelos went to the bar to demand service, papers tucked under his arm. Doctor Flint was not alone in touting maps and notepads wherever he went. The Greek needed to understand the Englishman in order to find him. He already knew so much about Jeffrey Flint; his disguises, his habits, his eccentricities, his vanities. Flint was extremely bright, had more friends than he deserved and grew more devious with every day that passed.

The Scotch Whisky was very expensive. Angelos ordered a double without glancing at his change, then leaned with his back against the veneer, thinking of old movies. Flint watched the movies, he claimed to be a connoisseur and would recognise this figure snorting whisky in a hotel bar. Angelos gave a grunt of self-congratulation as he saw through his prey; one can become too clever. Was it not an old cliché of detective films that a murderer returns to the scene of the crime?

The gaunt rock of the Palamedhi frowned down on the station at Nauplion. Flint looked up once more at its zig-zag steps and the crenellations running along the skyline, sensing the way the present was dominated by the past. A local bus from Leoferas 25 Martiou carried them close to a campsite and they walked the rest of the way. As the site was almost full, the gatekeeper gave them a bad pitch, one at the very extremity of the campsite, which suited their purpose.

Dusk was creeping around the hills and the sun had retired after another day of blasting the soil dry. In a niche of conifers bleeding resin, bats flitted around their heads as they struggled with the ex-army sandfly tent, its ropes, guys and rock-hard ground. Once the tent was imperfect but upright, the pair fell into their improvised bed, groaning, complaining of aches and exhaustion and the effects of the sun, comparing insect bites, and making soft puns and private jokes.

'Do you remember our first night in Nauplion?' he asked. 'Just you and I, outside Andreas' taverna . . .'

'Don't start on romance, I'm too tired.'

'This is not romance – it's research. Do you remember that old fellow who was snotty about me digging in the olive grove?'

'No.'

'His name was Costas – he brought that confounded pen back to our table.'

'If you say so.'

'Do you think Andreas would remember him?'

Lisa sighed. 'Imagine if you walked into your local in Leeds and found Fred the barman. 'Hello Fred,' you say, 'remember a chap called John who was in here seven years ago?'. 'What does he look like?' he asks. 'Dunno,' you say, 'it was dark and I was pissed at the time.'

'Point taken. But will you go and ask Andreas tomorrow?'

'If I wake up tomorrow. Goodnight Jeff.'

Lisa rolled over and fell asleep almost instantly. Flint lay by her side, so close, so distant.

Pushbikes did not require passports as surety. Jeffrey Flint laboriously worked his way up into the hills towards Palaeokastro in a slow, reversed imitation of his escape. It was a bitter homecoming to the dull whitewashed village and he was unsure what to expect. With taut calf muscles he passed the familiar red petrol pump, the house where the first bicycle had been commandeered, and the taverna Mikos. He cycled up to the taverna, and brought himself to a welcome halt.

Only two old regulars were seated outside the bar, the timeless domino game still in progress.

'Mikos?' he asked.

They indicated the rear of the building and Flint passed through to the place where Mikos maintained a walled vegetable plot. Mikos was beside the toilet block, fussing over his cesspit.

'Mikos, can I speak to you?'

Mikos looked around sharply at the voice, but clearly had trouble placing the face. Slowly he raised an accusing finger. 'You?'

'I need your help to find the killer of Sebastian Embury,' Flint said with as much courage as he possessed.

'You?' The finger and the accusation were still there. Mikos stood up and wiped noxious grey matter from his hands with a kerchief.

Flint launched straight into his sales pitch, allowing Mikos no time to work up anger, or to discover public spirit. He told him about Byron Nichols, the pen, the mystery witness, Athens, Owlett, anything to convince Mikos that there was a case worth investigating.

'Why did you come back?' Mikos said in a quiet, distrusting voice.

'Because I am innocent.' Flint brought out his passport as phony proof.

'Huh!' Mikos began to walk down his vegetable patch, towards a group of plane trees.

'Someone stole a bicycle from this village,' he said. 'And many years ago, someone killed my friend, Mister Embury. My guest!'

The crimes might not have been listed in order of importance. A wedge of plane trees hugged the interface of ancient and modern settlements, with twenty-three centuries of secrets lying buried beyond.

Mikos sat down in the shade, with his back to a low wall. 'Mister Embury was my friend, a good friend. The police say it was you that killed him.'

Flint sat a few yards apart, 'Not me – his killer is still out there and the police can't find him, or they won't find him.'

'Yes, yes,' Mikos already seemed convinced, but his natural suspicion fought against it. 'There is a story that you have been asking questions and seeking the truth. A man came around, yesterday night, asking for you.'

'Who? A policeman?'

'No, not a policeman. He was not from the Argolid, but an Athenian.'

Mikos continued with a familiar description and Flint began to feel cold beneath the shade. The ghost in a white Citroën, the smooth-speaking chic Athenian had out-guessed them and was already here. Lisa could not be told, it would destroy what remained of her endurance. Who was he?

'I did not like him,' Mikos continued. 'He told me you had changed your hair and that the girl Lisa now looked like her Greek mother.'

Flint felt the noose tighten around his throat. 'Did this man give his name?'

'No. No name, and he had no badge, but I saw he wore a very fine watch, a Rolex, in gold. He also had a gun.'

'What?'

'Here,' Mikos tapped his left breast, 'like on the television. He said you would come here and he

245

told me I was to telephone him at Hotel Daedelus in Nauplia.'

Daedelus! It could not be coincidence. Flint began to feel nervous once the gun in the shoulder holster had been mentioned: someone meant business. 'Was it the same man who came to see Embury in the car, the night Lisa came to dinner here?'

'I cannot remember, it was so long ago. I remember that the car was black and the men were not from Nauplion – that is all.'

Time was clearly running out – the man in the White Citroën could return at any time. Flint needed answers and asked his questions rapidly. 'Do you know who owns the olive grove at the top of the site?'

'The Government owns it; it is part of the city of the Romans. The Pinakoulakis family rent it and work the olives.'

'But it contains nothing special, no shrine, no extra site that only the locals know of?'

Mikos shook his head, confused by the line of questioning. 'You must ask Doctor Dracopoulos, he guards the site, he will know.'

'How old is Dracopoulos? Did he fight beside Stylanos Boukaris?'

'No, I think not.'

'So tell me about Stylanos Boukaris. Why is he so famous?'

'Everyone knows Stylanos Boukaris, the *kapitanos* from Anatoliko. He was a bold fighter against the Nazi Germans. When the war against the communists began, Stylanos would not take sides. He said he would not fight his brother Greeks and so put aside his gun and took up his books. My father was taught school by Stylanos, he was schoolteacher before he was *kapitanos*, did you know?'

Mikos described the familiar statue in detail.

'How did he die?' Flint asked.

'He was taken,' Mikos said with dramatic emphasis. 'One night in winter, the communists came for him. There was shooting in the hills and he was never seen again.'

'What of his son, Vassilis?'

'Ah.' Mikos gave an 'Ah' which was part respectful, part derisive. 'Great men should have great sons, but I do not like lawyers. Lawyers and politicians are not good for poor people.' Mikos then gave a wary look, 'But he is your friend?'

'I thought he was. I heard a story he had been wounded in the war.'

'Yes, he cheated death three times, he was known as lucky Boukaris.'

Three escapes from death? Vassilis had clearly lived in interesting times, as the Chinese would say. 'And is he a friend of Doctor Dracopoulos?'

Mikos made a 'pouf' sound. 'Lawyers and Doctors are the same kind of people; fine restaurants and big cars.'

'I need to know more about Dracopoulos, and about Stylanos Boukaris.'

'If you spoke Greek, you could talk to the widow Esfratiou,' said Mikos, nodding with deep satisfaction. 'She sweeps the church in Anatoliko and keeps the

247

statue clean. She knows all the stories from the village. She tells everyone that she was the last person to see Stylanos Boukaris alive.'

Chapter Thirty

Tents hold a special, warm intimacy. Lisa's head was over his heart. Flint heard her breathing begin to slow, assumed she was falling asleep and closed his own eyes.

'I hate bleeding-heart life stories.' Unexpected, Lisa's voice purred in the darkness. 'But for the benefit of your ego, I'm going to tell you why I could never love you.'

'Fine.' It was a long way from fine, but Flint was always a willing listener.

'I met this feller when I was at college. He was gorgeous, really gorgeous. He played in a rock group at weekends and I used to go along to his gigs and pretend I was a groupie. God, the things you do when you're young and stupid!'

Nostalgia showed through and her voice attracted sparkle. 'He asked me to become their singer, but I can't sing for toffee. I was absolutely in love with him, do anything for him, you know how it is. So do you know what we did? Do you know what daft stupid thing we did? We got married. I was at college, he was just doing a few odd jobs, but this was real love, Jeff, the sort you buy in teenage magazines. I worshipped him, he was so cool and so romantic and he loved me! Me, at last, someone actually loved me after all those years of being dragged around airbases and posted off to boarding school.'

She sighed. 'This is sounding like one of those awful 'True Confessions' stories, isn't it? I ought to shut up.'

'Go on, please, confess.'

Lisa said nothing for some time. A pair of voices laughed somewhere across the campsite. A car droned along the coast road.

'So, guess what happened next?' Her voice clouded. 'Baby?'

'No, well, only partly, but that's forgotten now, that would have been the end. No, he wanted to 'go on the road', travel around, make a name for himself. So, I went too; bye bye college, bye bye English Lit. We had a great time, for a year, it was terrific. Then reality hit us. His band was useless, they never stood any sort of chance of making it beyond college discos. So we went back to Devon, I got a job, he didn't. He formed a new band, but it wasn't the same, the fun had gone, and they were still useless.'

Flint resisted making any trite comments. Lisa had fallen quiet again. He thought she was crying, then thought he was mistaken.

'Ever been beaten up, Jeff?' Her voice was even quieter now, husky and flat.

He mumbled. 'When I asked the wrong sort of questions.'

250

'But you've never been beaten up by someone you worshipped?'

'That how it was?'

'Oh yes. I kept saying I'd stand up to it, but I was never ready. I would be tired, lonely, wanting him to come back to me. If he came back, he'd come back drunk, end of story.'

Then she added: 'I would have made a rotten mother anyhow.'

Flint had to guess at the detail, it was time for that trite comment.

'That's unforgivable.'

'Yeah, I suppose it is.' Her voice brightened, 'So, I waited until it became a pattern, waited until I felt better, then left him. All the lads and this tart they found for a singer went up to London one week to try to fix up some gigs. I brought a bloke from the market round, sold everything in the flat and bought a ticket to Cyprus. I found a job in a bar, got drunk a lot, slept with lots of people I didn't know and felt a bloody sight better.'

Total silence fell. Flint thought it was up to him to break it. 'So you were still married when I met you?'

'I was, and not ready for anything but a good night on the town. You were fun and sexy – still are – but look what you've got me into. I have a way of picking lost causes. I knew you were never going to be anything; I'd be sharing my life with Bob Dylan and Humphrey Bogart and Julius Caesar and Che bloody Guevara. I wanted my fat rich old man.'

'I'll introduce you to Vassilis Boukaris.'

251

'Yes, the bastard who repossessed my hotel. That's the only reason I'm still here. I don't give a stuffed tomato for Sebastian Embury, I want my hotel back.'

She was deadly serious and Flint suddenly saw a trap opening before him. Whoever had put pressure on Boukaris had a powerful card to draw Lisa away from him; perhaps her confession was a subconscious effort to unload her guilt in advance.

'So we're just good friends?' he said, with his mind following another track.

'If you like.'

Mrs Kondyaki opened the door cautiously. Scarface and a group of Athenian detectives poured into her Athenian flat. Half the neighbourhood knew an Englishman had been her guest, but the policemen shuffled inside and heard her story anew. Flint's known associates were refusing to co-operate: too many people were interfering in the case and Scarface was becoming annoyed. Jeffrey Flint and his accomplice were becoming more eccentric with every new revelation; the stolen and abandoned minibus was a further galling enigma. Flint was still in Greece, taunting the police, acting out some bizarre fantasy that he would clear his name. It could only be a matter of time before he made a mistake and was caught.

The Land Cruiser swayed from side-to-side as it lurched across the uneven ground of the campsite. Flint could hear an Al Stewart song growing louder as the vehicle drew nearer.

Flint gave Max a clap on the shoulder as he dismounted, welcoming him, thanking him again and again. 'As you can guess, I'm pleased to see you. Where are the rest of your team?'

'Ah, I think we might have a problem there.'

'Where's Jules?'

'The cops took him in, right after you left.'

Jules too. The only life raft for Flint's conscience was that it had been the police who found him first. 'You're sure it was the police?'

'I guess.'

'Pretty blue and white cars, sexy uniforms?'

'No, plain clothes . . . they just drove up in this long white car . . .'

'A Citroën?'

'European . . . they asked for Jules, Jules came out of his tent and they just pulled him into the car. I wasn't there . . .'

The life raft had been leaking badly and gently slipped below the waves.

'And everyone else?'

Max seemed to have lost his image as the great leader of men. 'I couldn't ask them. Hell, they had flights booked, they saw what happened to Jules. What was in it for them?'

'What's in it for you Max?'

The American hid his embarassment with activity. He opened his rear door and hauled out his rucksack. 'Aw, I said I'd help. I can't go back on my word.'

'Philotimo,' Flint said.

'What?'

'Greek pride. There's a lot of it about.'

'D'ya still want me along?'

'Yes, wonderful, pleased you came.' Flint's mind was fixed only on Jules and the multitude of evil fates that could overtake him.

Max had noticed a pair of bare feet sticking from the moth-eaten sandfly tent. 'Hey Elena, the cavalry's here!' He boomed, bending over to look within the tent.

'It's Lisa,' came the listless response. 'Hello Max.' The inert figure hardly moved.

Max went back to the Land Cruiser and turned off 'Year of the Cat'.

'Is something bringing Lisa down?'

'Ennui,' came a voice from the tent.

He frowned at Flint. 'So it's weird words day today is it?'

Flint spoke quietly, 'She's just pigged off, to use her expression. You can't blame her, I've dragged her across half of Greece and given her a police record.'

The American grimaced, 'So I guess I'm now an accessory after the fact.'

He found his mallet and bag of pegs, 'You'd better tell me your plan, Paul, sorry, Jeff. Hey I'll never get this right.'

'Oh, we're Alan and Susan now; we made up new names when we booked on here. Call me Jeff, remind me who I really am.'

'Okay Jeff, help me with this tent.'

Working as a pair, they began to assemble the state-of-the-art pup tent.

'So, Jeffrey, old buddy, you keep telling me that you have a hunch about this, or clues about that, but from here-on-in, how does your game plan read?'

Flint stopped pegging out the blue and orange tent and seemed to struggle with his thoughts.

'What I wanted to do was drive up to our site at Palaeokastro with your team, put a dirty great trench through an olive grove, and find whatever someone doesn't want us to find.'

'The body, right?'

'Possibly. But that plan's no good any more.'

'We can still do it, I've got a spade in the back, and a couple of picks.'

'No, Max, we're talking an area a good eighty metres square. I'm sure the bones were brought up by rabbits. The pen came from the edge of a water gulley a couple of yards away, and that could still be the biggest red herring ever invented. All the material could have been re-deposited from somewhere else, so we need to find the primary deposit. If there is a grave up there, I want to know exactly where it is before we give ourselves up to the cops. That demands a whole set of sondages wherever the trees allow it, and probably one decent trench when we find what we're looking for.'

Max looked thoughtful. 'Did your resistivity survey give you any leads?'

Flint shook his head. 'I've been through the data and there's nothing to get excited about; I'm not a great believer in technology.'

'Your boss must have thought there was something up there. I brought all your papers, why not let me

255

have a look, see if an old colonial can find your grave. If not, I brought my GSR.'

Flint saw that most of the Land Cruiser was taken up by the radar sledge and a computer. He may be a New Archaeologist, but could he trust an electronic toy to keep them all out of jail?

Chapter Thirty-One

After the heat of the day had died, Angelos climbed the back streets of Nauplion where he had heard of a modest taverna. Angelos wore a dull blue blazer and chose to sit in the dark corner behind the door, facing the bar. He ordered a light salad and what the place could offer by way of wine. As he picked at the feta, Angelos wished for a good bottle of French white, Chablis perhaps.

Angelos watched Andreas busy around his regulars. Only slowly did the taverna keeper notice this attention. He began to glance in the direction of Angelos, betraying increasing nervousness. Andreas was unsettled, even afraid, which was the intent. One taverna keeper had already frustrated Angelos. Flat-faced, foolish Mikos had stonewalled with the blank cunning of the peasant. It was not important, Angelos could return to Palaeokastro again.

Mosquitoes whined around the fly-killing light whilst local men came to sip at ouzo and play dominoes or jacks. Andreas glanced his way again. Angelos deliberately pushed a chair forward with his toe. The feet scraped on the floor, the open seat became an invitation.

Andreas wiped his hands on a grey-white towel as he came over slowly. Angelos poured a glass of Nemea wine and urged his host to sit.

'Tell me about Lisa, the English hotelier. Has she been back here?'

The answer was obvious from the manner in which the taverna keeper's eyes widened. Angelos broadened his smile and poured a second glass of wine. Andreas tried to shrug away his probing, but lacked the resistance of Mikos. Within twenty minutes, the wine bottle was almost empty, and Andreas' wife was running the bar.

'Sit,' Angelos said, as Andreas tried to stand, 'talk with me.'

Refusal was impossible, he knew it and Andreas knew it. More anecdotes regarding Lisa and her barely-remembered boyfriend tumbled from his lips. The one concerning a man named Costas and a golden pen seemed to be fresh in Andreas' mind.

'Costas who? Did you tell Lisa his full name?'

Andreas shook his head, 'It was so long ago, and Costas . . .'

That question had been satisfied and Angelos pressed on. 'Can you remember what was special about this pen?'

'It had a name on it – Byron – that was it. We thought this was a wonderful joke, Lord Byron, here. But it was not Lord Byron, it was someone else who lost the pen, the pen was not so old, the young Englishman said.'

Angelos reached into his blazer pocket and drew out

an envelope. From it tumbled a bundle of newspaper small ads. He showed them to Andreas.

'Byron F. Nichols, yes, that was the name on the pen!'

'There is another name in the advert.'

'Boukaris, yes.' Andreas looked less happy than he had a moment before.

Angelos watched him for a few moments before selecting a few bank notes to cast by the empty bottle. He stood up, walking to the telephone beside the bar. 'You should lay in some French wine,' he said over his shoulder. 'I'll be back.'

He dialled a number and found Vassilis Boukaris. 'Doctor Flint is in Nauplion,' was all he said, then replaced the receiver.

In the hour before dawn, Max drove Flint and Lisa through the silent streets of Palaeokastro and beyond to the Roman town. Pulling off the road into the olive grove, he hoped to conceal the Land Cruiser from view.

Flint dismounted amongst the olive trees and drew in a sweet breath of morning air. Only distant cockcrows disturbed the windless calm. Everything pointed to that location, the hunch that guided him through the puzzle said 'end here'. To refresh his own mind, and explain the situation to the other two, he marched down through the grove and onto the site proper.

'Whilst we worked down there, no-one bothered us,' he pointed towards the skeleton of the mill in the bottom of the valley. 'Embury excavated for three seasons without any trouble. Then he sent me up here . . .'

At that moment, archaeology seemed a distant, irrelevant occupation. An uphill walk brought them back towards the road, which maintained its course by both terracing and embankment. Flint noticed something for the first time. To the north of the new road lay the faint remains of the old, half buried in hillwash and overgrown with brambles and mimosa. It swung higher up slope in a wider curve, departing perhaps twenty metres from the straighter line chosen by American military engineers. The old road terminated at the gully: perhaps a feeble wooden bridge had once stood there. Just visible was the point at which it re-started on the far side, before it was overtaken by undergrowth.

Only a minute's walk along the road took them from one side of the olive grove to the other. Here, the natural ground surface fell away gently before it broke into the edge of the watercourse. Some twenty yards across, Flint remembered the orange dusty margins as a ragged tangle of desiccated weeds and cracked earth clods. Now they had been sealed by a concrete lip which effectively entombed whatever had lain beneath Flint's sondage.

The road was carried over the gully on an embankment, with a large concrete pipe at its base seeming redundant in this dry season.

'This is the new road on my map,' Lisa stated.

'Built in 1949,' Flint added.

'By Americans,' Max completed the pronouncement.

Leaving the road, they dropped down onto the apron surrounding the half-built taverna. Flint kicked at the concrete at the point of his sondage: he had dug into the edge of the watercourse and encountered his spread of modern rubbish.

'We don't know the agency of deposition,' he said, 'it may have come up from rabbit holes, or, the material could have been re-deposited from anywhere upslope of here.'

'Your grave could have been washed clean away,' Max observed.

'Oh God, Max, don't,' Lisa said. 'Let him be right, or his ego will never recover.'

'Let me be right, or I go to jail,' Flint countered.

Lisa glared at him, 'We all go to jail.'

'Hey guys,' Max held up his hands as if to separate the pair. 'No fights. Help me out with my gear and I'll see what I can find, but if olive trees used to grow here, the root pattern is going to throw a lot of garbage into the read outs.'

Flint knew all about the sacred olive trees, well over a hundred years old and planted in orderly fashion. He recalled no obvious gaps to betray where the planters had avoided underground obstructions. Embury had told him to look for trees which were stunted to indicate they were fighting ancient stonework for space or those so luxuriant to suggest their roots had found deep graves in which to feast. Of course, he had found neither.

Max was left in the shade of the unfinished taverna, with his radar sledge, a plasticised site plan and the book of survey data compiled a decade before. Lisa and Flint took the Land Cruiser a mile further up the valley to the village of Anatoliko, parking beside the statue of Stylanos Boukaris. It gave the date of his death as 15th February 1947.

'One day after Byron Nichols left Sofia in Athens,' Flint said. 'He was coming here, to tell Stylanos about the death of his son.'

The schoolteacher-guerilla gazed grimly over their heads, his round brow furrowed by concern, his moustache flowing in the mountain wind, his arm pointing back down the valley towards Palaeokastro.

Across a few yards of worn tarmac was the paved precinct of the church, too large for such a small village, with its whitewashed bell tower standing separate from the dark doorway. Lisa was first inside, Flint came next, eyes immediately drawn upwards by the blues and old gold of the ceiling frescoes. Six orthodox saints frowned downwards at his shorts. Mrs Esfratiou noticed the shorts too, and looked displeased.

Lisa quickly drew the woman outside and they stood in the sun, opposite the statue. Flint loitered as they began to talk fast and fluently, hands in his pockets, eyes half-closed against the glare of white walls.

'She was a girl when Stylanos died,' Lisa said. 'That was his house, that was her mother's house next door.'

These were the last houses in the village, low roofs jumbled together as the pair clutched each other and the hillside. Lisa continued to speak Greek, nod, point, question, smile and concur.

'She was the last person to see Stylanos alive. It was a winter's night, four men rode up on donkeys from the high road. Two were village men called Socrates and Elias and one was some bloke from Nauplion who rented out mules. The other was a British officer.

'Byron Nichols?'

'She doesn't know – he'd never been here before.'

More rapid exchanges in Greek.

'That night, Stylanos came out and greeted the four men. He had called out to her, telling her to run to her mother. Stylanos wanted two chickens slaughtered as his British friend was here.

'Not Vassilis?'

'Vassilis had returned a day earlier. He had been boasting of escaping from the fascists.'

Another twist to the tale.

Lisa continued to ask questions. 'When the girl brought round the chickens, it was dark and she heard men riding away. The house was empty. Later that night, there was shooting in the hills, so no-one went outside the village. Vassilis came back two days later, with a pistol in his hand, saying that they had run into a communist ambush and been scattered in the dark. His father and the other four men were all never seen again.'

'Bodies?'

'Never found.'

Flint gave a self-satisfied smile. 'When I spoke to Sofia, I asked her about Nichols' grave, and she corrected me. She said 'memorial'. I missed the point, but I understand now. It's time for a consultation with the Good Doctor.'

Doctor Christos Dracopoulos was taking coffee on

his veranda, reading the newspaper and not at all pleased when his wife brought the two visitors out to see him.

'I should call the police right away,' he said, eyes flashing angrily from one to the other.

'Emma Woodfine admitted that you drove her home after the dinner,' Flint stated, straight to the point.

'Okay, so if I did, it was a long time ago, who cares? What do you want?'

'We want to know why you lied to us,' Flint chose himself a chair and sloughed into it. 'Sebastian Embury was a good friend of yours. When he was threatened, you would be the first person to whom he would turn.'

Dracopoulos shook his head.

'And so you were. After all, it was your job as site guardian to ensure the survey went smoothly. So, you telephoned the Ministry of Culture to check his permission to excavate was still valid.'

He was clearly both shaken and angry. 'So, I did that.'

'But when we came here, you denied knowing anything about what Embury had found and you denied that he was in any trouble.'

Dracopoulos was thinking. He had an opaque face, one Flint could not trust. Wheels could be seen clicking and whirring as the next lines were fabricated. The Doctor turned to Lisa, who was leaning against one of the veranda pillars.

'It is time I helped you. Sebastian was my friend.'

Everyone wanted to claim Embury was his friend. He

264

had been an obnoxious boor, wouldn't anyone admit to hating him?

'Super,' Flint said, keeping his own suspicions hidden.

'Ask me whatever you want.'

Now the game had changed, Flint would have to sift his facts very delicately. Dracopoulos had reached for one of the cigars which would surely kill him.

'Did you fight beside Stylanos Boukaris?' Flint asked. 'He used to live four houses away, after all.'

A quiver of recognition passed across the face of the Doctor. 'I'm not that old, I was born nineteen thirty-seven; the family Boukaris moved to Nauplion after Stylanos was killed, I was only a little child.'

'Whose side was Stylanos on?'

'Stylanos was neutral – when the Germans were here, he was nationalist, he fought the Nazis and the communists. When the Civil War began, he would not choose sides. He was a great man.'

'But his men, his followers. They can't all have been neutral? I've read about this war; every family in Greece had someone executed or maimed or abducted. I can't imagine that Stylanos sat here playing the liberal and that all his men sat here too, swapping bits of philosophy about the ethics of neutrality whilst their families were being butchered? He was active in the Civil War, and so was his son Vassilis, we know they worked with the British and we know they struck deals with the fascists.'

Dracopoulos gave a shrug. 'This is ancient history. Why are you so interested in the past?'

'The past holds the key to the present – it's an old cliché.'

They asked about the night Stylanos died, but Draco-poulos' information had no doubt been obtained via the widow Esfratiou. 'You should talk to Vassilis, if you need to know more,' the doctor said, cigar in mouth. 'I can arrange it.'

Lisa suddenly rejoined the conversation. 'Today?'

'Yes, today, I think. He wants to meet you. Both of you.'

'Somewhere public,' Flint said.

'Andreas' taverna,' Lisa added. 'Do you know it?'

The doctor nodded.

'Two o'clock?' Flint chipped in the time.

'I'll try.'

'No tricks?'

'On my honour.'

'Fine, but before we go, tell me about the olive grove at Palaeokastro and why Embury thought it was so important.'

'I don't know.'

Flint got to his feet. 'What was that half-finished building supposed to be?'

'A taverna – why?'

'Didn't you object to the project? In England, there would be a stink if someone started building a transport caff on a scheduled monument.'

'The development was stopped – there was a mistake over permission.'

Flint's ideas began to coalesce around one point on the map, at one point in history. 'And who built it?'

'Korifi . . .'

Of course, Mikos had given him that information a month ago when the name Korifi meant nothing.

'When? The year Embury died?'

'I can't remember.'

'We can check.'

'Late that year.'

'Did they dig foundations, or is it constructed on a raft?'

'Just concrete. They could build more quickly that way; it would not disturb the site.'

'Quite.'

Chapter Thirty-Two

Flint and Lisa drove back downhill.

'Paleface speak with forked tongue,' Flint said. 'That notwithstanding, we know everything now.'

'We do?'

Max was sitting beside his sledge, looking at Flint's own plans of the site. Flint explained to him, and to Lisa, how he had shaded the site plan to show areas of different resistance; this showed the size and position of features concealed under the surface.

'I used heavy shading for pits, ditches and other loose ground. Light shading for ordinary ground and blanks where we find walls and rocks.'

Max and Flint sat side-by-side on the concrete, legs dangling over the lip of the gully. Lisa hovered by their shoulders for a few minutes then drifted away to find shade in the olive grove.

'It's real messy up here,' Max ran a pencil across the site plan just below the road embankment. 'This your the first transept right?'

'We expected the readings to be fouled up by the road construction. If you compare it with the second run, all this ground is denser than the natural soil.'

Max let his pencil follow the embankment edge. 'This must be spoil from when those guys laid the road. Then at the east end, your plan goes crazy.'

The shading grew heavier some two metres from the gully.

'If that was your first run, crazy readings are okay,' Max said. 'Lower down the site, things are so boring, normal strata, there's nothing to turn me on. These patches must be old tree root holes, but the rest of the earth looks real rocky. You say you field-walked this area? What came up?'

'Bones, bullets, old buttons and modern junk. You saw the stuff in the finds tray.'

Max pointed to the heavy area of shading beside the gully. 'It looks like there's some big feature right where we sit.'

'Would you say it's more road building debris?' Flint had already formed his own opinion.

'No.' Max thought long and hard. 'My gizmo is having a moody day, but it tells me that the debris is dense material, but under here, it's all loose. We're right by the gully: it could be an old channel.'

That was an inconvenient theory. 'If it was a channel, it would run all the way down the site . . . water cuts downhill, our gully would get wider with time, not silt up.'

'Okay, so we're sitting on a feature two to three metres wide by three to four long. It's overkill for a grave, unless they bundled a dozen guys into it.'

Flint felt his mind fall vacant and he drifted into a realm of ideas, where facts and theories crowded in after him. After a few seconds of trance-like realisation, he let out a huge sigh. 'Well, that's it then. That's what the town doesn't want us to find. Did you ever read about the Civil War?'

Max scowled, 'The War between the States?'

'No, here in Greece, just after Hitler's war. This whole area was a nest of guerillas of various factions, fighting over small villages. Communists against fascists against liberals, all happily murdering each other. Man against neighbour, brother against brother, and all the horrors you could expect; kidnapping, extortion, mass executions and mass graves.'

'Bullets and knucklebones?'

'And brass buttons, and an archaic fountain pen, it all fits!'

A long, slow laugh came from the American's lips. 'Jeez, that's an intellectual jump. But if that village had a guilty secret, someone would have dug up the bodies and made darned sure no archaeologists came rooting them up.'

'You're forgetting the road.' Flint tapped the map.

'Road?'

'It's our terminus ante quem: whatever happened happened before the road was built.'

'1949, right?'

'And we have a terminus post quem. Remember my pen? Byron F. Nichols wrote a book called *Arcadian Commando* in 1944 or '45; If the Byron F. Nichols who lost the pen was the same Byron F. Nichols who wrote this book and if the pen does in fact originate from this feature, we can date it to within four years.'

'I must go to this school of yours next semester. It sounds superior to mine.'

Flint flicked his fingers in his excitement to explain, 'We stole this book from the American Institute – sorry about that by the way.'

'Not quite murder one is it?' Max observed.

Excitement brimming over, Flint rambled on. 'Nichols never mentions this area in his book. He describes every blinking shepherd's hut in Arcadia, so if he'd ever been to Palaeokastro he wouldn't have been able to resist writing about it. Forgotten ruins are the sort of things which fired him up. So whatever happened, happened after Byron Nichols wrote his book, so we're into the Civil War. We know Byron Nichols was last seen on February 14th, 1947 and Stylanos Boukaris vanished a day later, with three of his men. Their bodies were never found.'

Max raised his eyebrows, 'until now?'

'Your guess is as good as mine, but let's say whatever happened, people thought the secret was buried and forgotten. They think the road embankment covered it up. They might even have helped put the damn road there in the first place, so there was never any possibility of the site being dug up. Except the gamble failed, Americans are like Romans, they build straight roads and the road misses the site by a few metres.'

'Whew!' Max looked askance at Flint, 'All that from a resistivity survey?'

'. . . and a month of bloody hard graft.'

'And what about this parking lot?' Max thumped the concrete.

'When I found the pen, the bad guys realised their mistake. They poured this concrete, laid a few bricks but never had any intention of completing the building. It serves its purpose. It will be fifty years before anyone bothers to break up this surface; by then, what's underneath will rate as archaeology and the pen will wind up in a museum.'

'The Palaeokastro Massacree Experience Centre?' Max suggested.

Flint slipped off the concrete lip and into the gully. Marathon had been a far off, dramatic battle, but the one he was forced to visualise had a squalid feel.

'Nichols went to Anatoliko to tell Stylanos his son was dead; I still don't understand that part of the story. Shortly afterwards, the merry men mount their donkeys and ride to here.'

In the distance, the stacatto rattle of a moped could have been a machine-gun. Flint imagined a group of mounted men crossing the gully in single file, probably on a plank bridge. He could see one rock, a hundred yards further up the hill, ideally suited to site a Bren gun, or other weapons thoughtfully provided by the British. The men would fall in moments, perhaps some sought refuge in the gully, but it was no refuge. A sniper behind the rock would have the gully in enfilade, turning it into a killing ground. One man had survived: Vassilis 'lucky' Boukaris. His story would be worth hearing.

The moped had drawn close and slowed down. Flint chanced one look over the gully lip then hissed 'Hide!' and dropped out of sight. Someone else had tried this before, he mused. He worked his way down the dry gully bed, then up into the olive trees. He could just see an ageing Greek man, in grey shirt, red necktie and black trousers, dismounting from his moped.

Max knew less Greek than Flint, but stood up and managed 'Yasoo' which seemed to anger the man. The moped rider started to jabber and gesticulate as he walked towards Max, threatening to kick the radar sledge. Max blustered and turned for support. Flint dodged from tree to tree, finding the man familiar as he shouted and pointed. He had seen this resentment before, one night outside Andreas' taverna.

Whatever Costas was saying ended in brooding silence.

'That's better,' Max said, flushed. 'Can't you speak American?'

'What you doing?' the man managed in thick and halting English. He seemed to be aware only of Max, so Flint slunk quietly towards the Land Cruiser. Reaching inside an open window, he took out his camera, unscrewed his 35mm lens and replaced it with his 90mm. The exposure he set to automatic, pulled out the telephoto and guessed at an f-stop. Max and the man were still arguing across languages. Edging back through the trees, Flint dropped to his knees, fiddled with the focus and found a good head-and-shoulders portrait.

Suddenly, Costas kicked the radar sledge. Max dived to rescue his equipment.

The Greek looked up at the heavy click of the camera, then swung a bony fist at Max. Max fell back and Costas delivered a hefty crack to the machinery with his toe.

'Hi Costas, smile!' Flint clicked the camera again.

At the sound of his name, the old man drew a knife from his belt and flicked it open. Max retreated six feet.

'Camera!' Costas must have been sixty, but he had a look of sprightly aggression about him. This man was used to wielding a knife.

Flint was aware of company to his right and sprang around. Lisa handed him a mattock.

'Are you serious?'

'Yours is bigger than his.'

'Size isn't important, Lisa.'

Costas had seen the mattock, and the spade which Lisa levelled, bayonet like at the height of his groin. Max raised his pencil as if it were a dagger.

An angry stream of fluent Greek abuse burst from Lisa's lips as she edged towards Costas. His dignity dented, the man uttered a few imprecations, then began to back towards his moped.

'Okay, okay. You all in big trouble now.'

Photographed three times more, he pulled his machine off its stand, mounted up and rumbled away.

'Friend of the family?' Max asked Lisa.

Flint dropped the mattock and ran to the top of the embankment for a final shot. The moped streaked downhill, disappearing into the houses. As Max came up beside him, Flint begged the use of a pen and scribbled the moped's number plate on his own fore-arm.

'Right team, gotta move fast!'

'Are we going to Andreas' after lunch?' Lisa asked.

'Only fully armed.'

Chapter Thirty-Three

Flint was bouncy and confident as they drove back towards Nauplion.

"'Ere we go, 'ere we go, 'ere we go!' he sang aloud, partly to fight against Lisa's terminal depression.

'Jeff, why the celebration?'

'We know whodunnit, whydunnit and whendunnit. That guy Costas is old enough to have taken part in the Great Palaeokastro Massacree and vicious enough to keep murder as a retirement hobby. It's down to town, find the pharmacy, make a few calls, then bingo! We can all go home.'

'Some of us don't have homes,' was Lisa's dry comment.

'It will all come out in the wash, as my Gran from Wakefield used to say. Once we're in town, you can drop me off. You two should scarper in case things go wrong. Forget the tents, just vanish until I've sorted things out.'

'What's going to go wrong, coach?' Max asked.

Flint grimaced. 'The bad guys know we're here and Nauplion is not a big town. Whoever killed Sebastian

Embury could just make his living that way, so I want you both to go.'

'You'll need me at the pharmacy,' Lisa said.

'Get out while you can. We've had our chance to escape, we may even have been allowed to escape the first time, to avoid the embarrassment of a trial. Someone sent me my passport, someone nobbled Owlett and Jules, and someone was following us in Athens. Remember the man at the Genaddion library? He was also at the British School, and the German School and he was at Miko's taverna the day before I went up there. White Citroën, sharp suit, putting the heat on everyone he meets.'

'You never told me he was at Mikos' place.'

'Sorry. I just didn't want to scare you.'

'Scare me: if someone's trying to kill me, I want to know about it!'

Max parked in the tree-lined square opposite the station. All the while he chattered nervously about the town, the Venetian fortress, the harbour, the sea, anything but the task in hand. The incident with Costas and the damaged machinery had wrecked his jovial spirit. For himself, Flint felt both fireproof and invisible as he climbed out of the Land Cruiser.

'See you Max, I owe you one. Get your data processed, then take it to the British Embassy. Give them everything.'

'Watch out for the guys in the black hats.'

Lisa kissed the American's cheek. 'Bye Max, you're a hero.'

'Lisa?' Flint asked.

'This is my home town,' she said, a hint of wetness in her eyes. 'I can't run.'

Max closed the door, and waved a road map as a form of farewell. With Lisa on his arm, Flint walked along Stakiopoulou to the pharmacy. The narrow streets were humming with morning life; one day he'd have to return and enjoy this town. Lisa stopped dead, dragging him to a halt.

Strutting down the pavement towards her was a policeman. His eyes were invisible behind the obligatory sunglasses.

'He's seen us,' she hissed.

'I'd hope so. They don't employ blind policemen.'

'Ass!'

The distance between them closed, the policeman drew closer, then passed within inches of Lisa's trembling arm. Flint forced her to maintain their pace towards the green cross suspended high on a wall. The policeman was behind now, shrinking into their past, but without warning Lisa dodged into the next shop doorway.

Flint dodged after her, smiling back at the ironmonger's stares. Lisa was looking up at the assortment of secondhand tools, pans and tin baths which dangled from wall and ceiling, pretending to be interested.

'You're being ridiculous,' Flint hissed.

'I feel ridiculous,' Lisa managed a nervous smile. 'Honest, Jeff, he was looking at me, looking right through me!'

'It's a practised art called undressing a woman with

your eyes. We letchers are good at it. He only looked at you as a sex object, not as an international criminal.'

'I'm too old to be a sex object.'

For a moment, Flint recalled the sophisticated Sofia Kionghis. 'You're never too old; come on, grandma.'

The pharmacy was busy with people seeking remedies for piles, sunburn and digestive disorders. It would take a hefty bribe to turn the four-hour photographic service into a one-hour service, but Flint was ever an optimist and Lisa had recovered sufficient nerve to sweet-talk the pharmacist into cooperation.

He left Lisa in the pharmacy and walked back to the Post Office. An infuriating hour was spent in a phone booth, wasting coins and sweat. The British Embassy was staffed by half-wits, Owlett was not answering his phone and Vikki's mobile number repeatedly gave the 'unobtainable' tone.

'Typical, huh? Why does this always happen?' Flint talked to hinself, for want of intelligent contact. He glanced at his watch; it was one-twenty, so he jogged back to the pharmacy. Lisa was leafing through the prints, smiling at the look of total alarm on Costas' face.

'Do you know anyone who would recognise him?' Flint asked.

'Andreas?'

'Not Andreas, someone else.'

She looked at him, closing one eye.

'You once mentioned you had a friend called Spyro,

a policeman. A married policeman? Vulnerable to a pretty face and a little blackmail?'

A grimace confirmed that Lisa clearly understood every detail of Flint's lastest stratagem.

'Will he be off-duty?'

She submitted with exaggerated weariness. 'Was your degree in how to be a complete bastard?'

They wound around four blocks of clambering streets, hugging the shadows, until Lisa found one particular side-street, where she stopped to gain courage and disperse her conscience. What did she owe Spyro? He'd had what he wanted. Flint shrank around a corner.

Spyro, his wife, three children and matriarchal mother-in-law lived in a noisome house on the southern slopes of the town. Lisa rapped on the door, which was answered by a small girl, quickly followed by a woman of about her own age. It was the first time Lisa had seen his wife. Dark and anxious, with an expression drawn thin by child-raising, the wife was instantly suspicious of this girl with the cosmopolitan accent.

The policeman appeared sharply. Unshaven, clad in vest and trousers, Spyro was not at his rakish best. His shock, when he recognised Lisa, quickly turned to defensive alibis which sent the wife inside. His face turned to anger, he grabbed Lisa's wrist and pulled her off down the alley, rebuking her in Greek.

'Lisa, go away, what do you mean? You will get me into big touble with my chief and my wife, now just go away.'

Lisa dug in her heels and pulled from the grip. 'Right,

I will, as soon as I can, but first, Spyro, you must do one thing for me.'

A fist clenched as he spoke. 'You are helping that English murderer. I will go back for my hat and my gun, then I will arrest you!'

'And I'll tell your wife about all the good times we had. Girl talk is such fun.'

'Pah! She does not care!'

Lisa detected heavy bluster. She knew the policeman was in thrall to his wife, intimidated by her mother and devoted to his children. Relatives crowded his life and the macho playboy vanished when he entered that dingy house.

'Honey, honey, honey, I worship your feet,' she mimicked.

He looked away in disgust, or embarrassment.

'Invite me inside,' she said brightly, 'Your wife and I could have a woman-to-woman chat about birth marks.'

'Lisa!' he raised his voice.

A shutter opened directly above their heads and an aged face peeked over a balcony.

'We could talk about your nice new police car, with its wide back seat.' She jabbed a finger at his ribs, 'Hey, Spyro, remember the night your aunt died, when you . . .'

'Lisa! In the name of St Gregory!'

'Why him in particular, is he the patron saint of adulterers? I just need to know about a couple of blokes. How about Doctor Dracopoulos, from Anatoliko: is he into anything dodgy?'

'Dodgy?' Spyro shook his head slowly.

'Smuggling antiques, robbing ancient ruins, you know?'

'No, I don't know.'

'Okay, what about Costas?' She handed over the photographs.

Spyro looked through them one by one, gently shaking his head when he saw the knife. The policeman rubbed his whiskers and gave Lisa wary glances between short sentences. 'Costas Zoides: I think he's a land agent for Korifi, you know those people, they own hotels. Costas rides around the hills on his little motorbike, collecting money from the farms owned by Korifi.'

Lisa smiled an insincere smile. 'Thank you Spyro, you're an angel.'

'Lisa, I hate the way you told my chief about me and you.'

She maintained her brazen expression. 'Sorry, I couldn't lie, could I? Not sweet little me.'

'Sweet! You are poison. Where is your English boyfriend hiding?'

'He isn't my boyfriend, thank you. And he escaped, didn't you read it in the papers?'

'You should escape too, Lisa. Go away before I remember my duty.'

'Bye Spyro.' Lisa stroked a knuckle gently down his sandpaper cheek. 'Fun wasn't it? Go back to your family now, give them my love.'

Spyro stepped back as if bit, then turned to check which of his neighbours had seen. Lisa scurried away, feeling dirty.

Costas worked for Korifi, the circle was squared, Flint was elated, giving Lisa a warm kiss, supposedly as a reward.

She pulled away from the passion. 'It's time we met Boukaris,' she said.

'No,' Flint replied.

'Why?'

'Because I've worked it all out now. I need to phone Vikki.'

'Vikki is a thousand miles away – how is she going to get my hotel back?'

'Priorities . . .'

'It's my priority!'

'Phone first, argue later,' he asserted.

Lisa said nothing as they walked back to the Post Office. Flint joined a two person queue for the telephone booths.

'I'm parched,' Lisa moaned, 'I'm going next door to buy a coke.'

'Get me one – and grab as much change as you can, we're going to need it.'

Flint found himself a phonebooth, and dialled Athens on the off-chance Owlett had re-materialised. He had one more attempt at the Embassy, then with dry throat looked around for his coke, and for Lisa.

Quickly he dialled the office number for Vassilis Boukaris. A secretary asked his name, but he refused to give it. The lawyer eventually came to the phone.

'Boukaris.'

'It's Doctor Flint here,' he said, 'We were due to meet about now.'

'We were?' asked the voice, with a hint of surprise.

Flint closed his eyes and would have shrieked aloud. 'Forget it,' he said hurriedly. 'I'll get back to you.'

Flint put down the receiver, then gave the aluminium booth a hefty thump. Lisa had her priorities. Only one man could give her back the hotel, but that was not the man she was going to meet.

Chapter Thirty-Four

Angelos sipped at the glass of Chablis, then sat back into the shadows. A woman had walked into the bar; rather wide-hipped, her floral pleat skirt rather dusty, her white tennis top marked with red soil. The weighty taverna keeper recognised her at once.

'Has Vassilis Boukaris arrived yet?' she asked with urgency.

Andreas said nothing, simply licking his lips, then wiping a drip of perspiration off his cheek. He looked directly at Angelos.

'Madam,' Angelos spoke in his clear, educated English.

She turned to face him. The dyed hair suited her, thought Angelos. He bared his teeth in a smile. 'Will you join me for a drink?'

The offer was declined in Greek. Of course; her veneer had to be maintained.

'I would like to talk; you are English?'

Andreas glanced from one to the other, as if this were one of Flint's old movies and a gunfight was about to break out. Had someone been playing a piano, he would have stopped.

'What will you have, Lisa?' Angelos used her name with deliberate familiarity. 'May I call you Lisa?'

The irritation in her face turned to chill fear and she took a few wary steps closer. 'Who are you?'

'Perhaps you could come and sit at my table. I have just ordered some wine, I hope you are happy with French white.'

'My name is Elena . . .'

'. . . Kyriacou, yes, I know. Now, come sit with me and we can talk about your friend Paul Adams, or is it Jeffrey Flint?'

She glanced towards the door.

'Don't run Lisa, I'm not alone. There's a very apt English phrase which describes your situation: rat in a barrel.'

Angelos picked up the car keys that lay beside the wine bottle and jangled them. He was pleased to see the way her face fell.

'Toyota Land Cruiser? I'd never buy Japanese, but that's the Americans for you. We have Max.'

The door again attracted her hope.

'I'm tired of the chase, Lisa. And so are you.'

'Vikki! It's all going horribly wrong.'

At last, Flint had found someone to share his growing panic.

'You must find Hugh Owlett, get him to drive to Nauplion and meet me, with someone from the Embassy, or try the Consulate . . . anyone. The Athens branch of the Salvation Army will do . . .'

The mobile line was disintegrating, whilst around

him, the hollow interior of Nauplion Post Office echoed with afternoon hubbub. A commotion in the street seemed to be growing, it demanded attention. The coins gave him just time to bawl the description of a rendez-vous. 'There's a pull-in directly below Acronauplion . . . its a Venetian fort. Six o'clock, seven at the latest . . .'

His last coins ran out, Flint dropped the telephone and darted to the front of the Post Office. Outside, the excitement was subsiding. Anxiously he began to seek English speakers.

'What happened? What's going on?'

A helpful red-skinned tourist told him. 'Four men . . .'

'. . . three,' his wife corrected, 'And the woman.'

'. . . and the man in the white car . . .'

'. . . I counted him in the four . . .'

Flint recoiled as if a sledgehammer had been smashed into his groin. He stepped back and faded into an alley-way, desperate for ideas. After a spasm of terror, he knew he must return to the street to confirm his fears.

Two Ray-Ban touting tourist police beside Aghios Spyridiou seemed bemused by the incident with the white Citroën. As Flint walked rapidly past the Byzan-tine church and deeper into old Nauplion, he recalled the disaster again and again. Lisa had tried to see Boukaris and bargain for her hotel, but Boukaris had not even known about the rendezvous. Dracopoulos had sprung a trap and Lisa had been driven away in the white Citroën. The police had not been involved.

As he lost himself in the tangle of backstreets, Flint was lost in conflicting thoughts. It would have been simple for the local police to halt the Toyota on its way into Nauplion, if Dracopoulos or one of Max's excavators had tipped them off. It would have been simpler, perhaps, to search the half-dozen campsites in the vicinity; Max had found them without trouble. If the authorities wanted them formally arrested, it would have been done.

Nauplion's enchanting charm had been extinguished in an instant. The exotic architecture now seemed alien, the ancient houses now haunted by threatening ghosts. Heat radiating from old stonework made his head throb, the light tired his eyes as he squinted from cold doorways. When shopkeepers looked his way, he felt a challenge instead of a welcome. He had never felt so naked.

Under his arm he carried a notepad and in his pockets was less than thirty pounds in drachmae. With his evidence and his chance of escape gone, Jeffrey Flint's thoughts turned to Lisa. Where would they take her?

'Bang!'

He threw himself against a wall as the shot rang out.

'Bang! bang!'

Two guns spurted noise from point-blank range, as a pair of small English boys burst from within a shop. 'You're dead mister.'

One of the terrorists fired a last shot to put Flint out of his misery. The cap exploded with a sharp crack and a suggestion of flame. Blue smoke caught the breeze and wafted towards the cowering archae-ologist.

'Sorry,' said the parent. 'Come on, you tykes!' He ushered the trainee assassins away.

The guns had been frighteningly realistic. Humiliated by his shock, Flint stopped to gather breath under the orange striped awning of the shop, where local tack, plus imported tack was draped for the delight of the easily pleased. One model .38 revolver in Taiwanese steel hung on its card sling. For the first time since turning ten years old, Flint wished he too had the comforting, powerful symbol of the gun in his hand. At long range he might confuse policemen or villains. Thrust into the ribs, the gun could intimidate taxi drivers or even, he realised, uncover the truth.

He took down the toy. It was a little underscale in his adult hand, but possessed that weight which carried realism. Flint the pacifist had once been Flint the small boy, touting a similar gun. It held a plastic ring of twelve high-powered caps, the most powerful on sale to children. For a moment, he regressed to childhood games on wasteland and building sites. He recalled the ear-splitting bangs of yesteryear, the whiff of gunpowder and the drifting blue smoke. He took out a handful of money.

Chapter Thirty-Five

Flint sat alone, high above the town, amongst the weeds and dusty herbs which roamed amongst ruins of mixed parentage. Greek, Byzantine, Frankish and Turkish stonework was slowly reverting to nature, settling once more into the hillside. From the top of Acronauplion, he looked down upon the rendezvous. A new road snaked upwards from the south of the Palmedhi rock, winding under, then over the ancient fortifications. Owlett could pull his car onto a short track just beyond the first bastion, then halt at a point unseen from the road. An extra hundred feet of elevation, plus a three hundred and sixty degree view, allowed Flint to watch for unwelcome observers and time his sprint for safety.

Six o'clock, said the clock tower at the western wall of the fort. His stomach rumbled. Lunch had been missed, again. Would Lisa have been given lunch? Was Lisa still alive?

A motorboat led a sharp v-ripple towards the southern shore of the peninsula. Out to the north, a ferry was manoeuvering around the island castle of Bourdzi. A green car stopped by the roadside. Flint stood to watch, his heart thumping in anticipation, but after a few moments, a hand emptied an ashtray out of the window, and the car moved off around the hill and down into town.

Seven o'clock. A lizard ran across Flint's foot and into hiding. The sun was dropping towards Arcadia in the west, lending the scene a surreal air, adding to his sense of detachment. The bell tower stretched a long finger of shadow towards him and Flint fidgeted on the stony ground. Night would come, but would Owlett come?

The mountains of Arcadia swallowed the globe at four minutes to eight. As the air fell quiet with the passing of the sun, he heard approaching voices and scrambled into an angle of exposed stonework. A pair of Greek lovers giggled past, seeking a patch of ground with less brambles. Flint crawled out and looked again at the empty rendezvous. Vikki had not found Owlett. Owlett was not coming. Owlett had set out, but had been delayed. Owlett intended coming but had been prevented. Owlett was waiting below the wrong Venetian fortifications.

What he needed now was a good lawyer. He remembered how relieved he had been when Vassilis Boukaris had visited him at Argos police station, but that act of charity could only now be explained as an excuse to see Flint cleanly ejected from Greece before too many questions were asked. As he thought about his lawyer, he remembered how Boukaris had a habit of touching his hairline. Too late, all the facts tallied: Flint could have wept.

Whilst it was still light, he stood and looked along

the northward road, where a construction site had been the scene of Sebastian Embury's death. A mile down the southern coast road lay a different objective. What the commando Byron Nichols might have called a soft target.

Villa Dafni was terraced into the hillside above the sea, close, but not too close, to other refuges of the comfortably flush. At any other time, the stroll along the coast road would have been pleasant. A few cars nipped past, but for most of the way only mosquitoes accompanied him. From the coast, he walked three hundred yards up a steep, poorly-metalled incline. Should things turn badly, he fancied he could bolt down the slope, flag down a car then poke the toy gun into the ribs of the driver as a final mode of escape. Escape to where was unclear.

Flint knew all about the house and its occupants. The details were written on one of his little cards.

Just past the villa, the road edge became an unfinished kerb and beyond this lay sweet scented pines with reassuring shadows. Flint slipped into the darkness of the trees, thinking, and watching. A ten-foot wall surrounded the house, which seemed quiet, and heavy wooden gates stood closed.

Could Lisa and Max be inside the villa? No was the sensible answer. Korifi owned warehouses, dark sheds, isolated cottages and unfinished chalets. The directors need not soil their own hands or compromise their own property.

With a quick bolt, Flint rushed across the road on

the balls of his feet and vaulted to grab the top of the gate. Ornamental studs of heavy iron served as footholds and he pulled himself over in moments. Within the embracing walls, a long garage block lay to the right, and dustbins to the left. Ahead, the white, two-storey villa glimmered on its terrace, with faint music from within; opera, perhaps. Flint chose to wedge himself behind two dustbins. The month had seen so much hiding and waiting, a little more would make no difference.

A little more waiting dragged into a little more. Two figures came out of the house, servants perhaps, making their way home through a postern gate. Flint moved along the left wall, and clambered up the terrace and looked over a shallow parapet which framed the patio. A dining table had been cleared and the French windows beyond were open, with only light curtains to deter insects. Flint crouched back below the parapet and lay still. Had burglar alarms got as far as the Argolid? If so, were they habitually turned on? Should he make his move now, or wait until the lights were out?

In the dark, listening to the cicadas and the sound of unwanted food slipping from plates, he became aware of movement off to the side of the house. A dark mass of Bouganvillea swamped the far wall, and below it grew a clutch of conifers and shrubs which formed a small apology for a garden. Flint strained his eyes to see motion to accompany the noise, but after ten minutes became convinced it had been a cat, or a rat, or paranoid delusion.

Upstairs, someone was moving about a bedroom, but someone else had just turned off the opera record. With one last nervous glance towards the conifers, Flint crawled over the parapet and advanced to the curtains. Partly transparent, they revealed a single figure filling an armchair, seeming to be brooding over his empty brandy glass.

Flint drew the toy gun. Pathetic as it was, it gave him confidence and it was the gun which led the way through the curtain and into the room.

'Don't make a noise.' Flint said.

The face was full, folded by years, creased by a sin that time could not erase. Boukaris had deep, black eyes which disappeared within his skull. His hair was unnaturally thick and black for one of his age.

His chest drew a few heavy breaths before he spoke. 'Mr Flint? I was expecting you.'

'Rubbish.'

A female voice called from within. Flint flicked his toy gun.

'I shall tell her to go.'

'Do it.'

Boukaris dismissed the voice, in a tone which carried no note of alarm. His words echoed in the plain, white-walled room and Boukaris looked at the gun. From fifteen feet, only a fool would assume it held no bullets.

'What is the gun for? Put it away. You do not frighten me.'

Jeffrey Flint had spent years cultivating the image of a pacifist, now he recalled the mean, Clint Eastood

297

look, hoping it fitted his own face. Unshaven, hunted, frightened, the new look carried credibility.

'Then take a seat, please.' Boukaris waved to a deep leather armchair.

'I'm not playing games.' Flint walked slowly across the terracotta tile floor, closing the internal door with his toe.

Boukaris gave another wheezing exhalation. 'So, you come to shoot me? It is not easy to shoot people.'

'And I suppose you should know. I have your life story, I know about the Civil War.'

'So you have been spying on me. You have been very clever, but you will not shoot. I have seen men stand before their bitterest enemies and be unable to shoot. It takes a special sort of man to pull a trigger.'

Damn the bloated bastard, Flint knew he was right. 'So you know about killing?'

'I fought for my country. I have seen death. But the war is history, even the communist executioners are allowed back into Greece. All the wounds are healed.' There was an element of pleading in his voice.

'And the dead are buried.'

Boukaris inclined his head as if to say 'please let it remain.'

'I want to know where Lisa is.'

'I do not have your Lisa.'

'You're a liar.'

'So, I am a liar and you are a murderer.'

'No, I'm looking at the murderer. You had Sebastian Embury killed and you had me arrested. I have the evidence, I posted it to the British Consul in Athens.'

This sounded like a good idea, Flint wished he'd thought of it earlier.

'You are finished, Boukaris.'

'You cannot threaten an old man,' Boukaris said. 'I am going to die, sooner than you. So you rob me of ten years of my life. You pay fifty.'

'If I'm framed for murder, will a second make a difference?'

The gun had a realistic double-action hammer, Flint pulled it back with a click, which to him sounded weak and tinny.

'I want you to tell me what happened in 1947.'

Boukaris showed no fear, only a deep sadness. 'That was so long ago.'

Flint levelled the revolver. 'Take off your toupee.'

Boukaris simply snorted and took a mouthful of brandy.

'Do it, or I shoot.'

'Yes, the British Empire. Do what we say or I shoot. Always the way, ha?'

Now Flint looked closer, above the bridge of the lawyer's nose, he could see the beginning of a thin white line. With a grunt, Boukaris removed the square of limp hair. His denuded forehead was disfigured by a long scar leading upwards and to the right where it divided in two, defining a Y-shaped region of dead scalp.

'Does that give you satisfaction?' Boukaris touched the wound, as if even the memory of it gave pain. Such an injury could lead to a lifetime of hatred.

'So that's what the communists did to you?'

'I escaped lightly. You cannot imagine the horrors I

witnessed when I was half your age. You read history, I saw history.'

'Do you remember Sofia Kiounghis?'

'Should I?'

'She was kidnapped, and rescued by a British officer named Byron Nichols and a boy with a scar on his forehead like the letter Y. Do you remember Byron Nichols? He remembered you, I even think he liked you and trusted you. Did you know how distressed he was when you nearly died?'

A dry hollowness began to undermine the words of the Greek, 'As I said, it was so long ago.'

'Let me get the story straight. You found out that Sofia was being held by the local branch of Organisation Chi and you led Byron Nichols to her. Once you knew how valuable she was, you betrayed Nichols and had the fascists pretend to lead you off to be executed. Only Nichols was too smart for your gang, he escaped and so did Sofia. Why did you betray him? Was it for money, or to impress Organisation Chi?'

'Angry Englishman. We should have been friends!'

Somehow, Flint thought that he was not the one being addressed. 'You killed Byron Nichols and you killed your father.'

Deep black eyes sank further into hell.

'Sofia told me why Nichols went back, he had one last job to do. He was going to tell your father that you were dead, correct? Then you reappeared, back from the dead a second time. Byron Nichols was a smart guy, he could put two and two together and you knew it. It

300

would be very convenient if he were to disappear and lo, he disappeared.'

'You have never been in a Civil War. You could never understand.'

'Oh I understand, facts lead to understanding. By an odd coincidence, your father vanished a day and a half after Nichols left Athens. But that's not so odd, is it? Your father would never have tolerated a son who was a traitor. So you brought your chums down from the hills and arranged an ambush, where, surprise surprise, you had your third miracle escape from death. You should have been a cat.'

Pain, bitterness, fear and anger suddenly boiled over as Boukaris' hands clenched on the brandy glass. It shattered.

'You are making this up!'

'You shot all of them and threw the bodies in a pit. Your big mistake was to suddenly discover decency. You couldn't strip the dead, not the man who saved your life, not your father's corpse . . .'

Boukaris gripped the chair, 'I shot no-one . . .'

Flint took out the golden pen. 'Behold, the treasure of Palaeokastro. There will, of course, be other identifiable artefacts buried under that convenient chunk of concrete. Your failing, Boukaris, was an excess of sentiment.'

When was Boukaris going to say something incriminating? Flint began to wonder. What the hell was he going to do when he ran out of insults?

'I bet it was a real big plus having a hero for a father. All those favours he was owed could be called in. All those debts of honour would be yours. His body was never found, so the myths grew. You couldn't spoil the glamour by having the bodies exhumed and you couldn't risk someone else stumbling on the mass grave in case reality contradicted the legend. Did you mean to kill Sebastian Embury or simply warn him off?'

The accused said nothing.

'So who did it? Your men? Your goons? Costas? The war is over, Boukaris. Plotting and kidnapping and killing, it's all over! Now tell me what you've done with Lisa!'

'Lisa, Lisa, who cares about Lisa?'

Flint wished the gun was real, wished he had the power to impose his will. His anger was rising, he was running short on empty threats. Pacifism was forgotten and he lunged forward in a fury, intent on battering Boukaris with the toy that would not fire.

'Where is Lisa? Tell me! Tell me!'

A rustling halted his motion. The curtains moved. A man with a gun, a real gun, a slick black automatic, advanced through the curtain. Flint dropped the toy instantly and raised his hands to shoulder height.

The moustached man in the blazer and tan slacks ran the fingers of his left hand up and down Flint's rib-cage and hips.

'Sit down,' the man kicked a leather pouf beside where Boukaris sat.

Flint dropped onto the pouf, hands on head. The intruder picked up the Taiwanese .38.

'A toy gun, Doctor Flint?' His English was immaculate. 'Rather foolish, but then there is a narrow line drawn between the fool and the hero.'

Boukaris demanded something in a flurry of Greek.

'Shall we keep the conversation in English?' The man said smoothly.

Boukaris had regained some of his composure. He smiled, a quiet, almost monastic smile. He looked at where the brandy glass had cut his hand, and watched a trickle of blood drip onto his armchair.

'They say you are a communist, Doctor Flint,' the intruder began. 'Ironic, isn't it Mr Boukaris?'

'I left politics a long time ago.'

'Politics is bloodless war – right Doctor Flint?'

Why was this hit-man quoting Mao Tse Tung?

'. . . and war is the politics of bloodshed,' the quotation continued. 'I suppose even a Marxist would appreciate that if one had wealth, position and family, one would not be willing to lose it all for some obstinate foreigner who likes digging little holes. One would suggest, even insist, that he dig his holes somewhere else. This has been a tragedy worthy of Shakespeare: by his vanity, Mr Embury brought about his own death. By his ambition, Mr Boukaris brought about his own nemesis.'

Flint was confused by the cross-play of incongruous images.

'Costas Zoides has kindly explained what happened to Mr Embury.'

'Costas!' Boukaris bellowed.

'He has signed a full confession, for due consideration

by the Prosecutor.' The man slipped the automatic back into his shoulder-holster. Reaching into the opposite pocket of his blazer, he drew out an identity card.

'Thymios Angelos, State Security.'

'White Citroën.' Flint murmured in awe.

Angelos gave a smile of self-satisfaction and the spell broke.

'Where is Lisa?'

'Elizabeth Canelopoulos and Maximillian Halleck the second are in safe hands, they have been relating an interesting tale. As have Dr Torpevitch and Mr Owlett.'

'You have Jules too?'

The smile on Angelos' face broadened. 'We are not amateurs, Dr Flint. Your modus operandi became obvious, after a while. I read Philosophy at Oxford, you know.'

He turned to Boukaris, but continued to speak English. 'We have some very useful photographs, wonderful charts drawn by a computer and a small bag of bones. Costas was very impressed by the bones. I think it would be very instructive if tomorrow, we could all drive to Palaeokastro and allow Dr Flint to show us how to dig a hole.'

Chapter Thirty-Six

Angelos was at the wheel of his white Citroën, throwing up dust on the road to Palaeokastro. Lisa and Max had already been sent to Athens, but Jeffrey Flint was being driven back to where the drama had begun, still unsure whether some complex twist was waiting to catapult him back into jail.

'I thought you were a gangster,' Flint stated. 'Some kind of hit man sent by Boukaris to hunt me down.'

This amused Angelos. 'He was not so powerful. He thought he was rid of you when he sent your passport. Then when you came back to Nauplion, I thought I would give him a friendly, but anonymous telephone call just to see what he would do.'

'Oh wonderful. Suppose he decided to have me rubbed out?'

'I don't think his friends in the police, even his son-in-law, would have liked another mysterious murder in Nauplion. You were safe.'

'Son-in-law?'

'You met him; he suffers from a very poor complexion.'

'Scarface?'

'Don't look shocked, it is a small town, he has friends and relatives in all the good positions.'

'So how long have you known I was innocent?' Flint asked.

Angelos grinned broadly, 'We became suspicious when we found you were in Athens. You were asking too many questions. If you had been guilty, you would have tried to escape, indeed, you would never have returned at all.'

'But if you knew I was innocent, why not just broadcast the fact, instead of sending people to tail Owlett.'

'We had to understand what was happening. The local police were making a bad job of catching you, then your journalist friends started writing about cover-ups. It did not look good.'

'So the newspapers embarrassed someone and that someone had your people find me?'

'Dr Flint, have you read about the Nazi occupation of Greece?'

'Yes.'

'A tragedy. Have you read of the Civil War?'

'Yes.'

'Another tragedy. You know of the Colonels' regime?'

'Yes. What point are you making?'

'So many Greek tragedies.' Angelos seemed to enjoy his own wit. 'We are the world's oldest democracy, so people say, yet we have had democracy only since 1974.' He took his eyes off the road. 'We have rid ourselves of the Junta, we are in the EC, we want our rightful place in the modern world recognised.'

'So?'

'Old ways die hard. Corruption, money, influence.' Angelos rubbed fingers and thumb together. 'That is the Greece of Vassilis Boukaris. It is the Greece we have to forget.'

The car sped past Taverna Mikos and on towards the olive grove. A police car stood idle and the area had been roped off, but no further action had been taken. Angelos braked sharply, his tyres grinding loose gravel as the car jerked to a halt. He pulled the handbrake with a vicious creak.

'Let us take a walk.' Angelos was grinning, but sincere.

Flint happily got out of the car, checked around himself for a few moments, then led the detective onto the square of concrete beside the rustling olive trees.

'What was Dracopoulos up to?' Flint asked, wanting all the facts squared.

'He wanted to be on the winning side. Mister Embury brought him a complaint that he was being harassed, so he passed it on to Athens. Mister Boukaris discovered this and Dracopoulos was told to keep quiet. Seven years later, you started asking questions, so the doctor tipped off his old friend. Finally, he let me know the whole story.'

'And he lured Lisa to Andreas' place?'

'Sorry, I asked him to do that; it was time to wrap up the case.'

Flint paused by the edge of the gully, stamping his feet on the concrete, below which, Max predicted the mass grave would lie. 'If I interpret the story correctly, there could be half a dozen bodies buried there. You'll be able to identify Stylanos Boukaris . . .'

'. . . by his wooden leg.' Angelos still held his Cheshire cat grin.

Flint scrambled down the side of the gully, explaining where he had found the loose bones and the pen. Angelos remained at the top.

'So when does the digging start?' Flint asked, looking up the broken bank for clues.

'That is not for me to decide.'

'Decide? You make it sound as if you're not going to bother.'

'Some things are best left undisturbed.'

Flint pointed an accusing finger. 'There is at least one dead Englishman and a heap of dead Greeks under that bank. They were murdered . . .'

'A long time ago. It was war, we cannot re-open such a case.' Angelos held his unflappable calm and secure expression. He waved away atrocity with one dismissive sweep of his hands.

'I suppose that wouldn't look good in the papers either, would it?'

'One can become a little too cynical, Doctor Flint.'

'So okay, you have a Statute of Limitations which says that you can't try people for war crimes, but what about Sebastian Embury? This site holds the motive for his murder. Opening this bank is essential if you're going to try the case.'

He was met by one of those Greek shrugs, an action which lost much of its effect when cushioned by padded shoulders.

'Find me a spade and I'll do it myself.'

'Come back to the car.'

Slowly, Jeffrey Flint's stomach began to sink. 'You're going to let Boukaris off.'

Angelos turned to walk away.

'After all this, you're going to let him off!' Flint scrambled after him, protesting and repeating his accusations.

On reaching the Citroën, Angelos opened the door and lay across the front seat. He pulled the local paper from the glove compartment and offered it to the incensed archaeologist. Angelos showed just a tiny streak of irritation.

'Do you read Greek?' he asked.

'No.' Flint took the paper and recognised the photograph below the headline. 'It's Boukaris, you have arrested him! What does the headline say?'

'Son of local hero takes his own life.'

'What?'

Angelos was still sitting in the car, giving attention to a smudge of dirt soiling one shoe. 'After we had taken a statement from Mr Boukaris last night, he said he was unwell and went to his room to fetch some pills. It appears that he had an old German automatic, a Luger nine millimetre. I would say it was probably one of his wartime souvenirs.'

Unflappable, Angelos wetted a finger and rubbed the shoe back to pristine blackness, whilst Flint absorbed the impact of what he had said.

'He shot himself? Jesus! That was a bit unnecessary.'

'In Greek we call it *philotimo*. In Latin it is *dignitas*; your honour, your respect for your own position in society.'

Many heavy hand gestures came with the philosophy. 'He had family and standing, he was the son of the war hero. In Greece, a man's first loyalty is to his family. What would his rich friends do when they discovered he murdered his own father? Vassilis Boukaris would be destroyed in an instant.' Angelos clicked his fingers. 'That man had lived with this crime for so many years and he chose the way he would pay.'

'So there will be no trial?'

Angelos shook his head. 'No trial.'

'But Boukaris didn't kill Embury with his own hands, he must have had help to steal the minibus then arrange the killing. Arrest his accomplices!'

'Who are they?'

'Costas for one.'

Angelos adopted a friendly, patronising tone. 'Costas was the last of the old fascist gang – Organisation Chi. He was there, that night Vassilis arranged to have his father ambushed, but that was the last killing he saw, Costas was the one who spotted you working in the olive grove, all those years ago; it was he who warned Boukaris. Last week, he was simply guarding the site in case you returned. He knows enough to be a useful witness, but he is not the murderer. Boukaris had business in Tripoli, with bad connections. There are plenty of people there who would kill for money.'

'And there I was, hoping for a nice, neat ending.'

'In police work, there are no neat endings and they are never nice. It must be like archaeology, no matter how much you dig, one can never uncover all of the truth.'

'You deserved that philosophy degree,' Flint said, allowing a wry smile to slip to his face.

'Your friend Mikos, the taverna keeper, what is his wine like?'

'Appalling.'

Angelos reached into the glove compartment again. Out came a bottle of Chablis. 'He will not mind if we use his seats whilst we talk. Will you join me for a glass of wine?'

Flint took one last look towards the gully, almost obscured by rustling olive branches. All the weight had gone from his shoulders, he could live again. 'Okay, why not?'

Flint returned to Athens the following day, to greet Lisa with a hug and to say farewell to Max and Jules at the airport. Owlett never wrote his exclusive story; he kept his press card and went to lunch with Angelos instead.

Two thousand eight hundred men are commemorated in the British War Cemetary off Leoferas Poseidonos. It is a little known, little visited corner of a foreign field where batallions of headstones stand in review before the sea. Britannia, as well as Poseidon, had once ruled the waves.

Sofia Kiounghis, Lisa and Flint stood around the grave that was not a grave.

Capt. B.F. Nichols D.S.C.
Missing in Action 1947

Missing no longer, mused Flint. 'Byron Francis Nichols, Captain. An English gentleman,' Sofia said. 'I try to come here when I can.' Sofia gave an embarrassed sigh, her face falling into anguish. 'All this is my fault, you know? All those people who have died; the boy Stephanos, brave Byron Nichols and his friend Stylanos. Now your friend.'

Flint winced at the thought of Sebastian Embury as his friend. In his next incarnation, perhaps. He took the pen from his pocket and passed it to Sofia. She had not run out of tears, one formed slowly then dripped onto her white silk blouse.

He turned his eyes away, wondering about those long, cold nights in the Greek hills, the privation and the cementing power of shared danger. He imagined a tale of a young, dashing English officer rescuing a beautiful, impressionable Greek damsel. With more careful editing, the plot could have had a heartwarming romantic conclusion.

Sofia suddenly snapped out of her introspection and offered the pen back to Flint. He refused it.

'Keep it, please.'

With only a soft thank you on her lips, Sofia slipped the keepsake into her handbag.

'How incredibly sad.' Lisa leaned back in the seat of the Gatwick Shuttle. 'Do you think they were in love?'

Flint sat opposite her, whilst outside the window

England arrived packaged as red bricks rinsed by rain. Mile after mile of terraced houses under a low sky brought adventure to a drab, familiar end.

'The romantic side of me would like to think so.'

'Romantic side? You have a romantic side?' Lisa scoffed, 'I know you Jeffrey Flint, I know you inside out. You like sex, booze, Bob Dylan, old films and even older archaeology.'

'At least I'm not shallow. Most guys stop at sex and booze.'

'I must have been mad getting tangled up with you.'

Flint had not seen her smile for a week, it was an encouraging sign. 'I was worried you'd double-crossed me in Nauplion.'

'I thought that I'd meet Boukaris on my own, see what he wanted . . .'

'That was brave.'

'No, it was selfish,' she said, bowing her head.

He knew what her motive had been.

'And, as it turned out, it was also incredibly stupid. If that creep Angelos had been a killer.'

'He wasn't, and we came through it,' Flint said. 'Look back and laugh.'

'Laugh? We should be having a wake for all those poor sods who died.'

'No, that's history, Lisa. Read the book, see the film. Brave men die, villains die, but fifty years on, we're all just archaeology.'

'And you say you have a romantic side!'

'I always thought I did.'

Her look mellowed. 'Of course you have, I'm only teasing. I do that too much, don't I?'

'A little.'

'Sorry.'

Flint looked directly into her nutbrown eyes. 'So, we're back in Blighty.'

'Back to Vikki,' she said.

Flint had become oddly reassured, once it was clear what shape the future was adopting. He had tried to resurrect something from his past and found that memories were best left undisturbed.

'And you?'

'See my parents, borrow some money, then go back to Nauplion and try again.'

Battersea Power Station, Chelsea Bridge and the distant spike of Founder's Tower, Central College caught his eye, then the train trundled slowly into Victoria. He helped her out with her trio of travel bags, then hoisted his fluorescent rucksack onto his back. A crush of humanity carried them along the platform and through the ticket barrier, until the current eased and they found themselves in space. Something was expected of the moment.

Lisa exhaled, then tightened her chin as she looked up at him. He leaned forward and their lips met. After a few moments, the kiss was at an end and she smiled and tweaked his cheek. 'Bye.'

'Have a nice life.'

Lisa picked up her bags and walked away towards the underground. Flint watched for a few moments before crowds obscured then engulfed her.